Shots Across the Bow

A Collection of Short Stories

By

Paul and Robert Gillcrist

iUniverse, Inc.

New York   Bloomington

Shots Across the Bow

iUniverse books may be ordered through booksellers or by contacting:

iUniverse
1663 Liberty Drive
Bloomington, IN 47403
www.iuniverse.com
1-800-Authors (1-800-288-4677)

Because of the dynamic nature of the Internet, any Web addresses or links contained in this book may have changed since publication and may no longer be valid. The views expressed in this work are solely those of the author and do not necessarily reflect the views of the publisher, and the publisher hereby disclaims any responsibility for them.

ISBN: 978-1-4401-3321-3 (pbk)
ISBN: 978-1-4401-3322-0 (ebk)

Printed in the United States of America

iUniverse rev. date: 4/2/2009

CONTENTS

PROLOGUE

usn

"Nothing is as exhilarating as being fired at without effect"
– Winston Churchill

Each of us, I'm sure, has done his share of foolish things. We have also needlessly put ourselves in positions from which graceful escape is impossible, and from which extrication is painful, embarrassing or both. With luck, many of those *gaffes* have been kept from the notice of friends and acquaintances. But, they remain forever indelibly emblazoned in our memories only to return at random times to remind us to be humble.

In the last few months, the usual reverie of our evening Jacuzzi/ chimenea sessions has been interrupted by such recollections. We are uncertain whether this unusual phenomenon is related to the approach of our senior years or whether there is another psychological reason. It has happened with such regularity that we decided to assemble some of them for a possible use thus far undefined. Many of these stories are humorous. But, many things are funnier in retrospect than they seemed to be at the moment they occurred. So, we tried some of them out on two of our brothers to see if this might be the seed of yet another "writing project." Their reactions were different. One couldn't recall any instances worthy of writing about. The other found himself convulsed with laughter and immediately began recounting any number of instances which had occurred to them both. That decided us.

So, here's our plan. We are going to assemble this set of stories and add to it as memories continue to percolate from deep storage. At some juncture we will put them into a more permanent binding, unedited and leave it on the coffee table for those moments when we think we need either to be amused or to be taken down a notch or two.

Below the title of each story will be a small symbol indicating which of us is the author. In Bob's case it will be a small usmc. In Paul's case it will be usn. There is one disclaimer. In a few of the stories the names of the protagonists have been changed to protect the innocent, or to insulate the guilty.

PART I

usn

THE EARLY YEARS

The Gillcrist family consisted of five boys and four girls. Paul was number four in the pecking order and Robert was number eight. The family first lived in Chicago, but moved to a small town in Westchester County, New York, called Pleasantville. It was a nice little town about a 45 minute train ride from downtown New York. The family spent its early years there with all of us attending the local Catholic parish. Bob was born in Pleasantville and I started kindergarten there.

In about 1936 the family moved again in response to the job market need of our father to a small town on the south shore of Long Island, called Freeport, about a one hour's train ride from New York City. Though not intended, Freeport's location near Jones Beach was to have lasting effects on all of us.

We moved into a rambling, three story frame house on a good size lot and with a wrap around screened front porch that was a magical sleeping facility during the summer months. Dad was in residential real estate at that time and I'm sure he and Mom decided that it was the perfect place for such a large family. The entire family attended the local elementary school, Our Holy Redeemer and with one exception the several catholic high schools in the vicinity.

Entrepreneurship, having been instilled in all of us, the boys shoveled snow in the winter, and mowed lawns in the summer. Nearly all of us found summer employment at the beach and most of us baby-sat year 'round. The particular block of Porterfield Place where we lived was populated by families of one or two children, no more. So, we are sure that our arrival was received with some trepidation by the quiet neighbors.

Mother and Dad went to great pains to insure that we were always on our best behavior when interfacing with the neighbors, but the presence of nine exuberant children had its effects both positive and perhaps, at times, negative. Most of the negative aspects were kept secret from our parents, if at all possible.

Tar Baby

usn

"Never get into a situation, where getting out is harder than getting in"
L.J. Steffens

For three or four consecutive summers Jim and Paul worked at a summer camp named, Dominican Camp, located on the east bank of the Hudson River half way between the towns of Staatsburg and Poughkeepsie, about 90 miles north of New York City. The years were about 1942 through 1945 and we were in our early teens. The camp was run under the auspices of the Diocese of Brooklyn by a Dominican priest, named Fr. William Whalen, a legend unto himself.

We started as applicants with the idea that by dint of hard work and performance we would be promoted after several years to the exalted rank of counselor. There was no pay involved.

My brother and I were essentially "pot wallopers" in the camp kitchen. But, it was an adventure. There was a swimming pool and there were all the activities one finds at most summer camps like hiking, outdoor sports activities, boating on the river etc.

About a half mile out into the river were some small rock outcroppings a few hundred yards long which were known whimsically as the Three Sisters Islands. One day several of us took one of the camp rowboats out to the islands to explore. We quickly became bored with exploring and decided to take the boat out into the middle of one of the islands' small coves. We took along some very large stones (ten or fifteen pound size rocks) with the idea of exploring the bottom of the cove. Visibility in the water was not more than a few feet, so our exploring promised to be a little scary. For some reason I was the first to go and, standing up in the boat with the stone clasped firmly to my chest, I took a deep breath and stepped over the side.

My descent was scary and far more rapid than I had anticipated. It seemed like an eternity before my feet hit the bottom but it was with a startling discovery. Instead of a solid bottom my feet sank into soft gooey silt all the way up to over my knees. Letting go of the stone I attempted to free myself from the silt only to find that it wasn't going to be quite that easy. In fact the clinging silt simply wasn't letting go of my legs. There was nothing against which to push or leverage myself. Stark terror instantly set in and the more I kicked and struggled the worse it got. I wasn't sinking any deeper into the silt but I was running out of air. When I tried to dig my legs out with my hands the silt seemed to grab at my arms. I felt instantly like I was dealing with some weird sort of underwater tar baby. By now I was frantic and my struggles became (in my mind) Promethean but useless. I was in total darkness, the water was cold and I was simply out of air and ideas. It was the most terrifying moment of my short life.

Finally, I decided that the only way to free myself was to swim out so I began to stroke with my arms as mightily as I could while, at the same time, kicking with my legs. It worked, and I gradually worked myself loose. My lungs were bursting when I finally broke the surface. As I lay in the bottom of the row boat gasping for breath with my legs covered with green primordial slime from the knees down I told my companions that this particular form of underwater exploration was not a good idea.

A Rung Too Far

Usn

"Human experience largely consists of surprises."
- Ogden Nash

The heavy, 26 foot wooden ladder was leaning up against the rear wall of our home in Freeport directly above the new back door. The year must have been 1949 because Dad had enlisted the efforts of Pat Tacke and me in cutting a second story window in the wall. Pat and I must have been on summer leave from the Naval Academy in our second year. I do not remember exactly what I was doing but the job required that I stand as high up on the ladder as I could. Perhaps I was cleaning out the second story rain gutter on the flat part of our roof. Pat was inside, on the other side of the wall making one of the vertical cuts of the window opening with a saw while Dad supervised the operation standing behind Pat. It was necessary that the cut be done accurately and carefully.

I was aware of what was going on but not as aware as I should have been. I felt a small vibration coming through my moccasins and into my feet from the wooden rung on which I was standing but paid no attention to it. Being at the top of a ladder, twenty feet above the ground, I was painfully aware of my fragility, and interested in getting the immediate assignment completed as quickly as possible so that I could get down from my precarious position. Finally, the vibration in my feet became so strong that I glanced down and, to my horror, saw that the saw blade which Pat was wielding so carefully but vigorously was extending in and out with the tip of blade sawing not only the wall but also the ladder rung on which my feet rested! In the instant of horror before I could move I saw that the saw blade had already cut halfway though the rung. It was only a matter of moments before the rung broke under my weight and gravity would take over. An instant later I was standing on the next rung down screaming at Pat and Dad to stop!

Dad, on later reflection, evidently regarded the incident as immensely amusing and reminiscent of a Keystones Kops comedy sequence. After carefully replacing the lacerated ladder rung, Dad called an end to the day's work, lit a Van Bibber cigar, and chuckled for half an hour over our Three Stooges performance. He probably salted it away in his memory for recounting to a more receptive audience than his son and the visitor from Idaho.

THE EMERALD MESSENGER

usmc

Nay, we'll go Together, down sir.
Notice Neptune though, Taming a sea-horse, thought a rarity,
"My Last Duchess" - Robert Browning

It was one of those days, when the surf was almost calm, when each wave approached the shore with such precision that for a hundred yards down the beach the waves broke as one long ellipse, making a distinct woofing sound as the air escaped from that long translucent green tunnel.

The sound of the breaking wave was almost subliminal, against a background of pitched voices of children at play, of raucous seagulls, and the muttering of the breeze as it ruffled umbrellas.

There were the scents of the beach too that day, of the sea itself, its flotsam and jetsam and of suntan oil and low tide.

The ambient beach music and scents were familiar to the old man, as comfortable as old friends were. And like old friends, these familiar surroundings didn't intrude into his thoughts.

The old man's thoughts were of his beginnings, of youth. So many years had past, so many of life's offerings had been plundered. It had been years since he last sat facing the sea.

For nine years as a young man he worked as a lifeguard at Jones Beach. In those days his eyes would wander over the swimmers as his mind wandered, miles from the guard stand he slouched on. It wasn't inattention, it was experience. The sea conditions, and the wind and tide were the precursors of trouble. A good lifeguard always assessed each swimmer as the swimmer entered the surf.

The young guard had been tan and tall and lean and able, and arrogant enough to presume immortality as a right. And so when summer came back to the Island each year bringing warm sun and humid breezes, he'd find a way to change his job and night school schedule and return to his job as lifeguard at the State Park.

The beach rejuvenated his soul, and the play that was part of the lifeguard job was like a multi-vitamin for the spirit. Young men have a minimum daily requirement for play, and the guard job certainly provided that.

The memory of that last year at the beach was particularly poignant. It was the year that he and his brother-in-law got out of the Marines, and decided to lifeguard for one last summer. It was a sort of farewell to their youth and to the boys of summer. They recognized the need, after their military obligation, to catch one last wave with good company like Barr and McGrath and Mannheim and Sulkies.

Through all the intervening years, wherever the old man was in the world, there were those subliminal tuggings, calling him back home to the sea. One time, high on a mountain above the Arctic Circle, as he pushed out of the evergreen timberline, an overwhelming scent shook his equilibrium.

It was the scent of the sea. It was so strong, so damp, so real that he turned puzzled and looked out over the foothills expecting to see the Bering Sea just beyond. But there was no sea, not for a thousand miles.

For the rest of that Arctic day, he pondered the scent. Had it traveled all that way to call him home? The question remained unanswered, but before too long, he was making a primal pilgrimage back to the sea. He traveled down through the Territory of Alaska, the Yukon Territory, British Columbia and on across the States, hiking and thumbing rides to eventually climb a wooden lifeguard stand and know he was home.

Maybe someday, science will discover a genetic memory strand in our DNA, a strand that is imprinted with the scents and sounds of the sea, embedded over thousands of years of living by the sea. After all, his parents and all their ancestors before them came from a wee isle, set in the western ocean. Maybe that would explain the gentle lure of the sea.

The old man's early memories of the beach were of playing in the surf as Coast Guard sentries strolled by in their blue woolen uniforms and white leggings, ammunition belts and rifles slung from a shoulder. All along the Coast, sentries waited, watchful, but that was during World War II.

Those childhood memories contained some humorous events too. There was the foggy day when a long boat of Brazilians pushed out of a thick fogbank and ground their bow onto the sand to ask the guard, who was only eight years old at the time, where they were. His simplistic reply, "You can't fool me, your right there in your boat" did little to help the lost South Americans.

Their ship, a freighter, was aground a few hundred yards out. It materialized like magic as the morning sun burned the thick fog off. The beachcombers all lined up along the shore covering their mouths and laughing.

Then, there was the day a sick whale struggled ashore pounding the surf with a few last desperate strokes of its flukes, its brave heart fighting 'til the end. That troubled the boy. It wasn't just the sick whale. It was concern for the many other beautiful sea creatures that no longer came to visit his shore. What had happened to cause this change? "What have we done?" thought the boy.

In his memories of boyhood, the old man remembered standing knee deep in the surf, enthralled as huge schools of porpoises cavorted within a few feet of him, showing off for him, but those delightful creatures were gone forever.

In darker moments he'd recall his first visit to the sea. It was the day after The Hurricane of '38. The boy's dad took him along on a trip across the marsh and barrier beach to view the destruction. Perhaps his dad brought him along to help him overcome his fear from the night of the hurricane.

The whole family was awake all that night, gathered in the living room. The power was out, so the family knelt amongst flickering candles. reciting the Rosary, as the house creaked and moved on its foundation and the wind howled, violently shoving huge maples to the ground. The little boy sensed that the family was in great danger, and sat trembling, crying.

By morning, the hurricane had moved off to Nova Scotia, leaving death and destruction everywhere. The boy sat in the car that next day looking at half-sunk bits of homes scattered across the marsh and barrier beach. The boy thought of the families who had crouched in those homes during the night, knowing that they were gone. The tour ended at the shoreline and the boy was frightened by the flotsam and jetsam he saw strewn along the beach, and especially of the might of the sea itself. He would always remember that hurricane and that day.

The old man smiled as he harkened back to that secret day when he learned to understand and love the sea. It was the year that a warm, generous young nurse in the neighborhood took him to the beach with her every day as a favor to his mom.

It was a quiet day. The surf was almost calm, and the boy had been searching for unbroken seashells. He had been following the irregular, foamy trace left by the receding tide, searching for nature's clues. Already that day he clutched two prizes. He found whelk eggs encased in what looked like a snake's skeleton and stingray eggs, hidden in little black pillowcases.

Then something caught his eye. It was floating a dozen yards out in the calm sea. It was a mass of seaweed tangled around a bit of flotsam. On an impulse he wadded out to examine this new find. Standing chest deep, he pulled the tangle toward him for a closer look. As the boy lifted the seaweed off the driftwood, his eyes lit up in confused delight.

There before him was a tiny emerald jewel. It stared back at him and cocked its head like a conspirator. The boy stood transfixed. He had seen the likeness of this creature on the state park signs and employee's uniforms as well. Everyone knew the emblem was a replica of a seahorse, but the boy had assumed that, like the unicorn the seahorse was only a myth, something those ancient mariners claimed to have seen long ago.

The little boy felt as though he was taking part in some religious experience. It was a sign. Very gently, he reached out, whispering to the seahorse, and touched it. The seahorse followed his finger with its eyes and as he touched it, the seahorse moved over with its pectoral fins fanning and slowly, gently wrapped its tail around the boy's finger. The pressure of the seahorse grasping him electrified the boy. Some sort of energy passed between the seahorse and the boy. Speechless, the boy stood in the surf and experienced a communion with this almost mythical creature.

As if by some miracle he suddenly understood that the sea was benevolent, it wasn't the evil force portrayed by the hurricane. The sea was a gift from God, as bountiful as America's farmlands. In that moment the boy intuitively knew that if this tiny jewel could exist in the sea, then all creatures could exist there as well. If such a defenseless awkward, slow-moving little creature could spend its whole life in the sea, then he had nothing to fear.

The boy possessed the native intelligence to keep his newfound brand of faith to himself. It would be his secret. With this new shield, he lost his fear of the sea and its monsters. In that instant of conspiring with the seahorse, a transfiguration took place. This was no sea creature. This was an emerald messenger.

From that day on, the boy's confidence grew as he saw beauty in the sea and its endless creatures. The depths of his acceptance kindled a desire to increase his knowledge and so he read anything he could find on the sea. A few years later, the boy and his brother built their own underwater breathing apparatus and began exploring the vast region beneath the sea.

Love is a melding of many emotions, of respect and understanding and familiarity and need. Through the years his love of the sea grew along with familiarity and respect, just as the boy himself grew. As a young man he served his country at sea. Later still, he learned to sail and over the years, plied the coast from Maine to Mexico.

Sitting by the sea, the old man mused, "Whatever became of the emerald messenger?" After a time the old man stood, his knees cracking painfully. He began walking along the receding surf line, his eyes ranging back and forth. Then he stopped and slowly picked up a limpet shell, putting it in his pocket. Farther along he found a broken sea scallop's shell. As the old man beach combed, his search slowly changed from an examination of the surf line to the sea just beyond the breaking waves. It was just out there that he had found the Emerald Messenger, so many years ago.

RIPTIDE

usn

"Beyond all things is the ocean."
Seneca 4 B.C.

Some time in the summer of 1942 my friend, Ray Riesgo, and I hitch-hiked to the beach for an afternoon of body surfing. For reasons I can't recall we chose to go to Point Lookout instead of Jones Beach. As I recall Point Lookout didn't have very many life guard stations. Anyway, it was late in the afternoon and this particular part of the beach was almost deserted. We were treading water just beyond the point where the breakers were forming. Our conversation must have become absorbing because all of a sudden I noticed that the water had turned several degrees colder. We looked shoreward and what we saw turned my blood cold.

We were easily three quarters of a mile from the wet sand! I could scarcely believe it. Obviously a rip tide had taken us out unbeknownst to us. At first we began to panic. The distance we had been swept was so great that mere stroking shoreward was simply out of the question. The good news was that our seaward motion seemed to have stopped and what we were faced with was a long, protracted swim to shore. We started stroking slowly toward the beach. Then we would stop every ten minutes and float on our backs for a while. I didn't say anything to Ray about it but I found myself expecting a shark to appear and make a ***hors d'oeuvre*** out of us. There was no one on the beach to hear us even if we could have yelled loud enough. When we finally made it ashore through the surf we just sat down on the wet sand exhausted and looked at one another. My recollection is that we had spent over an hour getting ashore. Of course we never told anyone about it but I can still remember that terrible feeling in the pit of my stomach when I first realized we had been swept out so far.

We got home a little later than usual that evening. I have always had a funny feeling that had I been swimming alone, panic could have taken over and I might not have made it.

We never told anyone about this.

LEXICON

usmc

"The music of the heart."
- Akenside

Many years ago, I attended a dismal, inner-city school. One day, while conversing with a classmate, he surprised me by using the word *brick* to describe a smooth, round stone that I found in a stream. I had carried the stone to school to show the science class an example of obsidian. The term brick was an example of the boy's experience. Gang borders, family, economics and other arcane inner-city influences defined his world. I remember the conversation still. His lost opportunities will always bother me.

Each day we should learn something more about the world, language, art, and ourselves. "Travel broadens," it is said. These are true words. I remember walking by a shop in Vienna, Austria, one day. It was obviously a cutlery shop. The sign above the window read, Messerschmitt. I thought the word meant a German fighter plane from WWII. I was curious, so I entered the shop and discovered a Brotmesser (bread knife), Küchenmesser (kitchen knife), and a world of words I had not yet learned. Every day, I looked about like a kid in a candy store. The words jumped out at me from all directions. I took the *Straßenbahn* (streetcar) from the corner by my brother's *Haus* and needed a *Fahrschein* to show the conductor. Driving the *Autobahn*, I came to an exit ramp. *Ausgang* it read.

I suspect that more important than learning words, is learning to love words and to seek them out. My dad never finished grade school, but my mother was a schoolteacher before marrying and raising nine children. I guess she could not resist the impulse, because on the kitchen wall was a blackboard. During dinner, my parents not only addressed our nutritional needs, but also our intellectual needs. Conversation was strictly enforced. If I tried to chat about a lost baseball, someone would remind me that was "Not of general interest."

There was another rule. Any sibling could challenge another's use of language. If I was challenged for using a word improperly, my dad would grin and say, "Get the dictionary." I would immediately lay down my fork and go to the library to look up the word. Next, I would return to the kitchen to report. After all the Bronx cheers and jibes died down, I was obliged to write the word and meaning on the blackboard. Since my age, intellect and standing in the pecking order did not augur well, I learned to keep my big mouth shut and listen.

It was commonplace for a sibling who was studying Latin to try words out on another sibling, or for one to ask, "*du beurre, s'il vous plait*" at the dinner table. There were Spanish, German, French and Latin words flying about like honey bees, at dinner. What a forum it was for learning.

My mother was a walking Thesaurus. She would frequently offer suggestions for more appropriate words than those we chose. She also enjoyed giving us the etymological background for words we used. I still have *Word Origins* by Funk, a gift she gave me fifty years ago, when I left for the Marines. I spent many an idle hour thumbing through it. The book is falling apart now, so I keep a rubber band around it. What follows is a sampling of word origins I still remember:

Grenade: exploding seeds. Origin pomegranate, French. One who throws grenades is a grenadier.

Admiral: a Saracen chief, Arabic. *Amir.*Commander at sea.

Assassin: derived from the habit of giving *hashish* to the murderer or terrorist a middle-eastern leader sends off to kill someone. The *hashish* eater is the *hashshashin.*

My parents gave us the gift of words, but more important was their gift of the love of words.

Trolling

usn

"Fate is the hunter."
Earnest Gann

The year was 1953. It was late summer and I was in the carrier qualification phase of naval flight training at Naval Auxiliary Air Station, Barin Field just outside the small town of Foley, Alabama.

My friend, Charley Craig and I were spending a pleasant Sunday afternoon at the beach at Gulf Shores snorkeling. There wasn't much of a surf, maybe two or three feet, and it was breaking just inside a sandbar which happened to be about 150 yards off shore. The water depth over the sandbar was about 20 feet, perfect for snorkeling.

I had fashioned a hand spear with a double loop of surgical tubing for propulsion. It was made from a rake handle and had a twelve inch steel point with a barb; perfect for sting rays which sat on the bottom covered with a thin layer of sand. The spear had a wooden pin driven through the shaft two feet behind the point and protruding about two inches out on either side of the shaft. The double loop of surgical tubing was run through a metal eyelet screwed into the back end of the handle. The trick was to gather the two ends of the loop through the outer fingers in my left hand, hold the spear between my left arm and body, then reach forward with my left hand stretching the tubing forward until my fingers could grasp the ends of the peg. All I needed to do was point the spear and release my grip on the pins causing the spear to shoot forward about eight feet. By retaining my hold on the tubing I could shoot again in a matter of seconds.

We were having a good hunting day and gave little thought to the larger effect of all the stingray blood we were putting into this particular portion of the Gulf of Mexico.

At some point, Charley experienced an equipment failure and returned to our beach blanket to effect repairs. I foolishly elected to remain over the target-rich environment of our sand bar and slipped into the reverie of the happy hunter paralleling the beach. I was a stranger in Paradise.

I glanced toward the beach to check my position relative to our beach blanket and was surprised to note Charlie waving both hands over his head and shouting something which I couldn't understand because of the noise of the surf. Charley was making no effort to come into the water, so I erroneously concluded it couldn't be too important.

It was perhaps a minute later when I surfaced from a dive and noted Charley still waving both arms agitatedly and beckoning me to come in out of the water. I caught a wave in and was standing in water up to my hips when I saw that he was pointing to my right. Glancing out in the direction he was pointing I saw something which froze my blood. Clearly visible in the next breaking wave was the outline of a shark. It was probably an eight-footer!

Charley recounted that the shark had been slowly following me and slowly closing the gap for several minutes. When I asked him why he hadn't grabbed his spear and swum out to get me all I got in reply was a glazed stare.

I never went snorkeling with Charley after that.

THE COBBLER

usmc

"No canvas absorbs color like memory."
- Willmot

In an album at home, there is a picture of my father. It is a black and white photo that is cracked and yellowed with age. The photo is of a stern young man in the uniform of an Army Captain. The photo is dated 1917. The Captain has experienced things that have transformed him. He is no longer the simple farm boy who traveled all the way to Church Street, New York City, to enlist in the Army as a Private and fight in France. That farm boy never dreamed of trench foot or mustard gas and chlorine gas. The Captain knew them well. I shoved that album into the back of a musty drawer, as I am sure the Captain did with his memories of that time.

Albums are fine, but I prefer mind pictures. Mind pictures have it all over albums. They never fade or crack with age and you don't need an album. I call them mind pictures, because they are such vivid memories. For example, even forty years later, I could pick out of a police line-up, the point man in a particular Viet Cong patrol. I even remember the hat and shirt he was wearing and the look of surprise in his eyes as he stepped out of the monsoon rain on that jungle trail.

What follows is a mind picture, shoved into some musty drawer, like the old photograph. Events spark the crisp memory with all the detail, the tenor of the voices, the scents and sounds, the backdrop of the cellar, and I have an instant picture from another time. And as the picture resolves, I see once again youthful, unlined, smiling faces and feel a sense of loss, of melancholy, or love, as I relive the moment in remembering those friendly faces and familiar places.

• • •

It's Saturday and Dad's day is chock-a-block. My four brothers are waiting out by the garage for haircuts. Dad has an old, dull, manual shears similar to sheep shears. Every Saturday, we line-up for a haircut, joking and laughing as the victim on the stool winces, because from time to time, with dull shears, Dad inadvertently pulls out a tuft of hair instead of cutting it off. However, before the shearing begins, Dad and I go to the cellar, to complete another task.

The cellar has whitewashed brick walls and locust trunks for lolly columns. It is curiously cool down there in summer and warm in winter. The cellar also has a special scent, a melding of aromas supplied by bins of green potatoes and dusty anthracite coal and shelves that line the walls with mason jars of preserved foods. Sometimes, one of the mason jars will spoil and explode, sending more scents to join the army of occupation. There is also a pervasive, transient scent, an essential element in my mind picture of hide glue.

My dad's workbench commands the far corner of the cellar, where in later years I would get my licking after mouthing off to the nuns. The Army Captain must have become frustrated with his obdurate, insubordinate son, realizing after a few episodes, that he might just as well be licking the locust lolly columns.

There are sheets of thick, tan cowhide hanging behind that workbench, and a bare bulb dangling above it, casting long shadows and meager light. The wiring for the bulb runs exposed on the cellar ceiling, consisting of two separate wires wound on white glass insulators to prevent the wires from touching and shorting. The wires stretch across the cellar disappearing in the shadows. The wiring for the whole house is similar, replacing the gas lamps with electric lights.

The ancient, decorative escutcheoned pipes for those gas lamps still poke through the walls and ceilings, waiting. They will have to wait a little longer, until the energy crunch forces us to go back to gas lighting.

Dad is standing at the workbench, cobbling my shoes at my request, and I stand by his side in stocking feet, acting as his assistant-cum-audience as he cobbles away.

The Captain loves to work with his hands. For such a big man, he does surprisingly intricate work. He is a man parsimonious in personal rewards, enjoying an occasional, brief interlude, smoking a nauseating Van Bibber cigar. He releases the smoke through his nose, watching it changing shapes as it drifts lazily above his head. That and a shot of whisky once in a great while seem to be the extent of his vices.

I am relieved that he is cobbling my shoes, because both soles have holes. I have been stuffing cardboard into the shoes for weeks. Dad is almost finished now and entertains me by humming a doughboy's tune from France, through a mouthful of shoe nails, puffing his cheeks and keening through his nose like a trombonist. The percussion section for his rendition of *Mademoiselle from Armentière* is a cobbler's hammer pounding a rhythmic rat-a-tat-tat cadence with the theatrics of a maestro, as he fastens a thick piece of cowhide to the shoe's last. The last is set securely on a black, cast-iron form that nearly matches my shoe size.

After the performance, in a pungent atmosphere of hide glue, he removes the shoe from the form and hugging it to his apron, carefully trims the excess leather with a truncated knife. He hands me the cowhide scraps, which get an immediate, tactile scrutiny. When both shoes are repaired, he gives them a quick dab of polish and swings into a rendition of, *We're all going calling on the Kaiser.* During his performance, Dad buffs the cracked, old hand-me-downs to a glassy sheen with much percussive snapping of his special buffing cloth, in imitation of the shoeshine boys at Grand Central Station.

Finally, Dad holds the newly cobbled shoes in his hands, admiring his work like a Dutch diamond cutter. Then with a grin, he kneels and gently slips them on my feet, tying them securely.

"No rest for the weary," I hear him sigh as he climbs the cellar stairs to begin the shearing. I clomp along behind in my stiff, slick-soled shoes, hoping he will begin shearing my older brothers first.

STURDY STOCK

usn

"Tough as a steak was Yukon Jake;
hard-boiled as a picnic egg."
Parramore

Sometime about 1944, Dad gave me the job of re-wrapping some condensate pipes on the furnace in the basement at '52. I distinctly recall crouching low over a metal tub alongside the furnace and dumping a large paper bag of asbestos powder into it. Of course, a dense white cloud enveloped my face, much of it ending up in my lungs. Then I added water and began to mix a thick goop about the consistency "pangcake" batter. Then I dipped a roll of three inch wide cotton-like cloth into the mix and began wrapping it around the bare spots in the insulation. Dad's instruction had been detailed and explicit but he was not personally supervising this particular job which flattered me. Instead he was outside in the driveway, waiting for something. I wrapped more cloth around the pipes until the layer of insulation was maybe three inches in diameter in the bare spots more or less matching the original insulation. I was proudly admiring my handiwork when I heard a truck on Porterfield Place.

It was just then that a truck backed into the driveway and Dad opened the small window over the coal bin next to the furnace. The end of a loading chute appeared in the opening. I heard the rear of the truck bed grinding up until a stream of coal rushed down the chute filling up the coal bin. The white cloud of asbestos dust was quickly replaced by a thick black cloud of coal dust much of which ended up also in my lungs. But this was not your average anthracite. I had learned earlier in the day that Dad had arranged to have an acquaintance named Ben Brucia deliver a truckload of industrial soft coal for a bargain price. Of course, Freeport's zoning laws did not permit the burning of soft coal in residential heating plants for obvious reasons but it was a bargain nonetheless.

Last night in my jacuzzi the memory rushed back to me from deep storage. As I puffed on my cigar, contemplating the stars, I wondered why I had not long since succumbed to either asbestos poisoning or black lung disease or a combination of the two. Mom's answer if she were here would, of course, consist of her two favorite genetic words "sturdy stock."

THE DAREDEVIL'S DUE

usmc

"Wisdom is seldom gained without suffering."
- Helps

It was a warm, humid Friday night in July, during World War II. Mark told his parents he was going to the Boy Scout meeting in the church basement, but he went elsewhere instead. A week before, he had seen one of the posters proclaiming that on Friday night, Joey Chitwood and his Daredevils would be at the stadium on the edge of the marshland, a few miles from his home. The poster suggested that Joey Chitwood had been kind enough to depart from his world tour to grace the boy's village with his show of derring-do and dented cars. The posters displayed a car leaping through fire and air, high above the roaring crowd, diving towards a row of derelict cars. Mark had not discovered girls yet. His only love affairs were with cars, preferably speeding cars. This show was the stuff his dreams were made of.

Mark was a war-lean, tough nine-year-old with a shock of black hair that never stayed combed. His wardrobe consisted of used, war-surplus combat boots and baggy pocket fatigues. All his pals went to the same shabby store in the village to buy the used, surplus Army clothing. They were the children of the Second World War and lived each day with the chatter of the ack-ack guns practicing on the barrier beaches just beyond the marsh, and the nightly air raid drills too. Wearing the used uniforms and turning in pieces of scrap metal found in the desolate wooded area near their homes was their way of supporting the war effort.

On Friday night, Mark skipped the Boy Scout meeting, heading for the stadium to see Joey Chitwood instead. He hiked the miles to the stadium and waited until dark. Once it was dark enough, Mark approached the rear of the stadium, working his way through the mosquito infested marsh, like the ghost of a British Commando, scaling the chain link fence undetected. Elderly volunteer firemen were stationed along the fence, acting as guards to keep out fare-beaters like Mark, but they didn't see the ghost.

Things worked out fine. Mark eluded the guards, as he had many times in the past and found an unoccupied seat on the 50-yard line. What followed was an evening of burning tires, hot exhaust and stunning impacts as the Daredevils raced old cars up wood ramps, flying through the air, and crashing them into everything conceivable. The war-weary crowd roared with enthusiasm with each act. The air was filled with sounds of racing engines, screeching tires, the boom of crumpling fenders and the smell of hot metal. Mark was mesmerized.

On the hike homeward, at eleven o'clock, Mark was euphoric. The evening had exceeded his expectations. He had not told any of his pals about this night of bacchanal revelry. It would remain a secret, at least until tomorrow. Mark's mind was still happily digesting the events, as he hiked along the highway in the dark, passing an occasional lamplight, haloed by the creeping, coastal fog. He was lost in thought.

By eleven the village was ready for bed and was quiet, except for the chorus of crickets and the wail of a distant freight train. As he hiked along, Mark became aware of soft footsteps behind him. The muffled steps drew nearer and some primordial instinct signaled to Mark. He maintained his pace and casually slipped his hand into his fatigues, grabbing his Boy Scout knife, which was as sharp as a razor. He took out the knife, opened it, and held it against his pants-leg.

It was probably a late traveling villager, or— it might be one of those Nazi saboteurs, who came ashore from a U-boat recently. *A Boy Scout must always be prepared*, he reminded himself. Mark was prepared.

"Hey, wait up," called the late traveler. Mark turned to see a slightly built, nondescript stranger skipping a few steps to catch up. The stranger smiled and said, "Where're you headed?" Mark lost all suspicion and enthusiastically told the stranger about The Joey Chitwood Daredevils.

"I'm one of the Daredevils," the stranger quickly volunteered.

Holy Smokes, Mark thought! *Fancy actually meeting one of his new Heroes. Wait until tomorrow,* he fantasized, *the guys will never believe it.* He grinned and began chatting with the Daredevil, and the Devil smiled back. They approached the wooded area in the gathering fog, sharing tales of derring-do, the stranger and the boy. Mark was delighted. What a coincidence. The two pals were getting along swell, as they left the last lamplight behind them. Then, the conversation took a strange turn. "Do you like wrestling?" asked the Devil, with a smile.

Mark did not know what to think of the question and was still forming a reply, as the Devil said, "Here, let me show you a wrestler's hold," and struck with lightening speed, locking Mark's arms over his head. Mark was stunned. Mark had been taught to respect his elders, but something was awry here. He was helpless. He didn't want to wrestle with an adult anyway.

The Devil smelled oddly. He was sweating, panting in Mark's ear and his breath was foul, as he forced Mark off the highway and into the deeper woods. Then panic erupted in Mark's stomach and he finally reacted.

The razor sharp Scout knife was still gripped tightly in his hand, unnoticed by the Devil. In a panic, Mark reached over his shoulder and struck the Devil, frantically, solidly, again and again. The Devil grunted and loosened his sweaty grip, and Mark twisted out of his greasy hands. Once free, Mark raced off through the dark, foggy woods. His heart was pounding loudly, sounding like the footsteps of the Devil in pursuit, but there was no pursuit.

When Mark reached his home, he was covered with sweat and sticky, drying blood. He stopped at the outdoor shower by the kitchen door and tried to wash away the blood and the night. Mark was frantic. He knew he had broken the law and might go to jail. He had stabbed a Daredevil and he did not know why it had happened. He was confused. *The police will be knocking on the door in the morning, and Mom and Dad will disown me,* he cried, head bowed in despair.

After the cold, sobering shower, Mark took off his soggy, bloody clothes and cunningly stuffed them under a load of soaking laundry in the old wringer washing machine. Then, he went to bed with his knife gripped tightly in hand, trembling, wide-awake, waiting. On through the night, Mark replayed the violent events, confused, expecting the

Devil to step through his bedroom door at any minute. Finally, despite his best efforts to be vigilant, he slept.

Mark awoke to sunlight shining through the window. All Saturday, he waited for the police to come for him. Each knock on the door made him wince, but the police never came. After a week of endless nights, Mark's fears eased a little and the following Saturday, his pals suggested a bike ride to the stadium. Mark felt secure with his pals around him and went along. At the stadium, Mark looked cautiously about and saw nothing, but a bit of newspaper tumbling down the empty ball field, pushed by the onshore breeze. Joey Chitwood and his daredevils were gone. A few days later, the posters were gone too.

The sun's arc moved lower in the sky and summer vacation ended. Back in the classroom, Mark found the knotty problems of arithmetic, competing poorly with his dread of the night, the darker side of life, and— retribution. Mark carried that burden of dark guilt for years, never confiding in a soul. Then one day, he discovered the truth.

THE BOWL AND PITCHER

usn

"Put your trust in God, my boys, and keep your powder dry."
Oliver Cromwell

The Spokane River ran right past the Gonzaga University campus then wended it's way in a southwesterly direction running through the main part of down town. As it went through the city it dropped several hundred feet through a series of rapids, one of which was named "the Bowl and Pitcher". The name derived from the unique cylindrical rock formation directly in the middle of the river rising ten or fifteen feet above the surface at normal water levels. The rock (pitcher) was perhaps fifteen feet in circumference at its base and the fast-moving water created an eddy (bowl) behind it that was perhaps ten feet lower than the surface of the water at the upstream face of the pitcher. The rock was tilted slightly downstream toward the eddy. Hence the name, Bowl and Pitcher. A few hundred feet upstream was a low footbridge and then perhaps a half mile downstream was a huge waterfall. Between the footbridge and the waterfall the river's course was swift and steep.

In the spring of 1947 the snow run-off from the mountains was particularly heavy and the river's level rose substantially; so much so that the river gave off a low but powerful sound of rushing water as it passed the university campus, and the lower portion of the city was flooded.

My friend, Bob "Sarge" O'Rourke, a WWII army veteran who lived in my dormitory, owned an army surplus five-man life raft. Another veteran, Lyle "Joe" Steffens, Dick Kelly, a non-veteran student and I were watching the river in full flood from the back of the dormitory one day, obviously bored with campus life at the moment. It was almost predictable that one of us came up with the idea of running the rapids in the life raft but I cannot remember which of us verbalized it. Joe is dead, I've lost track of Dick Kelly and Sarge O'Rourke can't remember. No matter; it was a grand scheme.

We reconnoitered the rapids in Sarge's new Studebaker for an hour or so considering all the possible scenarios; then drove down to the edge of the floodwaters at a riverside park. Here we unloaded the raft, waded out to the middle of a street, got in and paddled off on our ill-considered adventure. A small crowd had gathered to watch us and someone must have called the Sheriff's office.

By general agreement, Joe and I were in the stern, I on the left and Joe on the right. Dick and Bob were in the bow. We all wielded wooden canoe paddles. The current swept us along rather swiftly and I became vaguely alarmed at how clumsy we were at steering the craft. Our first hurdle was rapidly approaching, the small footbridge. The water had risen so far that there was no more then 24 inches of clearance from the top of the raft to the bottom of the bridge. We all had to lay flat to pass under it.

We were being swept directly at the Bowl and Pitcher now, and I called out to Joe that we should pass it on the left. Joe answered, "No, right."

I countered with, "No, left."

"No, right," was Joe's rejoinder as we ran smack, dead center into the huge rock. The bow of the raft rose up the face of the rock several feet, as Dick Kelly was flung halfway out of the raft and onto the face of the rock. We hung there for a moment then capsized and went around the right side, over the edge of the drop-off and tumbled into icy cold water.

My next awareness was that all was pitch black, but I was alive and breathing and kicking like crazy to stay afloat countering the weight of my logging boots and heavy jacket. The top of my head touched something cold and wet and I realized I was under the overturned raft. Coming out from under, I clung to the raft and looked around, counting heads as I did so. Everyone was there, gasping and hanging on for dear life. The sound of a siren caught my attention. There high above us, on the west bank of the river was a Sheriff's patrol car calling to us on the bullhorn to get out of the river. That was when I remembered the waterfall!

"Kick hard for the bank", I yelled. We were moving so fast that I began to doubt whether we could make the fifty feet or so to the bank before we would be swept over the cataract. The east bank was boulder-strewn and very steep, but away from the Sheriff. We climbed up the bank pulling the raft after us. At one point halfway up the bank, Sarge fell face down and began to vomit.

"Come on", I grunted, "It's only about fifty feet more."

Scratched, bruised and shivering violently we all collapsed on a narrow dirt road waiting for Sarge's car to come pick us up. I do not remember who was driving. But I do remember the police on the opposite bank yelling at us to stay where we were, and that we were under arrest.

My memory fails me as to how we eluded the police but I do remember the newspaper headline the next day with pictures of us in the river hanging on to the overturned raft, and clambering up the river bank. The article mentioned that people had attempted to run the Bowl and Pitcher rapids over the years and that we were the first to survive it!

THE SPOKANE CANNONBALL

usn

"Fortune favors the audacious."
- Erasmus

In the summer of 1946, at age 17, I arrived at Gonzaga University, Spokane, WA, in the Naval Aviation College Program, which paid my books, fees and tuition and a miserly stipend of $50.00 per month to cover food and other expenses. My official rank was apprentice seaman in the reserves. As far as Mom and Dad knew, I was on my own and self-sufficient. It quickly became clear to me that, if I wanted to eat, a part time job was needed…and fast. I got a job immediately, serving at the school cafeteria during meals, which paid for my own sustenance. Then, to additionally supplement my finances, I got a part-time job cleaning the offices at a nearby cement plant every Thursday evening after the plant closed.

There was a minor detail; I would have to walk the three miles to the plant each way, which would entail more time than I wanted to spend. I could clean the small office space in about two hours. It was a three hour cleaning job which I was able to accomplish in two by hustling.

The plant was located at a rail siding with one of the cement loading hoppers straddling one of the railroad lines. Each Thursday evening, as I was locking up the office, I noticed a freight train chugging laboriously up the track which ran north out of town and passed along the banks of the Spokane River just below the college campus.

My dormitory perched on a bluff overlooking the river (and the railroad track). Here, I thought, was the answer to my dilemma.

I would jog alongside the right rear side of a freight car and jump up grabbing a rung on a ladder and at the same time putting my foot on the bottom rung. Then I would scramble up three or four rungs and hang on for the five minute run to my jump-off point at the campus. Since the train accelerated as it headed out of town, it was going a pretty good clip when it passed Gonzaga. A large pile of soft coal, about twenty feet high, stood alongside the track just below my dormitory and provided a landing spot that was reasonably safe though not very clean. I would time my jump, hit about halfway up the side of the coal pile, then roll down to the ground, dust myself off while the remainder of the train passed then scramble up the bluff into the dormitory showers and clean up…simple!

This routine worked for several weeks until the train engineer caught on to my game. Each night, we would make eye contact when he chugged slowly past where I was standing. I waited until I thought I was out of his sight before beginning my run. On the night in question he looked at me knowingly as he passed with much more steam hissing around the pistons. When I thought it was safe I began jogging along the loose gravel which made up the roadbed. This particular evening I was wearing moccasins and my footing was not as secure as I ran; also the train seemed to be going a little faster than usual. The target rung for my hands was about eight feet above the roadbed; and the darkness and extra steam was making visibility a little degraded. When I launched, I got a firm grip with both hands and swung my right foot up to land on the bottom rung of the ladder. What happened next still rings in my memory with terrifying clarity. My right foot hit the bottom rung of the ladder and slipped through all the way to my crotch. It was so startling that I hardly felt the pain of the impact with the "family jewels." I looked down and saw the toe of my right foot touching the front face of the train wheel about six inches above the rail. A healthy jolt of adrenaline kicked in and I hauled myself up and onto the third rung of the ladder in a nano-second. As the train approached my drop off point it was going like hell.

The engineer was clearly showing me who was in charge and was going to teach me a lesson. Luckily, my jump landed me in the coal pile but the impact even with such a soft medium knocked a little bit of my breath from my lungs. As I stepped out of the shower ten minutes later my decision was unequivocal; I had gone on my last free train ride!

A Midnight Burling Contest

usn

"There's never been a bond, old friend, like this---We have drunk from the same canteen!"
C.G. Halpine – The Canteen

Located just below the Gonzaga University campus in Spokane Washington, at the river's edge, was a saw mill. Its cutting blade made an almost constant, high-pitched whine during operating hours. The mill pond was a collecting area in the Spokane River itself set off by a long string of huge logs connected at each end by metal eyes screwed into the ends of the logs and short lengths of chain. Logs coming down stream were guided into the collecting area by lumberjacks wearing logging boots equipped with spikes and employing poles with sharp hooks on the end. They would walk around blithely on the logs pushing, prodding and jumping from log to log with the grace and balance of ballet dancers. It is called "burling."

When loggers gather together at the end of a job to celebrate, there are contests to demonstrate various logging skills. The contests include cutting with axes, two man saws, chain saws, "topping" and, most fun of all burling. Two loggers jump on a free-floating log and get the log spinning rapidly with their spiked boots. Then they try to put their opponent into the icy water by stopping the spinning motion and reversing it. There is much laughter, much beer consumed and many soaking wet, rueful loggers watching their competitors get their just desserts. The danger was deceptive but ever-present. Each log weighed tons. If you fell into the water between two of them there was almost a certainty of being maimed, drowned or crushed to death. Loggers lived "for the gusto."

The beauty of our "mill pond" became clear to us when we returned from having given Sarge's life raft its baptism of fire in the Bowl and Pitcher rapids. There was a strict policy on the Jesuit campus which prohibited the consumption of alcohol. But, there directly below our dormitory, Campion Hall, was an off-campus haven where we could drink beer to our hearts' content from the haven of our life raft. Our inflatable saloon enjoyed all the immunity of a floating gambling ship. The "Jebbies" couldn't touch us, or so we thought!

So we had to test out the thesis. One night, after lights out (10:00 pm), Sarge sneaked out and came back with two six packs of cold beer. Four of us; Sarge, Joe, Dick and I slid down the embankment with our beer and the life raft. The water into which we waded was much colder than the beer but principle was involved in our bold defiance of the Jesuit rules. We had to crawl out of the raft and onto one of the logs which made up the containment ring, lift the raft over the log then crawl back into the raft. With all four of us standing on the log the precariousness or our circumstance came quickly to each of us. The log rolled and bobbed under the combined weight of four spirited college students, evoking some noise from all of us.

I saw instantly the light come on in the window of the end room in the dormitory, the one occupied by Mister Haven the Jesuit priest-in-training, our dormitory monitor. By now, however, we were all ensconced in our raft, albeit cold and wet, and we were enjoying our first seaborne beer. The light went out after a brief period during which we held our breaths. The second beer inspired a certain recklessness and we began singing our favorite drinking songs. This was turning out to be a glorious evening and everything any of us said seemed hilariously funny. The light came on again in Mister Haven's window and this time a flashlight appeared in swinging arcs along the base of the dormitory probing the underside of the crawl space. Again we held our breath but this time with much stifled giggling. The flashlight retraced its tour and the light went out in the monitor's room. Sarge suddenly decided he had to relieve himself and stood up to do his ministering. Harry Houdini, in his prime, would have had difficulty accomplishing such a balancing feat. Sergeant O'Rourke, now on his third beer, never had a chance. Over the side he went with a roar of laughter from all of us. We retrieved him and, our two six packs gone, we decided to call it a night.

The unplanned burling contest began when all four of us stood on the containment log to haul the raft across it, now two six packs lighter. One of the other three decided to play a game and began rolling the log back and forth and at the same time bouncing up and down. In a second all four of us, now laughing uncontrollably, were in the icy water. This time when the light came on and the flashlight began probing towards the river we knew we were in big trouble. Huddling down in shallow water behind a rock, we watched the flashlight beam searching the rock itself but we were lucky. It seemed like an eternity, during which the cold water and danger of being caught had a very sobering effect on our spirits.

My memory fails me as to how long it took us to get back into our bunks undetected, and for our core body temperatures to return to normal, but we all agreed as we said our good nights, that it had truly been a glorious evening!

PER LA FAMIGLIA

usmc

"Every man owes his coming into being, his nourishment and his training to his parents.
Likewise, the individual members of a family assist each other in regard to the necessities of life."
- St. Thomas Aquinas, "Summa Theologica"

There is an Italian dinner toast: "Per La Famiglia." When I first heard the toast, it seemed so fitting, so proper that I've employed it at family gatherings ever since. The toast best expresses the mood of these pages.

When acquaintances were informed that there were nine children in my family, they invariable ask, "How was it?" They meant that they expected there would be many differences from their childhood lifestyles, and wondered what those differences were.

We learned to adapt, referee, share, and so on. One spin-off of such circumstance was the sharing of everything. Music, food, art, language, friends, mindsets, politics, religion, the list was endless.

For example, when someone gave us some records of the Strauss' waltzes, we all listened to the "Blue Danube" and acquired a taste for Strauss. There was no choice. And in my memories of that big old house, there was always some activity in progress. No matter which room you entered, someone was engaged in homework, a scout project, music lessons, cooking, maintenance, song, sewing, or practicing conversational French, German, Spanish and let's not forget Latin. Passé du beurre, s'il vous plait!

"52 Porterfield Place" was like a small private school. The exposure was there. Through the years, I've noticed that each of us is a born teacher. Perhaps it comes from years of teaching each other about individual interests. In fact, this manuscript has a lesson in each chapter. Couldn't help myself.

That teaching extended to nutrition as well. We were also taught to eat what was placed in front of us. It might not be appetizing but it would be nourishing. In a subtler manner, music, art, literature, and so on were presented for our consumption because of their particular value. This wasn't chance, Mom was always thinking ahead.

At the dinner table for example, we could be corrected by another sibling. It was a right, If the topic one chose to speak on was inappropriate; someone would say "Not of general interest", and the conversation would take another turn. This was standard operating procedure.

Mother had been a schoolteacher, so the temptation was too great for her to resist when she found a blackboard. Dad mounted that blackboard on the wall near the dinner table. The blackboard served as a learning aid during meals. It also served as a community bulletin board, notice to mariners, memo pad, whatever.

There was a subnormal lad in the neighborhood named Petey, who would walk in through the kitchen door unannounced, say hello, and feel right at home. Petey would go straight to the blackboard, erase everything, all the notes, schedules and so on and begin to draw. He loved to draw on that blackboard. As I write, I have to ask myself, how it was that Petey fit in so well?

That blackboard was like my soul in a way. Many concepts were impressed on it in those formative years. Life's environment has since erased much, but like an old blackboard, if you look carefully, there are ingrained, shadowy and sometimes elusive images that cannot be erased.

All things considered, that young couple of yesteryear managed the raising of their family pretty well. None of us ended up a cropper. The family managed higher education, albeit, on the government or on our own hook at night. There are about nine Masters degrees. There are about fifty grandchildren, many of whom are professionals.

Some of the siblings made significant marks in life. John, a Navy Captain, the eldest, was the pacesetter. He set quite a pace. I've been trying to keep up ever since. Dan, an author and the youngest, has the most influential circle of friends, extending to the White House during two administrations. Paul, a legendary fighter pilot, picked as one of the ten most influential aviators of the century, retired an admiral and is now an author, television scriptwriter, actor and lecturer. Jim, another author, is the most prolific, with nine boys and a girl. Jim was a mathematician and needed to be with that family. Jim is also a gold medalist and World Champion in the Seniors Track and Field competitions, retiring undefeated. Sr. Eve, a Dominican, was an editor and now, at 82, teaches new citizens in NY's inner city. Mary, a nurse, is a gifted artist. Anne, as a single parent managed to direct her family through Harvard and into medicine. Frances, an educator, dazzled us all at a recent gathering with her authorship of an extremely sensitive and insightful film on the family. I'm proud of them all.

Once when asked if I ever had a pet as a youngster I replied that we couldn't afford pets, but there were nine of us, so I had eight pets all of whom had an intellect.

An acknowledgement of the virtues and concepts the family shared with me follows:

Dad practiced humility and a rigid sense of duty, Mom instilled curiosity, John - leadership, Eve - compassion, Jim - a love of nature and music, Paul - courage, Anne - constancy, Mary - forbearance and hope, Frances - humor and Dan, the caboose, - the notion that the last can be first.

PART II

SOMEWHERE EAST OF SUEZ

The line from Rudyard Kipling's poem, *Mandalay* has always engendered visions of its very content: palms swaying in the sea breeze, temple bells, the Irrawaddy, and more arcane visions, such as a small Buddhist altar. I saw an altar nestled among the roots of a banyan tree on a lonely jungle trail. It was a tiny altar with joss sticks smoking and a painted dish with an offering of shrimp for Buddha. Shrimp mind you, something that I never saw in any farmer's rice bowl.

Viet Nam was my Mandalay. I loved the country and the folk who toiled in the paddies. So it seemed proper to collect Viet Nam and Asia stories and lump them together under the unlikely title: *Somewhere East of Suez*.

MANDALAY

usmc

"What's done, is done. And what's won, is won. And what's lost,... is gone forever"
- Coulter

One warm, humid, Sunday afternoon, I met the rest of the crew at one of the nicer hotels in Saigon. The hotel was a typical earth tone tropical structure, with high ceilings, ornate terracotta escutcheons and bandings, topped with a roof garden. In front of the hotel, a cobbled area was set aside as a sidewalk cafe. The crew gathered, grouped several tables together and sat for a drink and a chat. The hotel was one of those frequently used for housing newly arrived personnel.

As the crew was relaxing and chatting, a cab pulled up and a pasty faced, nervous, overweight fellow got out. His eyes were darting about as if he expected to see a hand grenade flying his way at any moment. It was obvious to the crew that this was a newbie right off an airliner from The World.

The cab driver sat impatiently behind his wheel, waiting to be paid. The newbie was acting like paying the cabby was a final act in coming to Viet Nam. He still wasn't sure he wanted to do it. Besides, he was unfamiliar with the wad of piasters clutched in his sweaty palm.

The newbie's flight had probably arrived within the last hour or so. He reached into the cab and pulled out one of his bags, placing it on the cobblestones. Next, he turned back to the cab driver to pay him.

One of the undernourished little street kids saw his chance, grabbed the bag and ran off, struggling with the bag. The newbie spotted this blatant theft and raced after the kid.

The crew sat there, enjoying the show, shouting encouragement to the little street kid as he struggled to make away with a bag half his weight.

As the newbie was closing in on the street kid, the crew shouted after the newbie, warning him to keep one eye on the cabby. The newbie turned in time to see the cabby pull away, taking his other bags, in lieu of a tip. With an Olympian effort, the newbie turned and raced after the cab.

The crew was having a grand time watching the goings on. It was the best entertainment the crew had enjoyed in months. The newbie came staggering back, gasping for air, covered with sweat, head hanging. In that moment, if he had a gun, he would have used it on us all. He was seething with anger. On the other hand, the crew and I were hysterical, tears running down our lean, weathered cheeks as we laughed loudly, ruthlessly.

The newbie stalked into the hotel, *picked clean* within his first hour in Saigon.

Back in the turbulent '60s, I was a young construction engineer: tall and tanned the color of coffee beans by the tropical sun. Most of the staff, thought that I was too young, too inexperienced, when I arrived, but they soon changed their view, because of my single-mindedness about completing the tasks, no matter what was happening or who was shooting at you. That was what we were in Viet Nam for, to get the projects done.

The newbie's' fleecing was part of a phenomenon that occurs, whenever someone enters a new environment. The predators recognize the stranger's tentative steps, the furtive looks, the nervous response to normal background sounds, and so on.

The same thing happens on the Serengeti. The hyenas spot an easy, confused prey in a similar way. Then, afterwards, when the killing is done, the rest go back to the watering hole satisfied that the inevitable has taken place again, and the *weak sister* has been culled.

The crew had all been through the same gantlet. They all had learned that when they first walked the unfamiliar streets of Saigon. The urchins, living by their wits, had dogged the crew's heels too, looking for an opportunity. And the cowboys, the city thugs, had given them the once-over, trying to decide if they would make a killing or be killed.

My solution to the problem was to accept the street people and become a regular customer for things like the little packets of peanuts that the street kids rolled up in old newspaper, forming a cone. The urchins sold the cones to me at inflated prices, but I pretended I didn't know better. I liked the moxie of those little urchins and they knew it. The urchins would spot me as I clomped over the cobbled streets in my jungle boots at sundown, dirty, tired, my shirt white with salt. They would run to me, shouting, and stand, chatting and haggling, as I searched for change. The street kids would start to cajole me, clutching their newspaper cones in dirty little hands, lying about not having change themselves, speaking in patois: "You dingiedao! Number 10! Ten pi, ok? Sau! Sin loi, Charlie. Choi hoi!"

There was one gamine-faced little girl, about nine years old, who I particularly liked. She always wore the same black pajamas and threadbare shirt over her bony shoulders. She was tough, resourceful and upbeat, and would generally out-shuffle the others. I used to call her Tiger, which was *Cop* in Vietnamese. *"Cop dee dau,"* I'd call to her as we approached in the street.

Cop and I would usually meet in the evening somewhere on Tu Do Street near the Caravelle, the hotel favored by the war correspondents. We would stand there in the dusk as flatulent scooters whizzed by, horns pleading, soup seller's bonging, shouting over the street noises, haggling, six-foot-five versus three-foot-five.

After we completed our transaction, Cop would smile and run off, and I would watch her join up with two little wisps of boys. The boys would look up at Cop and she would take one in each hand. Then, the threesome would disappear into the gloamin'.

I would like to think that there now is a beautiful woman called Cop, with raven hair, streaked with just enough gray. I would like to see her and watch her nimble mind at work and that gamine smile too. And, I would like to see those two wisps, now, in a cleaner, greener land, when the mist is on the rice fields.

As Kipling put it, *"For the wind is in the palm-trees and the temple-bells; they say: "Come you back, you British soldier: come you back to Mandalay!"*

NUC

usmc

"Observations made in the cloister or in the desert will generally be as obscure as the one,
or as barren as the other; but he that would paint with his pencil must study originals,
and not be over-fearful of a little dust"
- Colton

From time to time, I experience something I call mind pictures. One of those mind pictures is an impressionist image of Vietnam: a commonplace scene that I always enjoyed. The background is the ever-present rice paddy, bordered by the rich and varied greens of the land. In the forefront is a young boy in shorts, about six years old, atop the shoulders of a truculent water buffalo with thick ebony horns. The boy is singing a folk song. In the boy's hand, a slender bamboo switch the boy uses to guide and control a beast 20 times his size — a metaphor of the War.

Someone once asked me what I thought of Vietnam. He expected me to speak ill of the country, but I fooled him. There were two thoughts that came immediately to mind in reply.

First, Vietnam gave me an opportunity to examine at first hand the closest replication of the Middle Ages that I would ever encounter. There were so many examples. Sanitation, food preparation and preservation, medicine, public safety, animal husbandry, transportation, illiteracy, opium dens, beggars, and all against a backdrop of bubonic plague, leprosy, and the ever present question: Is that spittle betel-nut or tuberculosis? It was a unique experience. The time spent in Vietnam makes my reading of the Middle Ages much more meaningful. I feel as though I have been there.

Secondly, the land and its country people were beautiful. The country folk used to take me by the hand and tow me around like a water buffalo, to show me a problem that needed solving. They would laughingly call me U*ng Vietnamese,* meaning that I was a Vietnamese, because I would always try to speak to them in their language. Incidentally, the language was unique because it used our system of letters. Nowhere else in the orient is that true.

In contemplative moments since Vietnam, I've imagined living in Dalat in the Thirties: before Japan's expansionism. In the Marines, we had an expression: G*oing Asiatic.* It was something that Marines occasionally did. They fell in love with some foreign land and stayed, never again seeing their homeland. If I had been in Indochina in the 30s, I would probably have G*one Asiatic.*

The rice beetle is another image that comes to mind when I try to epitomize Vietnam. That bug is the subject of awe when first seen by westerners. It is outlandishly large; growls like a small mammal and apparently eats rice. The rice beetle is a fitting companion to the myriad oddities of the land. It was a constant source of pleasure for an amateur naturalist to come across treats like the rice beetle.

The flora is interesting. One unique plant, common to that part of Vietnam, was on occasion the cause for alarm. This plant would instantly wilt if touched. Once touched, it would stay in that wilted state for about 10 minutes. Then, the plant would rise back up to its original state. Whenever I was on my own, walking a jungle trail, and saw the plant in this wilted state it told me that someone or something was moving along the trail, just ahead of me, out of sight.

The country folk were a constant source of amazement to me. I couldn't help liking them. A mind picture that I like to recall is of an event that took place at dawn; *as the sun came up like thunder, out 'a China 'cross the Bay.* Bill Dunlap and I were driving past a series of paddies in our jeep when I noticed an old man thigh deep in one of the flooded rice paddies. His pajamas were rolled up high; he was backlit by the blood-red glow of dawn. The paddy water created his twin. Together they were using a piece of aluminum from a downed plane to scoop water from one paddy, over the dike into the next paddy. At sunset, after a long hot day, we retraced our steps and I looked for him again. The level of the water was not perceptibly higher, but the old man was still scooping with measured strokes.

This mind picture was of more than a farmer at work. It was a mission statement of the people. This rice paddy was that old farmer's land. It was the source of sustenance for his family. He would do whatever was necessary to defend it. In his mind, the land and the people were inexorably connected. The farmer knew that the one was the wellhead of the other.

Occasionally, we would come across a man-made clay formation, a rectangular, low, wall. These formations were so similar to the burial sites I have seen in France and elsewhere that I recognized them as individual graves. The locations were always on a rise above the terraced paddies. My immediate impression was that the family placed the farmer's body in a location, which allowed him to watch over his fields. It was simple, tranquil, proper and beautiful. It said so much about the land and its people.

Modesty among women was quintessential. By mistake I surprised some women bathing one day and was surprised myself, when they screamed and covered their eyes. At least I think they covered their eyes. I happened to be looking elsewhere! The idea was that if they covered their eyes, they would not see the interloper and would not be embarrassed the next time they met him.

The women were earthy, in conflict with their chaste, modest nature. This will be a shock to some, but I often would stop to chat with the women on the Site. We had many of them working as common laborers. It was reported to me that the women wondered if I was proportionally large all over.

With this in mind, as I walked up to a group of female laborers at work, I'd stand there, hands on hips and shout the Vietnamese equivalent of "Does anybody wanna to get laid?" They would all shout back, "Me first, me first." Then we would all have a good laugh. I liked them for their humility.

About Buddhists: it was pleasant to discover the many, little altars they erected in the oddest places. One comes to mind. It was nestled among the roots of a banyan tree on a lonely jungle trail. A tiny altar with joss sticks smoking and a painted dish with an offering of shrimp for Buddha.

In the beginning, I was distracted by their habit of stopping for an opium break. They would squat and light up their pipes. Not all of them, but quite a few smoked. Later, I put myself in their place. Suppose I had to walk home in the dark, to my hut, having nothing for my family to eat that night. I would smoke. Or worse, if I was stopped by the VC on the way to the Site in the morning and told to steal two flashlight batteries, and was unable to do so, I'd be upset at the prospect of returning home.

What would I have done with my time, if I had *Gone Asiatic* and settled in Dalat? I have dreamt of it often, through the years. I would have bought a drilling rig. Mounted it on a four-wheel drive truck and traveled the back roads of Viet Nam, drilling water wells in the villages. Clean, *nuc* (water) is what the country folk need most. I had prior experience with drilling rigs and knew I could manage it by myself. I considered the idea do-able.

Funny thing! A few years ago, my wife, my sister, Eve, and I arranged for a well in a little village in the mountains of Honduras. It was easy! And, after a chat with one of my brothers about Honduras and the need for hand tools, he called Home Depot's home office and spoke to the CEO. In a few months, Honduras received 75,000 pounds of hand tools. It was easy!

THE SHOEMAKER

usmc

"So wise, so young, they say, do never live long."
- Shakespeare

Not long after one of the attacks on the Site, I happened to be talking to some of the troops about the charcoal-maker's hamlet to the northwest of the Site. Whatever prompted us to do it, I don't recall, but we decided to check out the hamlet. There were four of us as we walked the trail towards the hamlet.

The three paratroopers were soft-spoken, lean youngsters with eyes that were a hundred years old: so wise, so young. Their slant pocket paratrooper jackets were white with salt. Their jungle boots were in tatters. All the new boots seemed to go to the rear echelon warriors. All their weapons were clean and oiled though, and the paratroopers carried them like extensions of their arms.

The mission that hot humid day was to baby-sit the Site Engineer, a lanky guy with a high opinion of himself.

They were such quiet young men: those paratroopers. My personal conviction was that they would rather die than admit to any weakness.

One rainy morning comes to mind, as proof of this. It was just before a mission, a group of those young men were sitting in my Soils Lab; bantering; insulting each other; nervously covering up for their jitters. The door of the lab popped open and their sergeant stuck his head in to bark out orders to load onto the trucks for the trip to Bien Hoa and the slicks that would deliver them into battle.

One slim young man stood and walked out to the truck as in a trance, leaving his M-16 leaning against the wall of the lab. I spotted this enormous gaff and started after him with the M -16 held tight against my leg, in hopes of smoothing over this manifestation of his nightmarish fear.

The sergeant turned and saw me carrying the rifle and the paratroopers troubles escalated out of sight. I will always remember my anger with myself for not managing to cover up for him. You see, they were going out to fight and die. But I was staying in my lab; to run some soils tests.

When the sergeant walked up to the truck with the forgotten M-16, every man knew and understood. The truck was suddenly silent. Gone was the banter.

Getting back to the tale, part way to the village, the four of us moved off the trail to approach the little collection of huts and ovens from a different direction.

Just before we reached the hamlet, we came upon an open area. The open area was covered with chest-high grass. It was probably an old rice paddy. Once in the paddy, we spread out, line a breast, weapons resting on thighs and started across the open ground.

There were no domestic noises, smoke or movement that we could detect in the hamlet. This lack of normal activity made us even more cautious. Slowly, step by step, we moved towards the hamlet, pushing through the chest-high grass. The closer we got to the village, the greater the sense of anticipation. By then we were too far out in the old paddy to retreat if attacked. My eyes were boring into the hamlet, looking for some sign, an indicator, a warning. It was at that moment, gripping my weapon too tightly that it happened.

Maybe ten meters to our front, the grass rustled and movement was detected. It happened so fast! The four of us had been so intent on the hamlet that no one expected an encounter in the overgrown paddy. The kids, that's what those young paratroopers were, moved like lightening. Their reflexes were honed to a razor's edge, one operation after another, month in and month out. Those young paratroopers had become machines.

Guarding a nest in the tall grass had been a wood duck. The wood duck had burst from cover at sixty miles an hour and I had stood flat footed, incapable of the reactions that are absolutely essential for survival.

In that instant in the paddy, I realized that I had no business in this line of work. It was hard to accept, but an irrefutable truth. I was *too slow... too old.*

More to the point, I had committed a cardinal sin. A sin, that in the construction business results in being called, with disdain, "a shoemaker." The expression means someone in the building trades, say a carpenter, who does some brick laying and does it poorly. In other words, someone who does a poor job because it isn't what he was trained to do. The term comes from the expression, "A shoemaker, who strayed from his last."

My job was to provide support, not to join in the fray. Furthermore, those paratroopers did not appreciate being burdened by someone that was inexperienced and had no track record in combat. When will I learn?

Shit Happens

usmc

"There is no such thing as accident; it is fate misnamed."
- Napoleon

It's funny the way the memory plays tricks on the mind. The other day, at the behest of my brother, I was searching for photographs from my days in Viet Nam. The photos are few and far apart. Probably, I threw most of them out in a fit. What photos I did find were of friendly, unlined faces, but unfamiliar places.

In the background, there was nothing green, none of the verdant jungle I remembered. The land also appeared flat. These backgrounds puzzled me for a while. Then I concluded that the photos were focused on the faces and consequently, background became illusory. The photos and lack of detail in the background prompted the remembrance of a mystery.

The day of the mystery had started out quietly. There were no storm clouds or smoke or curious movements of the woodcutters on the neighboring hills. There was nothing untoward to report.

My air-conditioned office, a luxury that we wangled into the project, was set on high ground, maybe three hundred feet higher than the adjacent Michelin rubber plantation. Earlier in the day, I had sent out a survey party of Vietnamese to check out some problem in the area bordering the rubber trees.

The sudden rattle of small arms fire brought me out of the office. Down in the rubber trees, perhaps 1000 yards away, I could see smoke and dirty black puffs with a red wink in the center as rockets or mortars exploded, slamming into the green tops of the rubber trees.

This was alarming because my Vietnamese surveyors were in that area. I envisioned them being mowed down by the VC as another example to the populace.

Those surveyors were my responsibility and I liked them. We had been working together for some time. Whatever the stimuli, I hopped into the nearest jeep and headed for the Bien Hoa Highway.

I chose the jeep because it would have taken too long for me to walk the trails to the rubber trees. Besides, if I could find them in time, the jeep was just the thing for a quick getaway. The route out to the highway, then east along the highway to the track through the plantation, then into the plantation was quickest.

As I entered the rubber trees, I slowed to a quiet idle and crept along at a couple miles an hour. The firefight was over. There wasn't a sound other than the crunch of the tires and the beat of the engine. My better sense began to assert itself. Fear worked its way up my spine and my hair felt like it was standing up.

The jeep was too noisy, so I turned off the engine and got out. It was hard to orient myself once there were trees all around me. However, I couldn't go back without the surveyors, so I headed deeper into the plantation, moving from rubber tree to tree, thinking of Joyce Kilmer.

The rubber trees had been planted thirty years before by the French Colonials, back when the French ruled the natives without a glimmer of conscience. Every tree was scarred like an aged gladiator. The gladiators were in ranks, a double arms interval apart, patiently waiting their next wounding. They would wait forever.

There was a deaf-like silence, not even an insect buzz. Then, to make a bad situation worse, through the trees I spotted a herd of water buffalo browsing. There was no boy to mind them, which further heightened my anxiety. As soon as the buffaloes scented me, the bulls started walking towards me, lowering their ebony horns.

Only a few days before, some of the paratroopers had told me about an incident on their last operation. A water buffalo had charged a patrol and the whole patrol had emptied their M-16s into the animal without stopping it, before it had gored the point man. The paratroopers were spooked by the experience. So was I. The bulls kept coming, so I ran to the left to escape them.

Advancing warily through the trees, I expected to find the lumpy, bloody, bundles that were the bodies of my surveyors, grouped haphazardly together. After what seemed like a long time, slowly moving through the trees, in the silence, without finding any signs of the firefight, I gave in to my fear and jogged back to the jeep. Never did find out what happened. When I got back inside the wire, my surveyors were waiting.

At about that same time the staff sergeant stopped by to say that they had trouble. The officers were huddled around the communications jeep as reports came in on another company of paratroopers. It seems that the company was surrounded and had run out of ammunition. To make matters worse, the heavy weapons could not be brought to bear for some reason. The surrounded company kept calling for help until there was only silence. The paratroopers were stunned: an entire company of their brothers!

The paratroopers called the site of the massacre, Hobo Woods. Next day, as I stood at the construction site, the ground began to shudder and the skies rumbled like an approaching thunder storm, as B-52s dumped tons of explosives on Hobo Woods. It was only a few miles away. The magnitude of the forces at work was awesome. We never did find out how the massacre could have happened. It would be another mystery, something the paratroopers never talked about. We knew better than to ask.

Some time later I had another inexplicable event to deal with. The rattle of automatic weapons and the curious slap-pop of mortars brought me out of my office. Again, I jumped into the nearest jeep and headed for that area because my crew of Vietnamese was working there. This time they were working on a knoll. I slammed on the brakes of the jeep behind the knoll, and sprinted up the reverse slope looking for my crew. The crew was under attack by an unknown force.

The fire was intense, coming from the far side of the knoll, to the west. The mortars were exploding off to the front, but the small arms fire was heavy and seemed concentrated on the knoll, clipping twigs and tree trunks, after which the rounds tumbled, buzzing like bees. A round hit the ground just in front of me throwing earth and vegetation into my eyes.

My surveyors were all trying to make themselves as small as possible groveling on the ground. I lost my temper with them and roared at them and then, began kicking their collective butts off the hill. What in hell had prevented them from crawling back down the reverse slope on their own? Why did I have to come up to get them? What a bunch of clowns!

Perhaps my reaction was from relief that they were ok. Again, I never figured out what was going on. My guess was that a patrol of ROK troops from the unit to our west was probably making a sweep and spotted my Vietnamese on the knoll, mistaking the survey equipment for rocket launchers. The Koreans were crazy, always looking for a fight. They were capable of anything.

Here was another enigma, or as the philosophical paratroopers observed with a shrug, "Shit happens."

NIGHT SCENES

usmc

*"The room was bare and dark as death,
And each ferocious fighter could hear his fierce opponent's breath
And clutched his pistol tighter."*
- Service

For a while I lived with Dunlap and a guy named Royce, a young easterner. We lived in a villa, out near Tan Son Nhut, the huge airfield. The villa was on Trung Ming Yuan. We called the street "Truman." The two story villa was all masonry and tile, with no glass in the windows, just heavy grills, no screens. At night the anopheles mosquitoes (malaria) would alight on my body and draw blood. They would become so bloated, that they couldn't fly and would be crushed when I rolled over, leaving bloody smears on the sheet.

The Malay nurse on the Site insisted that we take Atabrine tablets to counter the Malaria. His reading skills needed improvement. One day, after weeks of consuming large doses of Atabrine, I asked to read the medical book on dosages. It turned out that he had misread the book and was administering about five times the prescribed dosage. We were a little suspicious because we were all turning yellow. That's always a good indicator; turning colors. 'Course he was yellow, so he didn't notice.

The villa was a stucco two story house with wrought iron grills over window openings. The floors were ceramic tile. There was the smallest of electric services, with the wiring plastered into the walls, no raceway of any kind. The kitchen had a cast iron range that was served by the universal fuel, charcoal. There was a cold water tap on the first floor which worked so long as the demand in the neighborhood was not too great. At night the demand was too great, so I'd scoop cold water out of the cistern and wash off.

The place was kept clean by an older woman called Ba. She was tall for a Vietnamese, very thin and exceptionally ugly. Names are strange in that a name can be anything. If someone is introduced as Joy or Happy, we accept that as their name. The name Ba, until the moment that I wrote this line, was not questioned by me. As I wrote the name, I realized that all the time I knew her, I was arrogantly calling her "Woman," that is what ba means in Vietnamese. How stupid of me.

Ba wore those black pajamas common in that country. Those pajamas were odd in that the women could slide one leg up as they squatted, relieve themselves, and stand up without a guy getting so much as a "peek." Bill Dunlap had a girlfriend named Nha who did nothing but pout. Ba worked for her. Nha treated Ba like an indentured servant. One day because Nha was bored, she went out and bought a baby. Wanted to look domestic for Dunlap, I guess. The little thing was a few months old and was entertaining for Nha for a few days. Then Nha got bored again, and discarded the baby, much like a child drops a toy. The baby lay in a corner, ignore, dehydrated, weakened by lack of food, like refuse.

Despite the daily uncertainty of providing for her own children, Ba took the baby home and cared for it. Ba kind of reminded me of my own mother the way she quietly nudged me to bring her food, or solve domestic problems. She would look at me and we would speak in patois, a mix of French, English and Vietnamese. Ba never complained; she would accept any considerations with a brief nod. I liked her and have often thought about her and the many other good, hard working folk I knew in Viet Nam. What has become of them? It's haunting me.

The villa was a nice arrangement but, I didn't stay long because of the lifestyles of the people there. For one thing, Dunlap used to abuse and beat Nha. It was often public and always loud. At night I could hear them in their room. One evening, as I sat reading, they had an argument and Bill hit her so hard with his fist that his watch broke. What I learned there was that a man could look and act like an ordinary person and be a wife beater. I liked Bill Dunlap, and have enjoyed the company of other men who later turned out to be incestuous, corrupt, defective. This is something that I am unable to reconcile.

It was my custom to sleep with a .45 cal. automatic under the pillow. One night in the midst of a deep sleep, I was abruptly awakened by the sound of shots. The shots sounded like they were right next to the bed. In the dark I groped for my .45 and couldn't find it. The shots were interspersed with Nha's screams and the tinkling sound made by shell casings hitting the tile floor. Dunlap was cursing passionately.

What to do? The bed was more of a pallet than a bed, so I couldn't even get under it. What a fix; shot in my skivvies; some end to it all. The options were limited, so I ran next door to Dunlap's room, not knowing what to expect.

What had happened was that Dunlap heard some noise in the night. He eased out of bed and came into my room to borrow my automatic. He neglected to wake me and inform me of this. Dunlap went back to his room which was second floor front of the villa to investigate the noise. There were some Vietnamese climbing the front of the villa intent on gaining entrance though his balcony. Whether they were VC, or just your garden variety burglar, we never found out.

What with disturbing his sleep and all, he decided to shoot first and ask questions later. When I entered the room the villains were sprinting down the street dodging the bullets. I took my gun back and told him he was a "horse's ass." Bill replied that he didn't want to disturb my rest. I had a bad case of jitters for the rest of the day. What I learned from the incident was that when surprised, people frequently don't react well. That is the reason for repetitive training.

On another night as I was sleeping fitfully, I heard a noise. This time the .45 was where it was supposed to be. The noise was on the first floor, so I slid down the spiral stairs on my belly. Moving along the wall towards the front of the villa, I saw the silhouette of a man. I crouched and steadied the .45. "Dung lai" I called, thinking it was a Vietnamese.

Fortunately I heard Dunlap curse and saw him swing towards me to fire his gun at the VC he thought just shouted at him. I shouted "don't shoot." Bill didn't.

The Saigon nights were often punctuated by automatic weapons fire. After the 11 pm Curfew, nobody was permitted on the streets.

Gun jeeps with sandbagged floors and .30 cal. machine guns moved through the dark, hunting. Whether it was the street patrols firing on shadows or clashes with VC, we seldom found out.

My nights became restless after many odd incidents. One classic incident makes me laugh today. The event took place after I found a place of my own. It was an evening when a group stopped by for a drink and a chat. We were lounging around my room enjoying ourselves, when the wizen little concierge came in. he kept jabbering excitedly and I couldn't follow him. The effort turned into a game of pantomiming and quizzing. As the gestures and pidgin progressed, a message evolved.

It was like "Wheel of Fortune." The message grew, along with our curiosity and finally, I took a stab. I asked the concierge if he meant that a VC had just placed a satchel charge against the outside wall of my room. The concierge nodded; yes. You should have seen the looks as we all dropped drinks, knocked over furniture and tried to get through the door together. As usual, the message was screwed up. The charge was placed at another location, a couple doors away; so much for "Wheel of Fortune."

There was a recurring dream that interrupted my sleep regularly. This became an exhausting, nightly event, after I found a place of my own on the edge of Saigon. The dream was strange. In the dream I would awake face down to feel people pinning my arms and legs down. They were quiet. They had come to lead me off to Cambodia, barefoot, bound. At first they were too strong for me, but with the adrenaline flowing full force, I would exert all my might and with an all consuming effort of will, grips would start to slip in the sweat. Finally, after a Herculean struggle, I'd break free and roll off the bed, soaked in sweat, gasping for air, exhausted, awake finally, and alone.

During an early dream, perhaps the progenitor, I awoke to see them by the door of the room. I grabbed my automatic and turned to fire but, they were gone. When I went to the door, it was opened as was the outside door. I never leave doors unlocked. Ask my wife, I lock doors all the time. She thinks I'm a little crazy. Maybe she is right.

BOOTS

usmc

"Grief has its time."
- Johnson

A few months ago, while puttering in my shop, I spied an old pair of boots. The boots were hiding behind some hardware, clinging to a metal shelf. They were white from sweat, scuffed and limp. In a flash, I could hear the rhythmic, thumping of helicopters and could smell aviation gas, hot metal, burning oil, and the thick, sweet scent of decay.

I remembered the day they dropped those boots from a chopper. Lt. Sullivan brought them to me. He was grinning, because my leather boots were falling apart in the tropical environment and I was holding them together with the wire from C-ration cases. The Lieutenant noticed my problem and presented me with a gift of proper jungle boots. They were green nylon, with black leather trim. The boots were light and dry, perfect for the climate, but they were the wrong size. With no option, I jammed my feet in, laced up, stamped hard, and in time the boots gave up and stretched to fit my hard feet.

For the next forty years, I wore those boots. I wore them when hunting or camping in the States. I climbed the Schneeberg in those boots. I recall some Austrian climbers passing us as we rested on the edge of a snowfield that July day. They saw the unlikely boots and exchanged glances. I looked them in the eye and the Austrians moved on. *Grüß Gott!*

There is a distant memory of boots, which has disturbed my rest for years. It is of a moment in time on the tarmac at Bien Hoa, against a background of feverish activity. Helicopters are ferrying the paratrooper into battle nearby, but the troops on the tarmac stand in silence, but for the beat of the helicopter's props. I remember nothing of the moment, but the platoon of whitened and worn, empty boots set in proper military order, heels together, toes at forty-five degrees, before the ceremonial formation.

There was a hot dry wind blowing across the airfield that day, and dust devils were marching slowly up and down the ranks of empty boots as if a review was in progress. As those dust devils passed, they left an offering of fine red clay on each pair of boots. I stood to the side, at respectful attention, blocking other thoughts, by imagining that the dust devils were performing some ancient, arcane ritual.

The events that led up to the ceremony had begun, for me, on a hill about 20 miles southwest of Bien Hoa. It was a week before and I was walking past a tight group of officers. They had gathered around the communication jeep. It was apparent that they were very upset. One slammed his helmet against the side of the jeep in frustration.

I quietly asked Lt. Dusty Rhodes, a friend, what was wrong. He shrugged me off, because he was listening to calls coming from another platoon. The voices were as far away as the moon. They were calls, asking someone to tell their wives that they had always loved them. There was a furious background chatter of small arms fire. NVA regulars had surrounded the platoon, a voice advised, and the platoon was just about out of ammunition. They were fixing bayonets, the last resort of warriors.

It was a place the troopers called *Hobo Woods*, over toward the Iron Triangle. Apparently, someone forgot to assign assets for the mission.

Forty years later, standing before the shelf in my shop, I made a long overdue decision. It was time to get boots off my scope. I drew my boots from the shelf, wrapped them neatly in brown paper. It was early morning, when I surreptitiously tucked them into the refuse can at the curb.

Irreconcilable Differences

usmc

"Here's to you, as good as you are,
And here's to me, as bad as I am;
But as good as you are, and as bad as I am,
I am as good as you are, as bad as I am."
    – Irish toast

"Remember to put the theatre tickets in your jacket," his wife reminded him, adding, "Let's not forget them like last month." With no recollection of where the tickets might be, Dan began pulled out drawers, and shoving the accumulation of useless junk about in a fevered effort to find the tickets. Then, in a musty corner, of a little used drawer, he found a faded photograph. He saw a much younger Dan; standing stiff-legged in sweat soaked khakis, fists tightly balled on hips, stone faced. Standing next to him, but an arm's length away was another khaki clad man in a hint of a wrestler stance, equally unsmiling.

The implications of the body language were clear. The two men were not comfortable being this close, or of having their picture taken together. They were not friends. The other man's name was Elwood Hudson.

Dan sat down; photo in hand and an inner voice asked *How could we have become such implacable foes? What happened? Aside from the incident with the Vietnamese women, we had no serious issues. How immature we were, or was it just that I was a poor manager back then?* Dan knew that today, he had developed the skills needed to handle Hudson properly.

Ann came bustling into the room waving the tickets. "I found them," she began to say. She saw her husband sitting looking off into the past, photo in hand. He was too far away to even hear her. For a moment, Ann stood watching, and then she touched Dan's shoulder, dragging him back to the present. Dan abruptly stood. "Sorry, I got sidetracked," he explained. Ann watched him slip the photograph gently into the drawer. "Come on," she said, "I found the tickets in my bag."

It all started in the darkness of early morning in Saigon, as a group of strangers climbed into the back of a truck. There were whispered introductions, handshakes, and jokes about *fresh meat*. They were all a little tense because they were going to re-start the job again, and they knew it was risky. Hudson sat next to Dan and they traded experiences. Both men had recently been discharged from the Marines and that would normally have been a strong bond. However, Dan had served one hitch and left the Corps, while Hudson had served 25 years with the rank of master sergeant. There was an irreconcilable difference in their views of the Corps, and later, other issues. Dan had found the life suffocating, while Hudson had reveled in his power and position, living the life of a medieval baron. Their views separated them like the Earth's poles.

At their first meeting, Dan did not know of Hudson's harrowing tale. Had Dan known, perhaps he would have treated Hudson differently, but that morning, Dan's only thought was *I'm no longer in The Corps, Master Sergeant Hudson, so kiss my ass.*

Hudson's tale took place a month before. He had driven to the Site with three other men to start the job. They left the highway, thirty kilometers from Saigon, following a dirt track back into the jungle to the site of the project. As they stepped from the jeep, they turned to look down the gun barrels of the Viet Cong. Their clothes and boots were taken and they were marched off to Cambodia, barefoot, bound, with nooses around their necks, hiding during the day, traveling by night. Then Fate took a hand, deciding the trail the VC party was traveling would be the same trail an American patrol picked as an ambush site.

The American soldiers stopped at an ideal bend in that trail. The sergeant ordered claymores set and placed the men in position. The light faded in the jungle and the men lay waiting by the trail, listening in the night. They would do so until dawn, without so much as a whisper. Hours later, the Viet Cong party rounded that same bend and the night exploded with gunfire and screams. After a time, the American patrol stood and started searching the bodies for weapons, papers or identifying insignia, and found Hudson lying under the body of another captive, stunned, but alive.

After a time to heal his feet, Hudson resolutely reported for duty and met Dan in the truck. Later, Dan would realize that here was a man's man, regardless of his other foibles

An incident a few weeks later further fueled the growing dislike. Dan needed ammunition for a handgun he carried. Hudson offered to find the ammunition for Dan, a sign of thawing of the relationship perhaps? In a day or so, Hudson presented the box of ammunition to Dan and said, "That will be one dollar for each bullet, a sum totaling $50 for the box." Dan was outraged. Hudson had not paid for the ammunition; it was a gift from Special Forces friends.

Time went by and Hudson arrogantly approached Dan to ask for Dan's liquor allotment. Hudson was a heavy drinker and Dan did not drink the hard stuff at all. Dan saw this as an opportunity to try once more to smooth over past differences and agreed to hand over the precious liquor at no cost. Hudson took this display to be a sure sign of weakness and the spiral of animosity continued downward. Dan mentally kicked himself for relenting. There were many other incidents and with each one, the two became more confrontational. Then, one evening, their dislike reached the violent stage, when Hudson set a trap for the women laborers at the site.

Hudson placed canned food where the women could see it. After the women picked up the cans and hid them in their clothing, Hudson stepped out from his hiding place and ordered the women to report to his villa that night to service him or be fired for theft. The job was critically important to the women, because although they only earned a few piasters a day, it helped to feed their families. Hudson stood there grinning with delight, expecting those women to walk 20 kilometers to and from his villa in the dark, and to do so after curfew, when they were at risk of being shot on sight! The women were cowed; nodding their heads and crying "Sin loi, sin loi!"

Dan happened to walk by at that moment and stopped to ask the women why they were crying. First, Dan gave the women the canned food and sent them home, then he turned on Hudson and they fought. The decision to use his fists instead of a one-dollar bullet was a very close decision. Dan was shocked by his own animosity. He had never before experienced such disliked of another human being.

A few days later, fate stepped in again. It was shortly before dawn. The sky in the east was blood red, promising another 105-degree day. Dan and his pal Curry, another of Hudson's foes, were driving to the Site, when up ahead they heard the sounds of battle and saw tracers arcing through the sky. They continued along the road, past scenes of other battles, of burned out vehicles, sandbagged checkpoints and rice paddies. They were aware that Hudson owned a terracotta villa by the roadside a short distance ahead: the scene of his nightly revelry.

The jeep continued along the road, drawing ever nearer to the sounds of battle. Hudson's villa was just around the next bend and as the jeep rounded the bend, the scene of battle lay before them.

On the right shoulder of the road was a platoon of ARVN troops with a tank in support, churning up some poor farmer's rice paddy. On the left side, in the jungle behind Hudson's villa was a force of VC. The fire was heavy, with tracers flying in both directions across the road, ricocheting into the sky like shooting stars. Curry drove the jeep right through the midst of the firefight without a scratch, except that as they passed the villa, the tank fired a high explosive round over the jeep into the villa, flattening it in thunderclap of fire and flying debris.

When they recovered their senses after the stunning muzzle blast and explosion, and reached the safety of the next bend in the road, Curry and Dan turned towards each other and laughed deliriously. It was the dawn of a new day.

PART III

REFLECTIONS

usmc

There is a folder on my PC called Unfinished Business. At the moment, it lists about sixty pressing topics, along with the bones of the proposed story or essay. Every so often, I'll reach into the folder and attack a subject. Sometimes the result of several hours of slipping into the zone and writing brings about an epiphany. Suddenly I realize that I never fully understood what took place in the woods that fateful day, thirty years ago, at least not until this moment.

Other times I simple open a file and rearrange predispositions and get them in the proper order, making it easier for me to understand my position on some issue. Soap boxing in some cases, simply expressing my conclusions, or sharing my experiences in other cases, is what this amounts too, mostly essays and memoir.

BEST LAID SCHEMES

usmc

"Best laid schemes oft gang aglee"

- Burns

The train slowed for the country station with groans, squeals, and a final, shuddering jolt as the cars all slammed to a halt. I stepped down from the perforated steel steps and stood taking in the scents and sights of the village. In the near distance was the three-story bank building, the biggest building in the village. During the war, the villagers manned an antiaircraft gun mounted on the highest roof of the bank. All night long, volunteer villagers stood by the cannon, wearing steel helmets, ready to fire on approaching German bombers.

In the distance, the bell tower of the church poked above the lush green maples that were the hallmark of the village lanes. Over my shoulder, the pretentious gold dome of the village hall gleamed like a temple, in the setting sun. I had been away a long time.

As I set off to walk the miles to our old Victorian home, I noticed another institution from yesteryear, leaning indifferently against the fender of his battered, old taxi cab. His hair was white now, his face lined and weary from the years of defiance. The confrontational stare had dimmed somewhat. He still had the stooped posture he assumed in bygone days as he stuck stubbornly to his choices and stayed in the village like a leper. I could never have done that. After his father died, Lowell Colby should have moved on. He had made his point.

Embarrassed, as I had often times been before in his presence, I tilted my head to hide behind the brim of my hat. Then, I left the station at a mile-eating pace. I'd be home in fifteen minutes. As I warmed to the pace, the angelus bell tolled, mournfully, echoing off the hills, beseeching the faithful, beckoning distant memories. It was six o'clock, dinner time.

My mom knew I was coming and would have one of my favorite meals ready. She had heard the Cannonball Express rumbling by, racing east, to meet the night like a lover. Mom lived alone now in that big house. She looked forward to the infrequent visits from her *brood* as she calls us. Somehow we had all left home and spread out over the States, unlike so many of my hometown pals: people like Lowell.

Entering the lane was like getting a long distance call from an old friend. The lush maples were huge now, creating a cool arcade, safe from the summer sun. The only jarring difference was the line of cars parked along the lane. Back during the war, everyone who owned a car put it up on blocks "for the duration." That included the whole village, with the exception of Lowell's father. No, not him, he was too important. While the villagers walked, Mister Colby drove his car, with the "A" coupon stuck to the windshield, visible proof he could still get rationed gas and tires. He would drive into the village just to get his shoes shined.

As the lane passed beneath my anxious feet, distant memories kept pace. The Colby home was just up the lane, a three-story Victorian house with a wrap-around screened porch and nine bedrooms. The Colbys only lived two doors away from us, but they were never friends. Lowell's father was pointedly polite to my parents, but he saw no gain in their friendship. We would never be in the same social or economic stratum.

How could he have known that as his privileged family tree became diseased and died, the sons and daughters of the poor Irish immigrants two doors away, would become world champion athletes, friends of Presidents and statesmen, editors, authors, even legends? He hadn't learned that timeless lesson yet that things change. I learned that valuable lesson early.

One day at the age of six, I stopped by to ask if Lowell could come out to play. His mother and another prominent neighborhood woman, whose son played with me, blocked my way, telling me that I was not fit company for their sons. "You're not clean-cut," they stated matter-a-factly, looking down their noses at me.

Blockaded by those daunting Man-o'-wars, I jibed and ran before the wind, quickly putting the nearest peninsula between the Colbys and me, vowing to make the necessary adjustments to my life, so that I could deal with other Colbys I met.

Mister Colby was an imposing figure of a man, a wealthy man, a man of power and influence. He wore a black homburg, sincere dark suits, and a neat mustache beneath his opportuning nose, but his image had a darker side. One summer evening as we played *Hide and Seek*, I crawled under their back porch to hide and was puzzled to find bags and bags of money hidden there. Next morning as he was picking up his morning paper, I happened by. I politely informed him of my find. The money was gone, when I checked, later that day.

Mister Colby's image was important. He slyly had his substantial liquor needs delivered with his groceries, so no one would know. He would never be seen in a liquor store. Mister Colby knew money made power possible and power made influence possible. The one thing that was most important on his list of essentials was lineage, his family history and that had been present in abundance in the Colby home in the past. In a large, sunny front room was a shrine to the past. One wall was decorated with a painting of a Confederate general. His grey wide-brimmed hat and saber rested on a shelf beneath the painting, completing his shrine. There were other shrines too.

Now, what Mister Colby wanted above all else was successful progeny, *sons who amounted to something*. When he had completed that final task, he imagined himself taking that victorious step towards immortality, with his own shrine in the room. He was willing to do whatever was necessary to further that end. We could hear him in his cups on quiet summer nights with the windows open, haranguing his two sons mercilessly. He worried them day and night, like a puppy with an old shoe. He made sure Lowell and Chase had every tool they needed to succeed. *What's the matter with them,* he would muse, loudly and angrily, *why don't they show some guts? Couple a pantywaists!*

Lowell once confided, "I dread weekends, because Dad is home all day, Saturday and Sunday and won't let up on me for a second." Chase, in a surprisingly candid moment observed, "You have a lot of fun at your house. You and your dad are always working together on the house. My dad does nothing. I see you and your brothers playing ball and singing on the porch and going fishing. It must be nice. My dad never lets up on me. Never takes me to a ball game. I'm afraid of him. I try my best to stay out of sight when he's around. Sometimes I hide in my closet to avoid him. It's nice in the closet, dark, quite, safe"

The boys, both of whom were of small stature were intimidated by his massive presence. Lowell and Chase struggled to meet his expectations. He cunningly pitted them against each other. In time the tactic drove the brothers apart. They became competitors for their father's approval. The pressure on the boys was constant and suffocating. Not once did Mister Colby shove his hand out with a big grin and say, "Put're there," by way of congratulation for a job well done. My dad used to do that. He made me feel like a million bucks. Next time at bat, I'd try even harder. Apparently, the notion never entered Mister Colby's mind.

After high school, Lowell and Chase attended Harvard as expected. In Lowell's mind, Harvard was that final step toward independence from his overbearing father. In time, Lowell and Chase graduated from Harvard Law as befitted the sons of a successful lawyer and politician. They were now ready to set the world afire, or so Mister Colby thought. He had already arranged positions for the boys as law clerks for prominent circuit court judges. After their June graduation, Mister Colby sat on his porch in the evenings, basking in the glow of self-satisfaction, rocking back and forth joyously. He had done it!

Then early one warm, humid July morning, two weeks later, Chase left home. He left unannounced, moving out of state and out of reach. "I have no respect for him," he told a friend, years later, when his friend remarked, "You never mention your father."

Lowell could have done the same thing Chase did, but he had a different turn of mind. Lowell had planned his revenge. *I'll show the bastard*, he vowed, assuring himself, *He can't touch me now*. Lowell chose to stay in the village for the rest of his dark days, driving the old, battered taxi cab for a living. Never once did he make use of his impressive education. One night, at The Elbow Room, I ran into Lowell. He'd had a few beers and loudly declared, "He wanted me to be a lawyer. I didn't. I wanted to be an engineer, like Mister Shoemaker, the eccentric inventor next door. Well, the laugh's on Dad!" I wonder if Lowell ever has moments of absolute panic in which he realizes what he has done.

I remember many an evening, sitting on our screened porch, enjoying the warmth, the banter and the songs of a summer's eve with family, until Lowell turned into the lane. Then we would fall silent with embarrassment, as he slowly drove his taxi past the home of his youth, while the old man sat in his rocker, hands resting on the cane between his knees, a stone face hidden beneath the brim of a Panama hat.

Icemen and Black Sheep

usmc

"The more sand has escaped from the hour-glass of our lives, the clearer we should see through it."
- Richter

A couple of years ago, my younger brother and I were sitting on the Club deck enjoying the view and a cocktail. There was a gentle breeze out of the northwest. We were sitting under the awning, looking over the harbor toward Stamford. A youngster at another table began crunching on a piece of ice as he prattled at his parents. The crunching of ice sparked a distant memory of an incident, which nearly shortened my younger brother's life. In the comfortable silence of Dan's company, my thoughts flashed back sixty years.

My pal Dickey Bates and I had learned to entertain ourselves on warm summer mornings, by jumping onto the back of the ice truck as the iceman raced through our shady lane on his customary rounds. What inspiration prompted the discovery I do not recall, but we found it fun to hop aboard and get an exciting ride down the lane. With the wind in our hair, the roar of the engine, and the soothing breeze on our damp skin, all our six-year-old senses were aroused. As a bribe, to keep us off the running board, the iceman would occasionally give Dickey and me a shard of ice to crunch on in the heat, but we felt that détente lasted only as long as the shard of ice did in the sun.

These events took place in the days before air conditioning and insect repellents, when we used iceboxes. During that summer of discovery, we endured more than our fair share of heat, humidity, and clouds of voracious mosquitoes drifting off the marshes with the onshore breeze. The screen porch was fine at night, as long as it did not rain, but during the day the porch was too confining for exuberant six-year-olds. So, riding the running board reigned supreme.

Then one day, Dickey and I invited my kid brother Danny along for a ride, probably because the twerp attached himself to me like a burr that day.

"Stick with me, kid and follow my lead," I ordered.

On that day, the plan was for us to stand over a storm grate ostensibly trying to retrieve a lost nickel, while we waited, steely-eyed and square-jawed to ambush the iceman. To a casual observer, we must have looked about as innocent as the James gang did as they loitered outside small-town banks in Kansas.

• • •

About Dickey. A few years ago, I stopped by for a visit with my mom. As we chatted and sipped tea, she acted as if she had a secret. Mom's eyes were flashing with excitement "What?" I asked.

She smiled triumphantly and said, "I had a nice chat with Dickey Bates the other day."

"That's impossible, Mom. The Bates left the village about sixty years ago," I stated emphatically.

I was very sure of the time, because I felt desolate, when the Bates left. Not because Dickey was my best friend, no. The feeling of desolation, now as familiar as an old refrain, was due to the departure of Dickey's little sister Betty. I had fallen in love with Betty and lusted after her with the tunnel vision of a pharmaceutical lab seeking a cure for acid reflux.

"It was definitely sixty years ago," I thought aloud, skipping why I was so sure.

According to Mom, she returned from the City, and took a cab home from the station. She sat up front with the driver as usual, because she was a democrat. Sometimes, I fantasized about my mom. I could see her with her wild, white hairdo, standing on the barricades, hurling cobblestones with the best of them, when the revolution begins. Anyway, Mom turned to the driver, started a conversation and recognized Dickey.

"How did you know it was Dickey," I tested her, hoping to catch her in an untruth, something she was always catching me in.

With a cunning smile, Mom stated archly, "He had one blue eye and one brown eye."

"Well, that settles it," I agreed, throwing up my hands in defeat, and we both laughed.

I always got a kick out of my mom's habit of sitting close to the driver and chatting it up. I recalled her trip to Ireland to see the land of her forebears. She was on a bus tour. Mom sat directly behind the driver every day. From time to time, she would lean forward and stab him with her finger, in that soft spot just behind his collarbone. The driver would jump in his seat and swerve all over the road and she would ask him another question. Eventually, the driver adjusted his rearview mirror to keep an eye open for the next stab, forgetting minor details like errant jaunting carts and cows.

One day Mom asked him, "All day we travel through the country and I see only white sheep. What happened to the black sheep?"

The driver's moment had arrived. He turned in his seat, as he sped down that narrow, windy country road, looked her in the eyes and replied through gritted teeth, "They all went to America."

Now that I think about it, Mom was preoccupied with unresolved issues of black sheep. She knew that every family had one. That wisdom made her days uneasy, as she mused, *Who will it be?*

Well, the James gang's plan worked like a Swiss watch. The iceman came and we hopped aboard for a thrill ride. All went well, until the driver inadvertently missed a customer and swung abruptly into a convenient driveway to go back to the customer. Without a pause, the ice truck started to reverse back onto the street again and Dickey and I jumped off safely. Little Danny however, was a novice and unwittingly, dropped directly astern. The truck immediately knocked down the four-year-old, who rolled underneath, out of sight.

My horror was such that I could not articulate so much as a syllable. I could not even breathe. All I could do in my state of terror was to point, white-faced, as Danny's head emerged and made contact with the double rear tires. By chance, the driver saw my frozen face in his rear view mirror and slammed on the brakes. The rear wheels were just starting to roll over Danny's head, causing the skin to break at the hairline on his forehead.

"That's definitely where you got your cowlick, Dan," I stated aloud, coming out of my reverie, alluding to the curious, clockwise swirl of hair on his forehead.

Dan was always quicker than I was, and recovered in an instant. After all, we had the same conversation a few times through the years.

"Like hell it is," he shot back. "I've always had the cowlick. Women like it. You're just jealous 'cause I'm better looking than you are. Besides, that was a UPS truck, not an ice truck. I aught 'a know. I was the guy under the truck, remember?"

Dan believed in going on the offensive. That is probably why he is so successful and influential.

Then he added, "Even today, I get cold sweats when I see a UPS truck. That proves it.

"Yeah, right," I countered, "all you ever saw was the underside of the truck, ya lunkhead."

We chattered on happily, enjoying the running argument and the view. Then I ordered another round in celebration of his life, looking with admiration at the man that Danny had become.

My thoughts turned to my other successful brothers, and I realized with a start, *Mom knew all along, which was the black sheep!*

NOBLESSE OBLIGE

usmc

"What do I owe to my times, to my country, to my neighbors, to my friends?
Such are the questions which a virtuous man ought to ask himself often."
- Lavater

It was one of those Long Island winter snows, a little sleet, several inches of snow during the night then turning to drizzle, by morning, the combined effect of which was the clogging of all the storm drains, creating huge murky puddles in the streets. Old ladies were seeking assistance crossing the intersections. Everyone was getting splashed by passing cars, no matter how slowly the cars traveled. It was a mess.

At the age of ten, I considered these weather conditions a challenge; a game. The blackboard had me down for serving at the 9 am mass that Sunday and Mom had made sure I was shined, pressed, combed and on time. On the way home after mass I was skipping and hopping the puddles, indifferent to the drizzle.

Up ahead at the intersection of Long Beach and Pine streets, a familiar figure was methodically shoveling the heavy wet snow away from the corner curb. Dad had set out after 6:30 mass, intent on clearing all the storm drains between our home and Our Holy Redeemer Church. "It was the right thing to do."

It's shameful, but I was embarrassed. We were poor. We were found wanting by the better class of citizens. Two years before, Mrs. Rainer and Mrs. Colburn had discussed the problem one day, on the Colburn's front lawn, by the Japanese maple, looking down their aquiline noses at me. Their sons, Harry and Lowell, were "clean cut";

that very term. I was not acceptable company for their sons. I stood there, mouth agape, unable to engage those two ships of war, so I cut and ran before the wind, putting a peninsula between them and me; later, creating an island.

On this gray drizzly winter Sunday, Mr. Rainer would be home in bed, reading the Sunday papers. He would never be moved to shovel out the storm drains, never. Why did Dad have to make a spectacle of himself? Besides, there wasn't even a drain at the north-east corner where I found Dad struggling. I walked past my own father, embarrassed and continued on home. What a horse's ass I was, but only a ten year old horse's ass. It's been fifty years since I denied Him and I am still disgusted with myself.

The sense of obligation, perhaps, "Noblesse Oblige," that Dad felt and instilled in all nine of us was in retrospect, a beautiful legacy. The storm drains incident was only one of many examples Dad and Mom both set.

Another example was set in the excitement of the early morning, as we all looked out at the newly fallen snow, one of us was surely going to be directed to go next door and shovel Bert's sidewalk, free-of-charge. It made no sense to me. But, Dad probably figure that since Bert was his engineering consultant, pro bono, the least that we could do was to occasionally do his walk.

The work ethic Dad instilled required that we shovel the entire walk; full width. Dad would march through the neighborhood after a snowy day, to inspect every walk shoveled by his children. Woes betide the child who had shoveled any walk that did not meet with his approval.

When we first moved into the neighborhood, the inhabitants were far from thrilled. We were a large, poor, catholic family of dumb Irishmen. And we had had the effrontery to insinuate ourselves into a wasp neighborhood. All that the father seemed to know was how to reproduce. Our neighbors neglected to look more closely and in an unbiased way at their new neighbors. Our parents resolved to give no excuse for criticism. A long list of dos and don't was enunciated. Always greet the neighbors politely. Always appear neat, if threadbare. Comport yourselves as though at home. Never cut corners, both geographically and in our work. We all followed the rules faithfully, through all the years. Well, almost all.

Had the neighbors been charitable enough to look more closely, they would have discovered a couple with intelligent, inquiring minds. A classic example of that intellectual capacity was displayed by my father when I was about ten. Somehow he acquired a copy of The Summa Theological of St. Thomas. As I recall, it consisted of three or four heavy tomes and a fifth book for the sole purpose of aiding the reader in understanding the other four volumes. With a daughter who was a Dominican, Dad was probably drawn to a Dominican thinker. Saint Thomas Aquinas was an extraordinary intellect. His work, crafted over a short lifetime, is truly a work of art.

Dad faithfully carried one of the blue volumes each day on the LIRR; day by day, absorbing the entire set. A true student, despite never getting past eighth grade, Dad took voluminous notes. The effort took years. When he had completed his study, Dad put Summa aside for a time. He then began all over again, since he was convinced, and rightfully so, that no one could absorb the Summa in one reading. He didn't realize it, but his crass son had noticed. Fifty years later, that son frequently carries a condensed Summa, in his attaché case.

Whenever anyone asks me about heritage, I can't help recalling my fathers admonition; "you are an American." He didn't ever want us to consider any alliance to another country. He expected all five of the males to serve their country generously and so we did. Loyalty, country, obedience to Caesar and God, these were the tenets to which we were all required to hue. His nexus was the soil; so fundamental. As we would sit to dinner, after saying Grace, Dad was likely to comment of the corn or beans, speaking of the sun and rain and horse manure that went into producing such good food. He loved the land and nature. In his later years, I'd stop by to find him absorbed by the nature programs of TV.

Leather was also close to his heart. This was a residual from the days when he cobbled our shoes. Dad hated to see unpolished shoes. It was an insult to the leather. Leather soles were the only proper way to make shoes. It took years for him to accept rubber soles.

Leadership was important to Dad. Not for its privileges, but rather for the obligation concomitant to leadership. He knew that his offspring were able to assume leadership roles. And so we have.

Acting in accordance with your convictions was something else that Dad demonstrated to the children. A simple but classic example was the "passing of the basket." Because of his conviction that a man could not act as an usher at mass and still honor his *obligation* to attend mass, Dad would go to early mass and then return to usher at his assigned mass.

The Church played a significant role in daily life in those days. It wasn't unusual for the Pastor to comment on some one or some family from the pulpit. Father Mahon, the Pastor felt that he had a license to do this. My recollections include two instances when Father Mahon did just that. What I will always remember was Dad's humility in this regard. He put up with the whims of the Church and it's agents like Gus Burns, without saying a word. There is no doubt that Dad would like to have passed a comment from time to time, but he held his tongue. Only once did I hear any hint of impatience. One day he grimaced and referred to Gus Burns as a "lummox." Dad chose his pals carefully. One, I remember and respected, was Mr. Mulooley. They would sit together at the Holy Name Society meetings and stoically endure the hyperbole of the Pastor and the "Leaders."

Ann, my wife, will on occasion, after observing my actions, say "you are so much like your father." What a complement!

REFLECTIONS OF A HAWK

usmc

"Pax vobiscum"

During the Vietnam War, there was extremely strong sentiment in America concerning our values, responsibility and global role. Some of us were "Hawks."

Even after all the years, I still feel a surge of anger, when someone presumes, that I share the notion that Viet Nam was wrong. Why was there such a divergence of opinion? What is the source of these individual convictions? Do I even need to provide a defense for my position? The reasons for the sea change in attitude are complicated by many factors. The purpose of the following is both exploratory and explanatory. It does not touch on all the elements of change, but I think I have found some closure.

About forty years ago, I had an interesting conversation with one of my boyhood pals. It was a lazy evening and we happened to hit upon the war years. A chance remark revealed that although he lived just up the street, went to school with me, and shared so many of my childhood experiences, he had no recollections of the hardships and anxiety we lived with during World War II! This astounded me. How could my pal not remember the rationing of food, for example? Later that same evening, I sat rehashing our conversation and realized I had a laboratory perfect setting to examine the divergence of opinion on the Viet Nam War. We knew each other for 30 years. We shared the same religious beliefs, girlfriends, adventures, teachers, jobs and level of education. How could this be?

As my pal and I grew, I noticed that we began disagreeing on a widening range of political issues. He was a dove. He saw no threat from Communism. Khrushchev never stood in the UN, pounding his shoe on the podium as if he was driving nails, shouting, "We will bury you." No, it was a misunderstanding. He explained Vietnam as a ploy by big business and so on. Diplomacy would always solve the problem. He felt that I saw a communist under every bush. "Peace at any price." "Better Red than dead," he advised.

After mulling things over, it occurred to me that those were formative years for both of us. The divergence of values came from our own brand of history, from our homes and family. He was an only son. He did not see three older brothers go off to war. His only contribution to his country was two years of typing reports at an Army camp in Georgia as a draftee. Those same formative year influences applied later, in Korea and again in Vietnam. There were many other influences in our early lives. Fathers, mothers, siblings, all helped form our thinking.

My remembrances begin with WWII.

It all started at the kitchen table one evening. The radio announcer was speaking in a hushed voice of an attack at some place called, Pearl Harbor. As he listened, Dad smolder with rage. Jim and Paul were voicing opinions, and Mom and Dad were giving the teenagers their attention. John was at the Naval Academy. Something out of the ordinary had occurred. I was five years old.

Suddenly, there was an Honor Roll in front of the Public Library. The list of service men slowly grew. The names of those who were not coming home highlighted. The front windows of the homes of all the service men displayed a cloth banner with a star to represent each man. Soon the banner at our home had three stars. Other families were less fortunate. Some banners had purple hearts. Some were black bordered.

If there was any doubt that there is a war on, one look at the bank was enough to change your mind. The bank was three stories high, the biggest building in town. On the roof in contrast against the blue sky was a sinister looking, black antiaircraft cannon. Dad had been a captain in the First World War and was assigned guard duty at night after a long day at his regular job. What they expected puzzles me, but these civilians would man that cannon through the night, discussing the war quietly, sitting in their WWI helmets. Imagine your average neighbor, manning a loaded cannon, at night, during an air raid, while searchlights roaming the sky!

The Pepsi Cola plant on the main highway became an airplane plant. My pals and I would stand in the doorway, mouths agape, and eyes like saucers, watching the workers building a single plane, piece by piece. There was not room for two planes. The scrap heap behind the plant held a variety of sheet aluminum scraps of myriad shapes. We would fill our pockets with the shapes and sit for hours trying to interpret the evidence.

Another local sample of the war effort was a plant just west of the reservoir that manufactured parachute flares. We would scour the shores of the "Rez" looking for expended flares so we could play with the parachutes. This making use of every square foot of manufacturing space in the entire country was an integral part of the war effort.

There were reinforced concrete bunkers along the beaches. The beaches were continually strewn with flotsam, which hundreds of torpedoed ships gave up. Those bunkers were the work of the Coastal Artillery. Their responsibility was to set up cannons at all strategic points along the coast and repel invaders. It was normal to hear the Ack Ack Guns firing away out at the beach as they held practice drills. On those occasions, when we went to the beach, there were armed sentries, Coast Guard sentries patrolling canvas leggings gleaming.

Who would have thought that one cold, misty morning a sentry would discover seven Nazi saboteurs among the dunes, just put ashore by a German U-boat? The saboteurs were hiding their explosives and funds. The Coast Guard web site has detailed accounts of what they called the Coastal Picket Patrol. The Patrol consisted of ordinary pleasure boaters and rumrunners, who patrolled in unarmed sail boats, looking for U-boats. Some of them found the U-boats. Who knows how many other saboteurs came ashore?

One evening, the house shook from a massive explosion at the Navy Yard. An ammunition ship blew up at the dock. More talk of sabotage and traitors. The FBI went around jailing suspected agents. The West Coast had a large Japanese-American community. We put them in concentration camps, and sent their sons to the European Theater to fight the Axis forces. The Country underwent a paroxysm of paranoia. An incident that my friend Marty shared is of him standing watch on a destroyer out of Pearl and because of a lack of familiarization with his automatic weapon, he inadvertently fired off several rounds damaging the radio antenna. Because he was of German extraction, he was court marshaled for sabotage! The claim was that he destroyed the antenna to prevent communications. Fortunately, his shipmates came to their senses. As an aside, the Country did execute service men found guilty of certain offenses, by firing squads.

To gather all possible support from the populace, the government employed psychological warfare. There were War Bond Drives with Heroes just back from the front, who talked about their deeds. This warfare of the minds and hearts was subtle and pervasive. All of these events fired the minds and imagination of us youngsters. A particular poster is vivid in my memory. It depicted a German storm trooper in a great coat and a coalscuttle helmet leering as he held his rifle high with a baby skewered on his bayonet!

Newspaper cartoons carried the psychological war message. One cartoon character called "Rosie the Riveter" comes to mind. The need for workers was such that women were suddenly occupying traditional men's jobs. "Rosie" was riveting bombers together. This departure from tradition was the source of the cultural explosion of working women that has echoed throughout my adult life, growing with each reverberation

"Delaney lights" will always get a laugh out of my brothers and sisters. It was not funny at the time though. Mrs. Tree, the air raid warden, would stand in the dark during the air raid drill, with her white helmet on, sirens wailing, and look for any hint of light emitting from homes in her area. She was the Truant Officer, had the lungs of a drill sergeant and invariable spotted a glint of light at our home. Mrs. Tree would shout, so the whole neighborhood could hear over the sirens, "Delaney lights"! The family would run all over the house checking trying to figure out where that glint of light was leaking past the blackout shades. The neighbors might think we were fifth columnist, trying to show a light to German bombers, to guide them to New York City. The notion of New York City being bombed was abhorrent.

Rationing began for food, gasoline, tires, clothing, all materials listed as critical. Most car owners did not have a priority, so they could not get any gas or tires. The patriotic solution was to put the car on concrete blocks for the duration. Those who were fortunate or dishonest enough to have a priority displayed a sticker depicting a capital "A" in their windshield. One of the spin-offs of this was the invention of hitchhiking! "Save gas." "Give a service man a lift." "Hitch a ride."

We gleaned every scrap of material for the war effort. One day my younger brother and I found an eight-foot piece of galvanized pipe. We turned it in at the local movie theater and got to see a movie free. We scavenged all the metal from junk piles in vacant lots. It became a patriotic act to conserve and recycle. The butcher actually gave credit towards new lard, if we returned a can of fat rendered from Mom's cooking. He weighed the can of rendered fat and we were credited accordingly.

As in every war, blood is in short supply. My dad, with three sons in the service and his own experience in the First World War was deeply committed. He was a repeat member of "The Gallon Club." During the war years, he gave five galloons of his blood. That equates to forty pints.

While the global struggle went on, there was on the home front, another fierce struggle going on. Mom and Dad had nine young mouths to feed. My mom made a deal with Himmel, the baker. He gave Mom flour sacks and Mom made drawstring underwear, positioning the manufacturer's big blue label on the back. Our underwear became known as *Iron Dukes*, in honor of the manufacturer. It was a little embarrassing on those occasions when we had to strip to our underwear for gym.

With food rationing, the government instituted coupons. Each of us had his own coupons for meat, lard, sugar, flour, soap, and margarine. In a given month, the allocation could be 10 oz. of meat, 6 oz. of sugar etc. Mom was responsible for coupons and sorted them out, planning our nutritional intake, with the cunning of a shylock.

The call went out for everyone to use all available land for "Victory Gardens." These gardens supplemented our rationed food supply. Dad sought the consent of neighbors to use their vacant lots. Being a farmer, Dad went into these gardens in a big way. To plant potatoes, as I recall, we would cut up the old potatoes that were sprouting, careful to include an eye in each quarter. These quarters were planted and produced our crop.

Mom carefully husbanded the bounty, which we enjoyed from the Victory Garden. She would send us into the lot to pick blackberries or maybe apples to supplement the food from the victory gardens. We would prepare fruits and vegetables and "can" them. The cool basement contained the mason jars of preserved foods. On occasion, one of the jars would ferment and explode, sending food all over the place. There was a bin full of potatoes in the basement. When I was hungry, I would eat a raw potato.

On the subject of labor, the farmers were in a bad way! Due to the war, the farmers did not have their sons and daughters to tend the fields. We did not have the itinerant labor we use today. As John Steinbeck later observed, "We weren't too proud to harvest our own food." The solution the Government came up with was to put the German and Italian prisoners of war to work in the fields.

It is hard for me to understand, how an intelligent person like my boyhood pal could have lived through those years, with no personal understanding of what the Country was going through. Perhaps, if world events do not affect you personally, they have little effect on your future decisions.

PART IV

FLYING THE NEST

usmc

Every spring the sparrows would build a nest outside the kitchen at home. My mother would watch and report on the progress of the chicks. Mom would observe squabbles, sibling rivalries and pecking orders, and the eventual culmination of the natural order of life, when the day arrived that the chicks flew the nest. That was the term Mom used, "Flying the Nest."

Those sparrows were a cosmos, reflecting the natural order in most families. The day arrives, whether planned or not, when the young chick teeters on the edge of the nest, hesitates, flutters its little wings and pitches into a nosedive that almost stops the parent's hearts.

In human terms, the nose dive can be quitting school, driving off to see the World, joining the Marines, or any of a hundred heart-stopping decisions that the youngster makes on his own.

All the parents reading this discourse can imagine the moment, when your own chicks finally fly the nest.

Augusts of Another Time

usmc

*"White clouds, whose shadows haunt the deep, light mists, whose soft
embraces keep, the sunshine on the hills asleep."*
– Whittier

The poor house orchard was behind our rambling, three-story home.
In August, the apples would ripen and begin to fall from the trees with
a soft thump. My job as a boy was to get up early on those August
mornings and wander through the orchard, shooing yellow jackets
off the newly fallen apples; gathering the apples in a bushel basket.
Then I'd sit at the trestle table in the kitchen, quartering and pealing
them for my mother. During the day, Mom would bake apple pies
and turnovers, filling the house with a savory scent of cinnamon and
apple.

By mid-August, our corn was as high as an elephant's eye. My
brothers and sisters would walk the rows, noisily rattling and squeezing
the ears, gather the corn. Then just before dinner, we'd have a corn-
husking contest, jostling each other's elbows, laughing and cheating.
The loser would have to do the dishes. After supper, the rest of us
would sit with our backs against the woodshed and smoke corn silk
cigarettes, blowing smoke rings and making earthshaking prophecies.

August was also the time when we would slowly move down the
furrows picking snap-beans, cauliflower, broccoli, and levering the
praetties out of the soil; unearthing them like diamonds. We had two
bins in the cellar: a big bin for coal and another one for potatoes. There
were also wooden shelves lining the cool stone walls. Those shelves
were piled high with mason jars of preserved fruits and vegetables.

Every once in a while, one of the mason jars would explode, spraying the wall with preserved fruit.

• • •

In later years, when I worked as a lifeguard, I discovered August was the month when the ocean telegraphed storms from as far away as 1000 miles, sending the best surfing waves of the whole summer toward those long sugary sand shores of the barrier beach. We body surfed those big waves with a sense of immortality that is peculiar to young men.

Late in August, the girl from the first aid station asked me to the end-of-summer beach party. She was a tall, dark, quiet gal. We had enjoyed each other's company since June and spent quite a bit of time together. We'd walk the beach, lay on a blanket sharing our sandwiches, talking about the coming fall and the future and relaxing in comfortable silence.

We joined our friends that night, drinking beer and building a big fire of driftwood. After midnight, we all ran into the surf for a symbolic baptism, before the start of fall semester. When the party waned, the two of us took a long walk down the beach, walking the surf line on the edge of the moonbeam.

The moon was a perfect harvest moon that warm balmy night, hanging so low and still. I turned to say something to her and we looked into each other's eyes. Her tan face was wet, glowing in the moonlight. We leaned together, our cold, wet swimsuits pressing. I slipped my arms around her waist. She was warm and soft. Her lips were burning hot. There was a scent of wet hair, a taste of salt and something else: a sense of discovery.

The surf gently lapped at our feet, and the Moon moved across the sky on its' predestined journey, exerting its influence on the oceans, the seasons, and continuity.

The beach season was ending, so Cynthia and I started roaming the City during the remainder of August and on into the fall. We walked from one end of the City to the other, hand in hand, but The Purple Onion in Greenwich Village became our *pied-à-terre*. Greenwich Village was a delightful discovery that summer. The impertinence, the iconoclastic attitude, and the freedom of expression were all the antithesis of my circumstance.

We met at The Purple Onion in the evening, where we drank beer, recited Kipling aloud and ate grasshoppers. Late in the evening, we'd take the subway to her neighborhood in Brooklyn Heights and sit for hours on a park bench at Penny walk, a park that overlooks the East River and the Manhattan skyline, listening to the faint sounds of the City's bustle across the water.

Cynthia and I shed our chrysalis that August. It was the end of many things and a new beginning too.

• • •

On another hot, August day, a lifetime later, I walked behind a horse-drawn caisson down a long, winding, sun-dappled country road, through the blackjack oaks and the pines of Arlington Cemetery. There was a special quality to the silence in the air that day: just the clop of the horse's hooves and the beat of the muffled drums. We buried John on a hill facing the setting sun, a flight of Crusaders thundered overhead in a Missing-Man-Formation; disappearing into the sky, and a bugler on a distant knoll played *Taps*.

IN SEARCH OF THE GOLDEN FLEECE

usmc

"Some bold adventurers disdain the limits of their little reign, and unknown regions dare descry."
- Gray

One day while rummaging in his workshop; examining half-finished repairs; blowing sawdust off fasteners and tools, Gil came across an old box of twenty-two caliber cartridges. The box was crumbling from age. The brass cartridge cases were verdigris coated. Fingering the brass rounds prompted a memory of a trip more than fifty years before.

In that memory, they were speeding along a desert road in Nevada; John Fitzgerald and Gil: free spirits; two youthful Argonauts in search of the Golden Fleece.

• • •

Fitz and Gil were tall, skinny and sixteen. Their attire was Levi's, tee shirts and sneakers. The Levi's hung precariously on their narrow hips. It was the summer that Jo Stafford was singing "You Belong to Me." Fitz and Gil were feeling their hormones and had decided to drive out to California and seek their fortune. When Gil mentioned his plans to his Mom, she nodded, "Fine."

For the first time in their lives, Fitz and Gil were unsupervised. Without the previous maternal guidance, their diet took an immediate turn for the worst. By chance, they happened upon an old building along the road. A big weather-beaten sign proclaimed, *War Surplus.*

Fitz and Gil wandered in and found cases of olive drab cans dated 1942, marked "Spanish peanuts." A case was about two dollars. It was plain to them that their food plan for the future was settled. It would be Spanish peanuts breakfast, lunch and dinner: a diet that would send a gibbons to the emergency room.

Fitz was a classic Irish redhead: never tanned, always burned, freckled, gangling. Under types, Fitz would be listed as a thinker: taciturn. At Chaminade, Fitz already knew that engineering was his chosen field.

Fitz and Gil were alike in that they were sparse with words. An example of that paucity occurred a few years ago. After a silence of thirty years, Fitz sent Gil a Christmas card. The inscription said, "Are we still pals?"

The following Christmas Gil sent Fitz a card with the inscription "Yes." Neither of them wants to clutter the postal routes with a lot of unnecessary correspondence about something self-evident.

• • •

That speeding car in Nevada, by the way, was a 1940 Mercury. The car had no seatbelts, no air conditioning, no automatic transmission, no radio, and no heater. If you wanted ventilation, you cranked the front windshield open, so it stuck out over the hood, and then you periodically picked bugs out of your teeth.

The Mercury was a tan coupe in which the pair had installed a big Ford engine. One day in Missouri, the two of them were challenged by some other teenager and in the ensuing race across Missouri; the speedometer pegged at one hundred and twenty miles an hour. The boys raced on into the night until their competitor quit or ran out of gas. That was a week or so into their adventure.

In the very first hour of their adventure, just as the boys exited the Lincoln Tunnel, Gil inadvertently happened to straddle a white painted line in the road. The time was four a.m. and visibility was not good.

Unbeknownst to Gil, that white painted line turned into a white painted concrete lane divider. The divider was only a couple inches high at first. However, in an astonishingly short time the divider grew to a height of three feet lifting the Mercury off the ground so the car skidded along on top of the concrete divider at fifty miles an hour sending up a shower of sparks.

Fitz was disgusted! The Mercury was tittering on the concrete divider, three feet in the air, all wheels off the ground. Their euphoria had evaporated in the blink of a sleepy eye. There they were, in the dark, the trip ended within the first hour. What a come down. Gil felt like two cents.

Then, along came a trucker. The trucker pulled his rig over and walked back to the two teenagers who were scratching their heads. The trucker suggested that they jack up one side of the car and shove it off the divider so one set of wheels touched the ground. Fitz and Gil got the car off the divider. Nothing seemed broken, so off they went again, the discouragement and disparaging words gone like drifting smoke.

• • •

Fitz's ability to think like an engineer was demonstrated by the effort they put into fuel economy on that trip. They only had $125 for their expenses, the sum total of their savings from summer jobs. In those days in Texas, gas was 15 cents a gallon.

In Fitz's opinion, that was a lot of money for a gallon of gas, so they decided to make the engine run as economically as possible. First thing they did, was to take the hood and lash it to the roof, so the air could cool the engine more easily. Then, they removed the fan belt. It was their feeling that once they got up to speed they didn't need the fan. Next, the twosome removed the accelerator plunger from the carburetor. They knew from taking the carburetor apart, that every time the gas pedal was depressed, that plunger squirted unnecessary gas into the engine. Fitz figured that they were in no hurry and did not need any jackrabbit starts. Their new driving style eliminated all form of rapid acceleration.

After those adjustments, the time to go from zero the 60mph was about ten minutes, but the car was getting 35 miles to the gallon. That fuel economy worked out to about 15 dollars worth of gas to travel from coast to coast.

Into the trunk of the car went their tools, spare parts, repair kits, fry pan, sleeping bags and so on. An abundance of self-confidence was placed in the front seat, seated side by side. Then, reluctantly, somewhere in the packed car, their guardian angels found room to sit down. Not once in that journey did the boys get a tow, push, repair, free lunch or directions.

• • •

The remembrance of that day, speeding across the desert of Nevada, was of Fitz at the wheel. Gil was seated on the passenger side, absentmindedly watching an exceptionally long freight train that was keeping pace with the car. The tracks and road were only a hundred yards apart and straight as a pair of arrows, for as far as the eye could see.

The train was made up of steel coal gondolas, and sitting on the side of one of the gondolas, legs dangling, was a hobo. It was obvious that with nothing but mesquite for scenery, the hobo was idly watching the two teenagers. That was when it happened.

The rifle lay on the back seat, loaded. The two boys had been using the rifle to shoot at the targets the Nevada Highway Department conveniently hung beneath the road signs.

The targets were a stroke of genius, saving the Department on sign repairs. It seemed that everybody in Nevada practiced their skill with firearms as they drove those boring, desolate roads.

The rifle was loaded, ready for the next sign, so Gil poked it out the window. Even at that distance, Gil could see the hobo's posture stiffen. Then, because the devil whispered in his ear, Gil swung the rifle in the hobo's direction. The hobo did an immediate back flip into the empty gondola and disappeared.

Then, after a pause, a small hairy hemisphere appeared at the top of the coal gondola. Gil imagined the hobo's eyes, furtive, frightened, so he squeezed off a round into the side of the gondola. There was a satisfying twang as the bullet hit the steel side of the coal gondola. The hemisphere disappeared, then popped up again at one end of the gondola. Gil quickly reloaded and the hairy hemisphere ducked as soon as the hobo saw the second muzzle flash. This turkey shoot went on for miles, with Fitz roaring with laughter.

Gil's theory was that for the first time in years, the hobo had something important to consider: his life! Against the background of the "tabogata- tabogata" of the coal cars, the Hobo's whole life must have passed before his eyes.

It was the sixteen-year-old's considered opinion that it would do the hobo some good, to review his life, examine his conscience. Thinking back, Fitz and Gil may well have given the impetus needed to turn around the hobo's life; a kind of *outward bound* approach to social work. Today, the hobo might be a captain of industry. All they could say in defense of their conduct was, "It seemed like a good idea at the time."

• • •

Shelter was where they found it. As Gil recalled, they slept in an abandoned uranium mine one night. On other nights they slept on a salt lake, under a bridge, by a crater-lake and always, high above them were brilliant starry skies.

However, they were not crass youths. They sampled the national parks, too. At Grand Canyon, the teenagers hiked down into the canyon in the noonday heat and found fossilized seashells from a former time when Arizona was on the bottom of some prehistoric sea.

At Yosemite, they explored El Capitan, and the falls and made an adult discovery. When the rangers put on the romantic "Fire Fall" display one beautiful crystal, clear night, Fitz and Gil came to the realization that they both would have preferred to be traveling with a lithe, blonde. In unison, they turned and looked at each other in disgust.

The pair never paid for any shelter on that trip. At summer's end, they stopped in Chicago to visit Gil's relatives. Gil's aunt, with a sniff request that they each take a bath. Even Gil was surprised at the color and texture of the ring around the tub. That ring looked like the plimsole line on a New York harbor tugboat.

In one of Gil's comical recollections, they spent a night near Dayton, Ohio, in a wooded area, retreating as far as they could from any sign of civilization. The night was quiet and they slept well. At breakfast next morning, they heard a distant whining noise. This noise grew louder and louder and closer and closer. At first, Fitz and Gil were just curious. Then, when the noise level reached about 150 decibels, they panicked, concluding that the world was coming to the end.

A moment later, an Air Force jet bomber passed over their heads at about thirty feet. Had they ventured just a few feet farther the night before, the two of them would have discovered that they had camped at the end of the runway of an Air Force base.

Nevada became a sort of proving ground for the old Mercury. During all Gil's years of driving, the blinding effect of the high beams of an approaching car has always annoyed him. You would think their experience in the desert would have changed that. The visibility in the desert is excellent. The headlights of an approaching car can be seen for miles at night. The blinding effect can go on for an equally long time.

That was just what happened one night. Gil flashed the high beams to indicate that they were blinded. Then after a few minutes, Gil flashed them again to no avail. After those attempts Gil got annoyed and decided to blind the approaching car with his high beams. It seemed fair to Gil. When this did not work, Gil pointed the car towards the oncoming car to give the full effect of his own lights. What Gil did not realize in that discreet moment in time was that the other car was parked well off the highway, out in the desert, with its brights on.

Gil discovered his error, when the mercury left the highway at 70mph. In an instant they were plowing through the mesquite, bounding over gopher holes on two wheels and narrowly avoiding the lava rock formations. After an eternity, with Fitz and Gil bouncing around inside the car, with the advantage of today's seatbelts, the desert dragged the car to a dusty halt. The two of them sat stunned. The shock was worse for Fitz since he had been dozing. Fitz thought that Gil had blown a tire, or fallen asleep. How could Gil tell him the truth? He still doesn't know. The Mercury was still ticking over and once they pulled some mesquite out of the radiator, they were off and running again, years older, none the wiser.

The tires were old and worn before they began the trip, and as the tires wore out, the boys picked old tires out of garbage dumps and mounted those tires on the Mercury. They did not make tires the way they do today, and so it was that the boys suffered an inevitable blowout.

Fitz was driving at the time and after the blowout, Fitz struggled to keep the car on the road. However, since it takes awhile to slowdown from seventy miles an hour, Fitz just barely tapped the brakes to bleed off some energy.

As soon as Fitz touched the brakes, the Mercury reacted like a wild thing, going out of control, flying off the road. Again, it flew into the mesquite in a shower of dust and gravel, miraculously landing on all four wheels.

That evening, the teenagers sat by the campfire trying to repair the blown tire. Tires had inner tubes back then. Finally, Gil rolled up in his sleeping bag for a rest under that crisp starry sky, and as he lay there, the earth started moving under him. At first, Gil thought that the diet of Spanish nuts was finally taking its toll. Then Gil heard the Mercury squeaking back and forth on its suspension system. When Gil turned to investigate, the car was rocking around by itself: an eerie sight. The next day Fitz and Gil hesitantly mentioned their experience to a gas station attendant. The attendant explained that they had experienced an earthquake.

The brakes on the 1940 Mercury were not too good either. One day in Texas, Gil was driving and miles ahead in that clear dry air, Gil spotted an intersection with a car waiting at a lonely traffic light. On the assumption that the light would surely change, Gil did not bother to reduce speed. Ultimately, Gil saw that some heavy braking was called for, if he was to stop in time. The Mercury slid up behind some old Texan's car, tires screeching and slammed into him.

The desiccated old Texan climbed out of his dented car dumbfounded. His first words were "Didn't you see me?" Gil acknowledged that he had indeed seen the Texan's car for miles and simply did not know enough to stop in time. The Texan looked at the New York plates, the two grubby teenagers, the old Mercury with the hood tied to the roof, shook his head with a grimace of disgust that reminded Gil of his own father and drove off without another word.

Fitz did the same thing on another occasion. When Fitz realized his error, he steered into the adjacent parallel drainage ditch to avoid rear-ending the car ahead. They roared down the drainage ditch to the intersection at sixty, and climbed the shoulder of the side-road. This climb, at sixty caused the car to leap over the side road without touching a thing. Back into the ditch and onward, then back onto the highway. Gil's mouth must have been hanging open in amazement. Fitz threw his head back and laughed uproariously. Such innocence! Such a sense of immortality!

• • •

As the adventurers were crossing the Rockies they stopped by a peak called Mt. Dana: elevation 12,500 feet. Fitz and Gil were admiring the view and chatted with the ranger. The ranger spoke of the climb to the peak of Mt. Dana as a challenge. The ranger claimed that the peak was a five-hour climb. With the arrogance of youth, they immediately decided to make the climb. The climb required no special equipment, just determination.

The pair started the climb immediately, going at the mountain with a vengeance; scrambling up like goats. The higher they climbed, the more things changed. The air was crisper, cleaner, and cooler. The clattering sound of the rocks they dislodged while climbing had a musical ring. The view was fantastic, especially from the peak. In Gil's excited state of mind, he was sure he could see Idaho and Wyoming to the east. The snow, hip deep at times, was a novelty in July. Their bodies were starved for oxygen in the cold, thin air. The exertion created a glow. The teenagers were dressed in tee shirts, jeans and sneakers.

Mt. Dana taught the pair two lessons. First, as they climbed they kept looked up at the side of the mountain above them. When they could no longer see the mountaintop, they assumed that they were about to crest the final slope. This proved to be untrue, time after time. Fitz and Gil would look up at blue sky and pour on the coals to make that final dash. With legs trembling, their breath ragged, their focus fuzzy, they would crest the rise only to find shelving, a plateau and another slope. Fitz and Gil would collapse in the snow sobbing for oxygen and lay there in a sweat for a few minutes. The lofty winds would gently cool their brow and suddenly they would be freezing. Hypothermia was not in their Lexicon.

Plateaus followed slopes, as they climbed for hours. The climbing of Mt. Dana was an analog that Gil has employed many times through the years. Life's problem solving has the same slopes, rock faces, fissures, bergschrunds and plateaus that they found on Mt. Dana.

The second lesson was that after the agony of the climb, the victory was sweet. It was a victory in the sense that the boys overcame the body's desire to quit and enjoyed the euphoria all climbers experience upon succeeding. Afterwards, the teenagers understood the symbolism of climbing.

• • •

There was another memorable experience. It was after an oven hot day in the Texas Panhandle as dusk was falling, that a biblical encounter occurred. A plague of locust was suddenly upon the boys.

Gil was at the wheel. The butterfly windows were pushed all the way out and the front windshield was cranked out too, to scoop in the cool evening air. Without any warning, Fitz and Gil were suddenly being violently pummeled in the face and upper body by huge crawly things. At that speed, they scooped hundreds of them into the car in seconds.

The locusts were about three inches long and as fat as your finger. As Gil applied the brakes, the tires churned the swarm of millions of locust crossing the road, into a greasy slurry. The car went out of control, spinning about. Meanwhile Fitz was shouting and swatting to beat the band. The locusts were inside their shirts, in their hair, everywhere!

Their adventure continued on a night in Oklahoma: Oklahoma, meaning red earth. Fitz and Gil had called a halt late one hot afternoon and found a track, which took them well off the main highway. They got a campfire going and heated some supper. As soon as the sun set, the boys noticed the loom of what appeared to be headlights of a car coming over the adjacent butte. To their surprise, up popped the biggest, brightest moon they had ever seen. In that crisp dry, air it was a delightful display of nature.

The neighborhood coyotes seemed to agree, and said so, one after another, howling lonesomely at the moon. Sitting by the fire, watching and listening to the concert in the flickering firelight was unforgettable.

One day the teenagers picked up a hitchhiker. He was a young cowboy who talked incessantly. His speech sounded like his mouth was filled with *corn pone*. Then, when the cowboy suddenly pulled out his harmonica, and rendered "Courtin' Uncle Joe," Fitz slammed on the brakes and they threw him out of the car— the boys had not yet learned that country western music was an acquired taste.

Approaching Santa Barbara, they pulled onto the shoulder of a desolate country road to rest. It was dusk. They were both exhausted and without any interest in food, they fell asleep. Fitz was asleep in the front seat curled around the steering wheel. The shoulder of the road was slanted, so they were sleeping at an angle. Gil's sleep was just below the surface of consciousness, luckily.

Movement outside the car, and the sound of clothing rubbing against the car by Gil's head awoke him. It was pitch black. Gil could not see a thing. Someone was very quietly trying the door handle beside Fitz's head. With his right hand, Gil grabbed Fitz and with his left, he groped for the rifle. "Hit the starter and go!" Gil shouted. Fitz had them moving in seconds. They never looked back.

• • •

Early one gray morning, while driving through Nebraska, they stopped at small, white clapboard, general store. The store was situated at a country crossroad. For miles in all directions, all there was to see was a wall of corn, about eight feet high.

Inside the store, a group of farmers were standing in faded jeans, their feet a furrow apart, discussing in hushed, anxious voices the meager two tenths of an inch of rain that had fallen during the night. The farmers' weathered faces were maps of the land they would work until they died: *dust to dust.*

The local radio stations discussed fertilizers and Brahma bulls. Fitz and Gil scoffed and guffawed then—not now.

Iowa was corn, but it was alfalfa too. All day long, the explorers drove by fields of rich green alfalfa. The farmers were marching across those fields, line abreast in Combines, like recruits in a close order drill. From dawn until dusk, and well into the night the farmers worked, using their headlights.

Fitz and Gil were so impressed by the farmer's industry, that they stopped late one evening and walked into the fields to find out what made this nonstop toil so important.

The farmers, as weary as they were, proudly showed the boys the contraption the Grange had invented to compress and dry the alfalfa. The process made the alfalfa look like black plastic rods, but it was stable, nutritious, and the cattle thought of it as some kind of TV snack.

• • •

The two crass teenagers did not appreciate it at the time, but that journey was an introductory course in America. It was a hands-on examination of this beautiful land. The land itself was an education: amber fields of grain, golden in the sun, and corn as high as an elephant's eye. The teenager's appreciation of music and songs was enriched by that journey too. Even literature was made more enjoyable. Reading Steinbeck's "Travels with Charlie" years later brought those youthful memories rushing back; a vicarious delight; a second adventure.

Their adventure awakened such a thirst in Fitz and Gil that they shared many another exploration of America afterwards, and since reaching maturity, they have traveled to many places. Recently, Fitz sent Gil a letter postmarked, *Zanzibar.*

The Teenagers' fledgling flight was not only a bargain, time well spent, but it also created a mindset. Fitz and Gil have been exploring places, ideas, and people ever since.

RESPECT

usmc

"He who respects others is respected by them."
- Mencius

When he scrunched his eyes up real hard and squinted, a VW beetle looked kind of like a turtle— especially since he'd had a couple of drinks. Now a police cruiser didn't look at all like a rabbit, but he seemed to recall that one of the policemen in the cruiser had a big pink nose.

The pursuit of his VW beetle by a City police cruiser was a classic example of Aesop's fable of *The Turtle and the Hare*, with the Volkswagen representing the turtle and the big police cruiser, the hare.

It is funny the way the mind works, he thought. *If it's somebody else who has a brush with the Law, it's easy to be critical,* he subconsciously added. For example, whenever he read about some young man in Harlem, or East New York, who was shot as he ran from the police, his initial reaction was the same. *Why run, unless you're guilt,* he questioned? *It seemed so stupid.*

The thought process had begun one day in an idle moment, sitting on the commuter train. For no apparent reason, he remembered a Homeric police chase of his own making, just a few short years before. As the memory flooded back, he shook his head and shifted in his seat in discomfort as he marveled at his own stupidity. As the train moved ahead, his own train of thoughts gathered momentum, and he recalled other occasions when he had done the same stupid thing. He was shocked at his youthful conduct and whispered a silent, fervent prayer of thanks that his father had never found out about his son's antics.

His father would turn over in his grave if he found out that the family name was entered on the police blotter. That's what his father called it: *The Police Blotter*. He could hear his father saying, "If one of my sons ever gets the Delaney name on *the blotter*, don't bother coming home, 'cause you won't be living here anymore."

Kevin was his name. He was a six-foot tall young man of 35 years age, with good looks and the intelligence to hold a position as CFO in an up and coming new company. Kevin got his Bachelors at Columbia and then went back for a Masters in Finance. He was an upwardly mobile guy who had his own condo in the City. Regarding marriage, Kevin had made of his mind to wait until he met the right girl first and was in no particular hurry to do so. Life was good and he worked long hard hours. He instinctively knew that a good marriage and a good executive position conflicted.

Kevin considered himself an all around, stand-up guy. His own personal self-evaluation was as honest as he could manage. He pledged allegiance to the American flag without reservations. He obeyed the traffic rules. Kevin knew the value of worship and besides, he didn't want a confrontation with his mom, so he attended church services on Christmas and Easter, *That should cover it*, he mused. Kevin loved his country and watched the parades on Memorial Day, but he involuntarily shivered when he thought of the notion of a *draft*.

At his weekly poker game, Kevin never peeked at another player's cards, unless the player was downright careless. He wasn't a slave to fashion, preferring to wear Dockers and no socks, except if he went to his parents for dinner.

In his own estimation, Kevin's greatest moral triumph was in hewing to a policy of never telling his date that he loved her, no matter how promising the evening appeared. Yes, he considered himself a stand-up guy.

Sitting there patiently on the commuter train, our man Kevin reconsidered the young Harlem man's plight. He decided that maybe the young man wasn't so stupid after all. Kevin suspected that the real reason why young men sometimes run when confronted by the police on some minor mischief is a gut refusal to put themselves in the hands of a force that they do not respect: a force that traditionally shows no respect for them.

In Harlem, showing a lack of respect is referred to as d*ising*, and is derived from the word disrespect. On occasion, d*ising* has been the reason for some of the violent deaths of young men in Harlem. The young men have very little, other than their own self-respect. Don't dis anyone.

As he sat on the train, Kevin tried to collect his thoughts, to make sense of the phenomenon. He speculated that his own tendency to run dated back to an incident at the age of eight.

Kevin and his pal had wandered into the rear parking lot of the village and observed a ladder leaning against the back of a two-story shop, just begging to be climbed. Out of curiosity, the two kids climbed to the roof and stood looking down on Main Street from a new perspective. It was an adventure.

Their adventure was interrupted by one of the village policemen. He grabbed them from behind and arrested them. The two boys were rudely, roughly dragged down the ladder in front of an audience of neighbors and presented to an old woman that positively identified the two as the pair who burglarized that very shop the previous night. The old woman even identified their clothing as the same clothing that they had worn during the burglary. *We are headed for Sing Sing Prison,* Kevin had thought

What a nightmare! Kevin's mind went blank. The boys were shoved into the back seat of the police car and taken to the police station to be arraigned.

Fortunately, the desk sergeant suspected a mistake in identity. The boys were released after what seemed like a lifetime. The two alleged perpetrators walked out of the police station somehow sullied and violated. There was no apology, and to compound the injustice, they had to trudge those long miles home in the gloaming.

Justice is blind and so too was that old lady, but that childhood incident probably triggered Kevin's reaction that fateful night.

It was a warm summer night, about 2am, and he had just dropped off his date at her home in Hollis. Heading east on Hillside Ave., in good spirits, in his brother's yellow VW beetle, Kevin approached an intersection and saw the traffic light several blocks ahead, turn red.

This all happened back in the days, when the City had a rule that you were to stop at whatever intersection you occupied when the traffic light, blocks ahead, turned red. Kevin considered the rule silly except during the rush hour traffic and especially so at 2AM, so he drove through the deserted intersection and moved on the two blocks to the real traffic light.

While waiting at the light, Kevin happened to look to his left and spotted a police cruiser idling in an alley. Two burly city cops were slouched down, visored caps down over their eyes, supposedly asleep. The practice was commonly referred to as *Cooping,* back then.

As Kevin watched, an arm suddenly shot out of the driver's window and signaled him to pull the VW to the side of the road. Apparently the cops hadn't been asleep, and had seen Kevin move through the intersection while the light was red.

What first annoyed Kevin was the attitude of the cop. He was too lazy to even sit up and look properly paramilitary. *Sit up for Christ sake*, Kevin thought to himself.

In that instant, Kevin envisioned a long night in the police station, as a pawn, while two lazy cops sipped coffee and filled out some paperwork. *I suppose I'm to be their ticket off the streets and out of harm's way for the remainder of their shift* he fumed

The light turned green and Kevin's mind went red in the same split-second. He floored the VW Beetle, skipping away. *Let the games begin*, he raged.

The earlier comparison of the turtle and the hare was no exaggeration. His brother's VW Beetle had a small engine, while the police cruiser probable had a 300hp engine. This chase was going to be over in seconds.

The two cops sat up in amazement at his chutzpah, as Kevin raced away into the night. The police cruiser swung out of the alley and into the traffic, lights and siren going, and in that nanosecond when the two cops were looking at oncoming speeding cars, Kevin made a snappy right turn onto the nearest boulevard, heading south. The boulevard was steeply downhill towards the next main street and the VW made good time. Maybe, because of the hill and the fact that he turned all lights off, the Beetle got an extra couple of miles an hour.

In his rearview mirror, Kevin saw the police cruiser, lights flashing and siren wailing shoot through the intersection behind him. They hadn't seen his snappy turn and were proceeding along Hillside Avenue at a mile a minute.

The next main street came up in no time and Kevin reasoned that the two grumpy cops were calling in the details of their chase. It was going to be a busy neighborhood in a matter of minutes.

Kevin felt a pressing need to take the quickest route to the City Line, but the police cruiser was ahead of him. Kevin found a big lumbering Cadillac up ahead and tried to hide the beetle behind the Cadillac.

In a moment, the police cruiser came racing back west, all aglow. They almost missed him. The cop who was driving did a double-take upon spotting the partially concealed yellow beetle and slammed on the brakes, slewing the cruiser around cutting into the oncoming traffic and Kevin did it again.

The Beetle is so slow and so low to the ground, that he was able to snap it around the nearest corner as both cops were looking to avoid a collision with the oncoming traffic. Down an unknown side street he raced, switching off the lights and again in the rearview mirror he saw the police cruiser roar through the intersection, calling in their disposition again.

Up 'till that moment, Kevin had not even thought of the consequences of his actions. He was totally committed to avoiding *The Blotter*. Now, Kevin began to acknowledge his stupidity. He was reminded of a street truism: *The longer the chase, the longer the beating. Well*, he thought with the arrogance of youth, *they'll have to catch me first.*

Whizzing through stop signs, on down narrow, darkened side streets; the turtle hurtled through the night, compounding the earlier transgression, while the radio traffic heated up.

The other police cars in the vicinity were also out looking, in hope of snaring the Turtle before their brother officers. The area near the City Line became very busy. The Turtle dodged, parked, hid and evaded, onward into the next county where Kevin slowed and turned the car's lights back on.

Kevin happened upon a tavern that was still opened. He parked around back, and strutted in for a frosty mug of beer. Kevin sat there smiling, but he also felt a little guilty about the other, poor, innocent, young man in a yellow beetle, that the cops hauled into the precinct in his place. "Perhaps he should have run for it too." Kevin reflected. "Maybe the next time, he'll know better!"

PART V

THE SERVICE

usn

Of the six males in the Gillcrist family, our father and the five boys, all served their country in the military service. Dad was in the Army in World War I, sons John, Paul and Dan served in the Navy and sons Jim and Robert served in the Marines.

John saw action in World War II and Vietnam. Jim saw action in Korea, Paul saw action in Vietnam, Bob served as a Marine aboard the carrier, Wasp, and later as a civilian engineer in Vietnam; where he saw more action as a civilian than as a Marine. Dan, served as a submariner on deterrent patrol off the Russian coast during the Cold War. Due largely to the many rosaries said by Mom and Dad; none of their sons was injured by enemy fire.

OK Corral

usn

"You may fire when ready, Gridley."
- Admiral Dewey

In 1955, upon returning from my first cruise, I received orders from VF-191 to an organization I had never even heard of; the Fleet Air Gunnery Unit, Pacific, located, of all places, at Naval Auxiliary Air Station, El Centro, California. All of our flying was done over the desert areas of Imperial Valley and the Chocolate Mountain Gunnery Range, a vast, trackless desert and mountain terrain. Survival for a downed pilot in such circumstances would require resourcefulness and equipment. We all carried a survival kit of our own construction which would help keep us alive for the time it would take for a rescue effort to find us. It had to be small enough to be easily carried in a flight suit or "G" suit pocket and it was intended to supplement what survival equipment was carried in all parachute packs. Our survival school training was the genesis for these personalized kits.

I decided that a handgun would be a good addition to my survival equipment. In those days the Navy did not issue survival handguns. So, I ordered an inexpensive used handgun from a mail order magazine. It was a .455 Webley revolver formerly in use by the British army for many decades. I even went to Mexicali and had a left-handed leather holster made so I could carry it slung over my flight suit and under my right armpit.

As mentioned in episode #13, the weapon had a break action which permitted rapid re-loading. The break mechanism was operated by a powerful spring lever which had two functions: locking the break mechanism and holding the firing pin away from the magazine face whenever the trigger wasn't pulled back. Because of this "fail safe" safety device I always kept a round in all six of the revolver's cylinders. After all, what could go wrong?

One day, I went out to man my airplane for a gunnery flight and did my standard walk-around inspection. Then I set the Webley, contained in its holster on the wing root while I climbed the boarding ladder. The gun lay on the wing root within easy reach as I mounted the ladder. As occasionally happens, when my added weight was put on the ladder, the oleo in the left main wheel shock strut was depressed a half an inch or so causing the slope of the wing root to increase slightly. When this occurred the Webley and holster began slowly to slide outboard and forward toward the wing's leading edge. I tried to grab it but was too slow and it slid beyond my reach and inexorably away.

I knew exactly what was going to happen and watched helplessly as it reached the leading edge of the wing and dropped about eight feet to the concrete parking apron. Realizing that the loaded weapon represented a hazard, I held my breath and turned my face away from the direction of the gun. It was a silly thing to do in retrospect, but the reaction was instinctive. When the gun struck the ground there was a loud report as the "most powerful handgun in the world" fired. It took me a moment of self assessment to be sure I hadn't been struck by the bullet. Then I climbed back down the boarding ladder to see what, if any, damage had been done by the stray bullet.

Search as I might I never found any clue as to where the bullet went. Suffice it to say, that when I reported the incident to higher authority, I was scheduled to make a safety presentation at the next AOM (all officers meeting) to explain the hazards of handguns on the flight line and the wisdom of leaving the chamber under the firing pin empty.

GETTING THE POINT

usmc

"Not only strike while the iron is hot, but make it hot by striking."
- Cromwell

All the platoons in The United States Marine Corps Recruit Depot, Parris Island had one thing in common, a guidon, as a means of identification. The guidon bearer was generally a small recruit, since the big recruits were generally in the front squad of the platoon. The comparison of the short guidon bearer guiding the big Marine of the first squad had a theatrical effect.

The guidon bearer for Platoon 356 was a cocky little guy. Years later, while riding an elevator in New York City, Don turned and there he was, standing by Don's shoulder, just as short and twice as cocky.

The guidon bearer's function was to carry the guidon; a hand polished wood staff with a brass spade on top and the platoon burgee, a red triangular flag with *356* emblazoned in gold.

The platoons were paraded each day on the Battalion parade ground, creating an atmosphere that begged for comparisons. One platoon might march better than another. Some platoons looked more *squared away* than others, or an occasional platoon might have a boogie rhythm to its march.

There were also daily competitions between platoons. The purpose of all the competition was to engender a sense of pride, of being the best, of having accomplished the extraordinary.

The guidons told the story of the platoon's ability, its accomplishments, its standing amongst the other platoons, because atop the guidon the streamers won in contests were placed. Almost all platoons had at least some streamers, secured in place by the brass spade. A few exceptional platoons' guidons were festooned with streamers.

Platoon 356 had not a single streamer secured atop its guidon, proof positive that it was a platoon of non-performers. For some of the platoon's recruits, this absence of streamers really grated on the nerves.

And, just as there was a shortage of almost everything else at Parris Island, in 1955, there was a shortage of spades to screw into the tops of those guidons. Platoon 356 might not have any streamers, but it did have a shiny brass spade or as the guidon bearer called it: a point, on their guidon. It was necessary for the guidon bearer to remove the spade and put it in his pocket whenever the platoon went indoors, say for chow, because it was the custom for all guidons to be placed in a rack at the doors of buildings. To leave the spade on the guidon while in that rack, was to invite its immediate loss.

Well, the day finally arrived that the Platoon lost the point. The guidon bearer simply forgot to unscrew the point when he went into the chow hall. He came to Don immediately with the problem.

The guidon bearer came to Don because by that time in boot camp, the individualists and self-sufficient men stood out amongst the recruits. Don was a man who fixed problems for the Platoon. He *expedited* things.

Pete was his name, but he preferred to be called Don. He was fair-haired, blue-eyed, well built, quick with his hands and quicker with a smile. Don was a natural salesman: a people person. All the recruits liked and respected Don.

Platoon 356 had been losing contests to the other platoons all along and Don was fed up. He considered this loss of the guidon spade, the final insult.

Without another word, Don went hunting. At a jog, to appear on an errand, he moved through the other company areas, opportuning.

It was late October, but South Carolina could still muster a 90-degree day with little effort. Because Don had screwed his determination up to full throttle, it felt like 190 degrees. Don resolved not to return without a spade. That's all there was to it.

Well, God was good, because in a relatively short time Don found a platoon in formation, in front of its Quonset huts. The platoon was standing at attention, stomachs tight, chins tucked, sweat streaming, being harangued by their drill instructor (DI). The guidon was nowhere in sight.

Jogging around behind their Quonset huts Don peered through the rear windows, shading his eyes, nose pressed against the screen, searching for the hut with the guidon in it.

Sure enough, there it was leaning against the front wall by the entrance of one of the huts. A quick look over his shoulder and Don ripped the screen and forced the rear window.

During the fifties, there was an exercise, a form of harassment, which recruits endure as soon as they arrive at Parris Island. It was informally referred to as *Inzeezes an' outzeezes*. The harassment consists of rushing into and out of the Quonset huts as quickly as was humanly possible. The DIs were known to put recruits through this nonsense for hours at a time, in and out, in and out. The unmilitary command for falling out of formation and returning to the Quonset hut was *Get inside*, given with hubris.

When the DI gave this command, the boots were expected to run over each other in order not to be the last one into the Quonset hut. The last recruit in was likely to be punished. The recruits learned to disappear into the huts in seconds, sometimes taking the door off the hinges in the process.

Inside the Quonset hut, Don was frantically unscrewing the brass point from their guidon when he heard the command: "Get inside!"

Without a second to lose, Don sprinted for the rear window, unscrewing the point as he ran. There was no need to look over his shoulder to know what was happening. First, the violent bang of the door followed by gasps of surprise. There were expletives and shouts, "He's got the point" and the pounding of boots, all of which were mere background noise. Don's whole being was concentrated on the window. His stride stretched to the limit, and Don lunged through the window landing in a tight roll, coming up at a run.

What followed was probably Don's personal best sprint time ever, since a thorough beating was the price for losing the foot race. He knew from experience that this platoon had several good runners. Platoon 356 had competed against them in the past.

Fortunately, the window slowed them down. It was too small for more than one man at a time. The first *boot* out the window wasn't the fastest. Don's subconscious mind was thinking that it must have been an odd sight as he sprinted through the other company areas like a blur, with the whole platoon strung out behind him in pursuit. He clutched the shiny brass spade in a white knuckled grip, determined not to give in or give up for anything.

Rubbery legs and rasping breath were dragging him down by the time Platoon 356's Quonset huts hove into view. The drab galvanized steel huts never looked better. Those non-performers were suddenly Don's brothers, his saviors. Platoon 356 was sitting on the ground and wash racks cleaning boots, chatting, and waiting to see if Don would come home with the goods.

Someone spotted Don staggering along with his entourage. In a moment of desperation, Don held up the brass spade like a religious icon, for the platoon to see. It reflected the sun and in that flash, they knew what to do. The Platoon had been getting the dirty end of the stick for far too long.

Platoon 356 surged forward with roars of glee. The Platoon was composed of New York area recruits. Many were street fighters from the inner city. For once, there was a contest that they were familiar with!

There were skirmishes, black eyes, and bloodied noses. The other platoon began retreating. They weren't cohesive enough. They were too strung out and exhausted from the foot race. They knew that they would never see the point again, not on their guidon anyway. The DIs looked out the door of their hut and never said a word.

Platoon 356 had a point again. The spade didn't screw on right because it was the wrong thread, but it was all theirs.

Of far greater importance, Platoon 356 had fought its first winning battle. They were suddenly comrades in arms: brothers. Platoon 356 had actually won a contest, though no streamer would be forthcoming. They had become *a team* in those few short moments. In the remaining hot, humid weeks of boot camp, Platoon 356's guidon began to collect authentic streamers. Platoon 356 also developed a noticeable *strut* as it marched across the parade ground.

COJONES DE BRONCE

Usn

"It is a far, far better thing that I do than I have ever done"
Charles Dickens

How could I ever forget him? He did a very courageous thing, putting himself in great jeopardy, and for me, and he did it with such casual grace that contemplating it now, 41 years later, still makes my throat constrict.

It was a rather pleasant spring day with sunny skies, balmy breezes, a blue sea and a bluer cloudless heaven. What more could a carrier pilot ask for? Then, of course, there were those god damned sea snakes! As I walked forward on the flight deck toward my airplane, I looked over the starboard catwalk at the surface of the Tonkin Gulf. It almost made me sick. As far as the eye could see there were hundreds of thousands of sea snakes, sinuating through the water in clusters of a dozen or so. They ranged in size from about two feet to five feet. Of a yellowish green color, they swam just below the surface of the water with only their heads sticking out. Our intelligence officer had briefed us on them before we arrived in the Gulf for the first time and told us they were the most poisonous of all reptiles on the planet. The thought of parachuting into the water filled with those hideous things made my stomach churn.

Our flight headed inbound to a highly defended target in the Hanoi area of North Vietnam, and the year was 1968. The mission was photographic reconnaissance to assess the damage that had been done by a strike just thirty minutes earlier. Since it was such a highly defended target, I made the decision to go in as photo escort armed with four vice two Sidewinder air-to-air missiles. Our normal load-out was two of the deadly missiles, one each mounted on a single pylon on either side of the airplane's fuselage just aft of the cockpit. The reason for this was aircraft weight. Our tired, old F-8E Crusaders had grown in weight over the years from structural beef-ups and the addition of electronic warfare equipment and deceptive electronic countermeasures devices. The weight had become a problem since each additional pound of gear meant one pound of fuel less with which we were allowed to land back aboard ship.

At first it didn't seem to matter much. It was nothing more than a minor operational restriction with which we had to abide. But gradually, as the airplane's empty weight increased, we began to realize that our number of landing opportunities was decreasing by one for every 200 pounds of increase in empty weight. At night, a landing attempt used up three times as much fuel. So, for every 600 pounds of increase in the empty weight of the airplane, one less attempt to land was imposed. (In 1974, back in the Pentagon, I did a study for my own personal interest. Using the A-4, F-8, F-4 and A-7 as examples, I found that, on average, a Navy tactical carrier airplane grew in empty weight at the rate of one pound per day of operational life. The accuracy of that rule-of-thumb was startling.)

So it was with careful consideration that I opted for the four missile configuration because, after all, we were going into MiG country. Who knows? I might need the extra two Sidewinders. As was the standard practice, the photo pilot flying an RF-8 took the flight lead. I was his escort and his protection should the North Vietnamese decide to send out their MiGs. We "coasted in" about 20 miles south of Haiphong going at the "speed of heat" as usual and I found that, because of the drag associated with the extra missiles, I was using a lot more afterburner than the photo plane.

The target, which was a railroad bridge between Haiphong and the capital city of Hanoi, was heavily defended, but we already knew that. Nevertheless, the quantity of flak was startling as it always is. They were waiting for us, knowing that it was U.S. policy to get bomb damage assessment after each major raid. I was flying a loose wing on the photo plane, scanning the area for MiGs, of course, but also for flak because I knew that Ed would soon have to bury his head in his photo display shroud for the few final seconds of the run to be sure that the bridge span was properly framed in the camera's field of view. Neither he nor I wanted to mess this run up and have to come back another time. That would be too much! During the actual picture taking part of the run, when the photo pilot was too occupied to observe flak, I made it a habit to be in a strafing run at the most likely source of flak in the vicinity of the target. It always made me feel better since just sitting there being shot at is always unpleasant and unnerving.

Just as Ed settled down for the photo portion of the mission, which took an eternity of about five seconds, I heard a low SAM warble (radar lock-on) followed immediately by a high warble (SAM launch), and my heartbeat tripled in an instant. I was on Ed's left flank and saw the SAM lift off at about four o'clock and only maybe ten miles away. There was a huge cloud of dust around the base of the missile as it lifted off and leveled almost immediately as it accelerated towards us. There was nothing I could do but call it out knowing that Ed would have to break off his run at the very last minute. (I think the North Vietnamese knew precisely what they were doing). There was no way Ed could stay in his run because the missile was accelerating towards his tail at a startling rate. My mouth was dry as I keyed the microphone.

"One from Two. SAM lift-off at four o'clock, ten miles. Break hard right now! " Ed broke and I did the same, feeling the instant onset of at least nine G squeezing the G-suit bladders on my legs and abdomen. The SAM roared on by us just as another high warble came on in my headset. This one I didn't see and that really bothered me. "No joy on the second one, "I shouted into the mike. "Keep it coming right, Two. "Then I saw it and it scared me badly since it was now off my left wing and coming at us fast. "Reverse it left and down, "I shouted hoarsely over the radio. Watching it pass to our left and explode about 200 yards away, I saw that we were skimming the treetops and called out to Ed. "Two, let's get out of here!" I heard two distinct clicks of a microphone, and knew that Ed agreed with me. The water was only a few miles away by this time and we were headed straight toward it. The two Crusaders thundered across the beach at perhaps a 100 feet in full afterburner and doing in excess of 600 knots.

About 10 miles off the beach, when we knew we were outside the SAM and flak envelopes, we came out of burner and commenced a climb. Ed's voice came over the radio, sounding apologetic and sheepish. "Two, from One. I missed it! "We both felt badly. Bomb damage assessment of the bridge from the previous strike (half an hour earlier) was important, and we both knew it. Another strike would be launched within the hour to go after it if the bridge span was still standing. As we passed to the seaward side of the northern SAR (search and rescue) destroyer, I suggested that we report in to the ship's strike operation center and ask them what they wanted us to do; I was already fairly sure what the answer would be. We orbited at 15,000 feet over the gulf as Ed checked in and reported failure, and asked for directions since the strike seemed important to them. Panther Strike told us to wait while they checked with Task Force 77 for further directions. As suspected, after waiting what seemed like an eternity, they told us to go back and try again. After the photo run had been completed we were directed to return to the ship as fast as we could so that the results could be analyzed and another strike launched if necessary. At my urging, Ed requested that an airborne tanker be made available for us upon our going feet wet, and back we went. And they were waiting for us!

Ed made a similar approach, using a different ingress route, and this time, flak and a SAM warning notwithstanding, we got the pictures. We both over flew the bridge in excess of 600 knots, and made the turn toward the Gulf via a preplanned route that ran on a southerly heading just west of Haiphong and then almost due east to the water over a relatively unpopulated area. Just as we approached the target, my low-fuel warning light illuminated, and it shocked me. Nonetheless, we continued our egress from the target area as planned and went feet wet at a low altitude and a high speed.

I was elated because I was sure it was a successful photo run and neither of us had been hit. This time there hadn't even been any SAMs launched, just a radar lock-on. Ed had plenty of fuel remaining and began his climb at full power with the intent of hurrying back to Panther. I kissed him off and, looking at a fuel gauge that read only 400 pounds, I headed for a rendezvous with the tanker who had dropped down to 10,000 feet 20 miles southwest of the northern SAR destroyer. As I began my rendezvous with the tanker, my mouth was dry. With only 400 pounds of fuel, my engine would flame-out in just 15 minutes. This was, I thought ruefully, cutting it too damned close. The tanker had been refueling some A-4s in the air wing and been vectored to the northern SAR destroyer by the ship when we asked for a tanker just before going back in for the second run.

Naturally, I was extremely happy to see the tanker, and was equally anxious to get plugged in. When I told the tanker pilot my fuel state, his voice suddenly sounded a little strange. He was extremely apologetic and explained to me that he had just given away all of the fuel in his buddy store. I was shocked! How could this have happened? Somebody back at the ship had really screwed up by failing to tell him to hold at least 1,500 pounds for me. A cold chill crept over me. There was no way I could get even halfway back to the ship with only 400 pounds of fuel.

It is worth spending a few words of explanation on fuel and what it means to a carrier pilot. In any fleet squadron, there is SOP (standard operating procedure) that dictates landing back aboard ship with a reasonable fuel reserve to take care of emergencies like a crash on deck, bad weather, malfunctioning recover systems or a recovery delay for any of a dozen other reasons. For example, the low-level fuel warning-light comes on in the cockpit of an F-8 Crusader at 1,100 pounds remaining. No carrier pilot who wants a long, safe career should ever be caught airborne with that light illuminated. There is a similar light in the A-4 that comes on at about 1,100 pounds. So, to find oneself 125 nautical miles from the ship in a Crusader with 400 pounds of fuel is not just critical, it is way past critical! The stuff of which nightmares are made, which still makes one wake up from a sound sleep with sweat dripping off one's forehead.

By now we had joined up and were climbing to cruise altitude for our return to the ship, except I was not going to make it. It was a strange feeling, one of finality. It was all unreal. And again I thought of those sea snakes. We leveled off at 20,000 feet and, with my fuel gauge now reading 100 pounds, I began to prepare myself for ejection. We were flying close together. The lower my fuel reading, the closer I flew to him. Perhaps proximity to a friendly face made me feel comforted.

The A-4 tanker pilot throttled way back to match a maximum endurance profile for the Crusader. Since getting back to the ship was out of the question, we were buying me some time before I flamed out in just a few more minutes, but every minute now seemed very precious. The tanker pilot's head, which was only 50 feet away from mine, turned to look at me for what seemed like a long time but was probably only 20 seconds. Then I saw him look down in the cockpit. A moment later the propeller on the nose of his tanker buddy store began to windmill in the air stream. This was the driving mechanism that reeled the refueling basket in and out.

The buddy store consisted of a fuel tank, a refueling hose, a take-up reel and an air-driven propeller to deploy and retract the basket. The fuel tank contained 300 gallons (2,000 pounds of fuel) when full. The tanker pilot also had the capability of transferring fuel into and out of the tank from his own internal tanks. It was the tanker pilot's responsibility always to retain enough internal fuel to get back safely to the ship. I found it curious that the propeller was turning then was startled to see the refueling basket reel out to its full extension. The pilot then looked over at me and transmitted over the radio.

"Firefighter Two Zero Four, I have just transferred 500 pounds of fuel into the buddy store. Go get it." I couldn't believe my ears!

"What about you?" I asked, almost afraid to do so.

"You'd better take it while you can," he warned ominously as though he were already having second thoughts. I slid back into position and prepared to tank. Never was my tanking skill so necessary as at this moment. There could be no missed attempts. My last glance at the fuel gauge showed 100 pounds. I resolved not to look at it again. The sight made me physically ill.

The in-flight refueling probe on a Crusader is high on the port side of the fuselage just aft of the pilot. In actual measurements, the tip of the probe is exactly 31 inches to the left of the pilot's eye. Therefore, the inner rim of the refueling basket when the probe is centered in it is only about a foot away from the canopy. The basket seems to float around like some wayward, feathery entity whenever one tries to engage it with the probe. In actual fact, the probe, for all its airy movements, is in the tight grasp of a 250 knot gale. The air stream grips it like a vice. Therefore it has all of the resiliency of a steel rail. If it so much as touches the canopy of a Crusader, the result is an instant and violent implosion and fragmentation of the Plexiglas into a thousand tiny shards that end up everywhere inside the cockpit. To say that tanking is a touchy evolution is the understatement of the year.

Needless to say, my technique on this particular tanking attempt was flawless and the tip of the probe hit the basket in its dead center with a "clunk" that resulted in a small sine wave traveling up the hose to the end of the buddy store. It is a comforting sound and sensation that one can feel in his pants and right hand. It is the next best thing to sex!

The very act of tanking of course uses fuel. It therefore took me about 100 pounds to get the 500 pounds, which left me with a net gain of 400 pounds. Now my fuel gauge read a much more comfortable 500 pounds leaving me feeling in "hog heaven." I disengaged and slid once more out to the right side of the tanker. We looked at each other and there was an unspoken understanding in the tilt of the tanker pilot's head that he had bought me some time, perhaps only 15 minutes, but a very precious increment of life nonetheless. Experiencing no small amount of guilt, I felt compelled to ask him the obvious question.

"Can you make it back?" The answer was slightly delayed.

"I'm not sure," he said but quickly added. "There's another tanker up here somewhere. Maybe he's got a few pounds to give." The tanker pilot then inquired of the ship about the tanker that had been sent north to tank the BARCAP (barrier combat air patrol). They came back quickly and informed us that he was indeed returning at maximum speed to rendezvous with us. The voice that told us this was more mature and sounded more senior. I suspected immediately that, recognizing that they had screwed up this matter royally, they had put the first team on the problem. (On a carrier at sea, everyone is in training for the next higher notch on the ladder.)

We droned along still at maximum endurance, watching our fuel gauges and the distance measurement device on the TACAN display. It was really simple mathematics, the kind naval aviators learn to do quickly in their heads. My fuel flow gauge told me the engine was burning fuel at the rate of 2,400 pounds per hour (divide by 60 converts to 40 pounds per minute.) My airspeed indicator told me my speed was 300 knots. Indicated airspeed decreases as altitude increases at the rate of two percent per thousand feet. Therefore, at my altitude of 20,000 feet my true airspeed would actually be forty percent higher than what my indicated airspeed indicator read (40 percent of 300 equals 120, which when added to 300 equals 420 knots true airspeed. Divide 420 by 60 and it comes to seven miles per minute. If I am burning 40 pounds per minute, then each mile I traverse through the air cost me six pounds of fuel). By cross-checking the distance measuring equipment reading on my airspeed indicator that tells me how far away the carrier is, I corroborate that my ground speed is roughly what my true airspeed is, meaning little or no wind effect to worry about.

So, no matter how often I ran the numbers through my head it told me that my engine would flame-out long before I ever got to the ship. Again, I thought of those damned sea snakes. Our only hope was that the other tanker had some fuel left to give. Moments later a target appeared on the left side of my radar scope, 30 miles away and converging. A few moments later, my tanker pilot, who had eyes better than I, called out somewhat excitedly, "Tally Ho the tanker; 10 o'clock, 15 miles." The several minutes it took for us to complete the rendezvous seemed like forever, during which we were informed that there was 1,400 pounds of "giveaway" fuel available. My tanker pilot said, "Firefighter, you go first and take 800 and I'll take 600, okay?" What could I say? My fuel gauge again showed 300 pounds.

Of course, the ship gave us priority in the landing sequence. We made a straight in approach with the tanker taking interval on me at about 10 miles astern. The sight of the ship steaming into the wind with a ready deck is one of the most beautiful sights in all of my memory. The LSOs seemed to understand our sense of urgency. We both caught the number two wire and taxied forward for shutdown. The arrestment felt great, and the feel of the ship under my wheels felt wonderful. The blast of warm air that filled my cockpit when I opened the canopy tasted like pure oxygen. Life was beautiful at that moment! As I climbed out of the cockpit, I felt a sudden and enormous exhaustion. Then I took one last look at the fuel quantity gauge. It read 100 pounds!

On the way from the airplane to the ready room I took a short detour to the edge of the flight deck and scanned the sea for the snakes. Strangely, there were none to be seen!

Five minutes later, while finishing the filling out of the maintenance "yellow sheet" in my ready room seat, I took a sip of steaming hot coffee and relished the moment. Then I got up, walked over to the duty officer's desk and pressed the lever on the 19 MC squawk box. "Ready Room Four, this is Ready Room Two, Commander Gillcrist calling. Is the pilot of Four One Four there?" The answer was immediate.

"He's listening" said a voice.

"Young man," I said. "You have cojones of brass. I owe you one." The now familiar voice of the tanker pilot came right back.

"No problem, Skipper, glad to be of help. It's always a pleasure to pass gas to a fighter pilot. I'll collect at the bar in Cubi."

"You're on," I finished.

I never got to pay off the debt. Three days later, that fine young man was literally blown out of the sky by a direct hit from an 85mm anti-aircraft shell! The three salvos from the Marine honor guards' rifles jolted me in much the same way that the violent 85mm explosion must have done when it ended that young man's life. For the first time in my life, as I stood at attention, saluting with the bugler playing taps, the tears coursed down my cheeks. The flight deck was heaving slowly in mute response to a gentle swell. Then the Marine honor guard tilted the catafalque up. The coffin slid out from under the American flag and fell into the sea.

THE PARABLE

usmc

"Give them great meals of beef and iron and steel, they will eat like wolves and fight like devils."
- Shakespeare

Platoon 356 was the "F Troop" of Parris Island. Whether by design or chance it contained more than its fair share of foul balls, non-performers, and outlaws. The platoon had too many guys who didn't have a *full sea bag*. Chuck was one of them.

One day, as the duty guard was standing watch on the platoon clothesline, three recruits from another platoon, came running by. Two of the recruits cut the clothes line and ran off with the platoon's freshly laundered clothes. The third, the toughest, fought the guard to allow his pals time to escape. This organized theft was commonplace at Parris Island. When the Drill Instructor (DI) found out about the theft, the already battered guard was given another battering.

Within a day or so of the laundry theft, Sergeant Stryker, a Napoleonic, truculent, wee-little-man was lecturing the platoon in the company street when a recruit from some other platoon ambled by. Sergeant Stryker grabbed the recruit by his rope (all recruits had a rope around their necks, with their locker key on it). With his victim firmly in hand, Sergeant Stryker began a harangue on company area security. He explained that the earlier theft of the clothing was a direct result of strangers wandering into Platoon 356's area. The platoon was instructed to punish any interlopers. If they did not do so, they would be in deep trouble with Sergeant Stryker.

As an example of the kind of punishment the platoon should mete out, Stryker took this poor soul's helmet and struck the recruit across the face. Sergeant Stryker used the edge of the helmet, not the customary rounded top, so the recruit was cut to the bone of his skull, severing the muscle, causing his face to sag. The platoon was unable to stop the bleeding. An ambulance had to be called and this is where Chuck came in.

"Chucker Boy" as the DIs liked to call him, was always in trouble. He was a tall skinny thug from Bayonne. His most prominent features were his multiple broken nose, facial scar tissue from a hundreds street fights, and dirty blond hair that grew in tufts. Punishment was a daily event for Chucker Boy. As time went by, some of the platoon began to think Chuck liked punishment.

Their suspicions regarding Chucker Boy's romance with pain were confirmed when the Platoon was on special assignment for a week. Chucker Boy got in a fight with a recruit from some other platoon. Chuck was badly beaten.

After the fight was called, he told the victor that he would be there same time next day for a rematch. Next day Chuck was badly beaten again. He began to lose his facial identity. The following day Chuck went at it again, and on, and on until the Platoon was reassigned, never once winning a single bout.

Years later, at Madison Square Garden, Chucker Boy, then known as "The Bayonne Bleeder" took on Muhammad Ali and was beaten again. Chuck was euphoric; probably had an orgasm.

Anyway, when an investigation team came to find out what had happened to the poor soul who Sergeant Stryker injured, the platoon all denied any knowledge of the event. Then, Chucker Boy spoke up, surprising them, and told the investigators the whole story.

As a direct result of Chucker Boy's testimony, Stryker was court marshaled.

The other DIs shook their heads, thinking, *Platoon 356 was about as organized as a herd of cattle. They didn't measure up. They never seemed to get the point.*

The following day, the Senior DI, a Staff Sergeant named Merlin Jones, marched the platoon into the company area and climbed up on top of one of the concrete wash tables. These were tables on which the recruits stone-washed their clothes with cold water in all kinds of weather.

Sergeant Jones was a veteran of the Pacific and Korea. He limped because it was rumored that he lost most of his toes in Korea. Sergeant Jones had a phlegmy voice, probably from all the Beechnut chewing tobacco he used. Sergeant Jones would deliver a harangue to the platoon in a loud voice, then spit, and then continue with the harangue again.

Sergeant Jones was a lean, ancient, ridge runner from West Virginia. He always wore starched fatigues, bleached white from sweat and the Corps in general. One day, as part of the hygiene syllabus, Sergeant Jones lectured the recruits on the difference between "clean dirt" and "dirty dirt," an interesting and colorful differentiation.

On this particular day however, Sergeant Jones, after staring at the platoon for fifteen minutes, preached the following parable:

"Once upon a time, there were these piss ants. They wandered around the parade ground aimlessly day after day, doing nothing constructive. This aimless wandering went on until one day one of the piss ants found a huge pile of shit.

This enterprising piss ant gathered all the other useless piss ants around him and explained that if they could only learn to work together, they could bring this prize home and profit from their cooperative effort. Under their new leader's guidance, the piss ants heaved mightily and by working as a team, were able to lift this pile of shit onto their shoulders.

Then, off they marched, with the leader counting cadence. They did quite well for a while aided by antenna signals from their leader who rode atop the pile of shit.

The signal system was simplicity itself. A wave of the right antenna meant turn right oblique. A wave of the left antenna meant turn left oblique. What could be simpler?

As the piss ants approached their nest, they started down an incline at the edge of the parade ground and since they were tired and the load was heavy, the piss ants began to stumble and stagger, running faster and faster. Soon, they were in a headlong scramble down the incline, madly trying to control and not drop the pile of shit.

Their leader, recognizing the problem, was frantically waving both antennae. Now, all the piss ants saw him frantically waving both antennae, but did not have the presence of mind to figure out what this meant.

In the end they fell down and were covered in shit.

After a long silence, their leader managed to calm down long enough to explain through gritted teeth, that when he waved his right antenna, it meant turn right oblique. When he waved his left antenna, it meant turn left oblique, but goddamn it! When he waves both antennae, it meant one thing: *THIS SHIT HAS GOT TO STOP.*

With that, Sergeant Jones hopped of the wash stand and stalked off.

As green as the recruits were, all of them knew who the piss ants were, with the possible exception of Chucker Boy.

After that day, the platoon began to focus on teamwork, and started to improve their performance in the daily competitions against the other platoons. Platoon 356 developed some measure of pride. The Platoon finally began to see the point of Boot Camp.

EVEL KNIEVEL

USN

"Fasten your seat belts; it's going to be a bumpy ride."
Mankeiwicz

The year must have been 1969 and I was making one of my many solo trips across the United States attendant with a permanent change of station from San Diego to Washington, D.C. I put Nancy and the children aboard an airplane and then headed east in our second car, a bright red Volkswagen Beetle. The route began on Interstate 8 and I was crossing the Arizona-New Mexico approaching the Powder River Canyon.

The scenery was spectacular and by mid-afternoon I had begun the dizzying descent to the bottom of the canyon when I came upon a sign that told me there was a scenic viewing area ahead. The road curved right and I crossed the centerline headed for the viewing area with a little more speed than I would have wanted but there was oncoming traffic and I had to make my move quickly or hold up the traffic following me. As my car crossed over the shoulder and onto the gravel surface of the viewing site I headed for a set of logs set end-to-end which constituted a primitive guardrail at the edge of a sheer drop-off of several thousand feet to the bottom of the canyon. I began early to apply the brakes to slow down and was horrified to note that the brake pedal went all the way to the floor with no brake pressure at all. Now, it seemed that I was hurtling at break-neck speed toward the flimsy guardrail and certain death. Actually, my speed was probably only 30 miles per hour but with only 50 feet of gravel surface between me the guardrail my speed might just as well have been 90.

With my heart in my mouth I reefed the wheel hard to the right and yanked up on the emergency handbrake with all of my strength. The car began to skid as it swung to the right and gradually came to a stop just as both left wheels touched the guard rail amidst a cloud of dust. Two elderly couples who were standing maybe 100 feet farther down the guard rail turned to look at me probably wondering who this cowboy was. I enjoyed the view long enough for my heart rate to return to normal, then slowly drove to the nearest service station to get my brakes fixed.

JOHN GLENN

usn

"One of the most underestimated of all political resources is personal attention."
Doris Kearns Goodwin

How could I ever forget the time I landed my T2V-1 jet trainer at Marine Corps Air Station, Cherry Point, on a re-fueling stop and enjoyed an unexpected fifteen minutes of fame? It was 29 May 1961 and I was on what was called an "out and in" cross-country logistics flight from Naval Air Station, Patuxent River, Maryland.

While the transient line crew was re-fueling my airplane I walked to the "greasy spoon" cafeteria in the terminal building and ordered a hamburger and cup of coffee. An ancient DC-3 taxied up to the terminal and began disgorging what looked like older women in civilian clothing not unlike what tourists wear. The crowd entered the cafeteria and one of the women spotted me sitting alone at a table in my flight suit and headed directly toward me. What in the world have I done, I wondered?

"Major," she purred excitedly, "Would you autograph my itinerary for me please?" I was stunned. She explained that she was part of a group of high school educators taking advantage of a summer orientation program offered by the U.S. Air Force, visiting various military bases, and had no idea she would run across the famous John Glenn! I wrote a glowing comment to her and signed "John Glenn" with a flourish. In no time my table was surrounded by a cluster of giggling, gushing school marms pushing their itineraries across the table for me to autograph.

When all of the autographing was over they left me alone, thrilled that they had met a celebrity. (In 1957 John had achieved fame by setting a cross-country speed record in an F-8 Crusader.)

There is a slight facial similarity between John Glenn and me and once again, in 1965, my wife, Nancy and I were approached in a San Diego restaurant, by an older lady in her cups who mistook us for Annie and John Glenn despite my protestations to the contrary. It was embarrassing to Nancy. But, there in the flight line cafeteria at Marine Corps Air Station, Cherry Point, it seemed like an innocent deception and it gave the school marms something to talk about for the rest of their orientation tour.

I wrote John a letter explaining what I had done and hoped it wouldn't bother him. He didn't respond.

Thirty-four years later I was doing research for a book on the F8 *Crusader.* I made an appointment for an interview with Senator Glenn in his Washington office. His secretary advised me that the best she could do was fit me in for a 20 minute slot on his busy schedule. The purpose of the interview was to get his account of his famous flight from California to New York to set a coast-to-coast speed record. He was most animated and when my time was up he blythely waved a pontifical arm at his frantic secretary and we talked on and on. The interview lasted at least two hours. When I finally left I believe I had made a mortal enemy out of his secretary. When the book, a coffee table sized tome, was published it featured a full-page photo of John Glenn with a forward by him.

It was after his much-publicized second trip into space in 2006 that I had occasion to write to him. One of my seventh grade students wrote a wonderful account of the flight, having traveled to Cape Canaveral to observe the event. Her essay won first prize in my creative writing course contest. I enclosed a copy of her essay. Senator Glenn was gracious enough to write a very personal note on a picture of himself which I received promptly in the mail. It was a surprise during the award ceremony and her father showed up unbeknownst to her, resplendent in his naval officer blues. Moments like that are unforgettable.

NAP TIME

usn

*"There's a Providence sits up aloft,
To keep watch for the life of poor Jack."*
Dibdin

It is one thing to suddenly wake up and find yourself at the wheel of a speeding car. It is quite another to have it happen in an airplane. All of us have, at one time or another, had a momentary nod off in a car. If it is only half a second, and a bob of the head is the catalyst to complete and frightening awareness of the terrible danger into which we had just placed ourselves. We nevertheless get a sickening sense of guilt for demonstrating such stupidity.

Sometime in the spring of 1954 I was on a cross-country training flight with a squadron mate. We thought we were hotshots and, at the same time, "bulletproof." Permission to "borrow" two of the squadron's twelve airplanes for the weekend was considered precious and was based upon the stipulation that we get them back to the hangar at Moffet Field by Sunday evening...or else!

But, in our flight planning we had gone too far; exceeded our prudent limits; and ultimately put ourselves and our airplanes in jeopardy. Extrication from our predicament could only come with additional risk, and we took it.

That's how we found ourselves, at ten p.m. arcing across the great western plains at 40,000 feet headed for our destination, Moffet Field, in Sunnyvale, California. It was our fifth flight of the day which had begun sixteen hours earlier, dodging weather as we headed westward. We were dead tired, having long since burned up whatever adrenaline reserves which are called up by flying at near the speed of sound at 40,000 feet. As was our policy, my wingman, Robin McGlohn, and I swapped the lead with each leg of our flight. On this last leg Robin was leading and I was his wingman. A millions stars lit up the sky…it was like a dream.

The startling awakening occurred and, of course, fear rushed over me like a bucket of ice water dumped over my head. Everywhere I looked I saw white lights. Straight over head the lights looked different from those I viewed from the side of the canopy and downward. It took a moment for me to recognize that the lights overhead were farmhouses and dwellings in small towns. In other words I was inverted! Not completely, but nearly so.

A quick glance into the cockpit, at the instrument panel, told me that the airplane's nose was 30 degrees down, my wing attitude was a 120 degree bank and the plane was just going supersonic! I made a panic recovery to wings and nose level and began the long ascent from 26,000 back to 40,000 feet wondering, as I did so, where in the world was Robin? Also, I wondered just how much I should tell him about the last few moments of my flying career. How long had I been asleep? Who knew? Instinct told me to keep silent about my lapse of consciousness.

"One, I've lost sight of you. Blink your lights, please," I transmitted.

"Wilco," Robin answered and I searched the sky above me for the telltale blinking lights among all the stars. No luck.

"No joy, " I transmitted, noting that I was now climbing past 35,000 feet. The era was before airplanes carried anti-collision lights. One could only blink lights by depressing a button intermittently causing all external lights to go on and off. Suddenly I saw him almost directly above me. Apparently, during my maneuver I had gotten slightly ahead and below him. "Tally ho. Joining up from six o'clock," I called exultantly.

Thirty minutes later we started a long descent into Moffet Field. I had learned a big lesson from that flight but chose not to pass it on to Robin after all.

THE NORWEGIAN LADY

usn

"A fool there was and he made his prayer,
Even as you and I,
To a rag and a bone and a hank of hair.
The fool, he called her his lady fair.
We called her the lady who did not care,
Even as you and I."
Kipling – "The Harpy"

It was during the 1971 deployment of U.S.S. *Saratoga*, (CV-60) that, before in-chopping into the Mediterranean, the carrier battle group took a short detour into the North Atlantic to participate in a NATO joint exercise. I forget the name of the exercise, but I will never forget the beautiful Norwegian woman whose image became forever connected with our ship and its embarked air wing.

There was to be an exercise planning conference in Oslo, just before the start of the operation. As much as I would have wanted to attend, the air wing was at sea, so I sent LCDR Fred Wright, the air wing operations officer, to represent me. It has always been my belief that the CAG belonged on board when the wing was flying. But, before an elated Fred departed in the COD bound for Oslo I gave him one directive, to bring me back a memorable souvenir of Norway. Little did I realize that the "souvenir" would become an icon in the Sixth Fleet for years to come. Three days later Fred placed in my hands a cardboard mailing tube about 36 inches long and two inches in diameter; soon after the COD brought him back to *Saratoga*. There was a mischievous smile on Fred's face as he admonished me to open it up only after I retired to my stateroom that evening.

Several hours later I opened the parcel in my stateroom and was astounded to find a 24" by 36" color poster of a beautiful Norwegian woman. What made the souvenir so startling was both what she revealed and didn't reveal. She was standing with her body facing the camera, feet slightly apart and head turned to her right in profile. There was an expression of extreme rapture on the classic face. She wore a black armless and legless wet suit with a zipper running from neck to crotch, and had unzipped it to a point about six inches below her navel. She was holding the suit open exposing her breasts. Painted on the open expanse of skin was a colorful depiction of a burning World War I biplane in a vertical dive and trailing smoke and flames. The nose of the airplane seemed about to enter the unexposed portion of the suit where the zipper ended.

The overall effect of the piece of op-art was, to say the least, breathtaking. Of course, I hung the poster on the steel wall of my stateroom and waited for comments at the next meeting which I sometimes held in my room for small groups of staff or squadron commanding officers. It was difficult to maintain eye contact with my visitors after that.

The air wing commander was required to maintain an air wing command presentation for briefings to "visiting firemen" when necessary. Oftentimes when the carrier visited foreign ports the carrier group commander, a two star admiral, would put on a "dog and pony" show for the visiting dignitaries. In preparation for our port visit to the beautiful island of Palma de Mallorca in the western Mediterranean the admiral asked to see my command presentation which he hoped to include in his presentation to the Governor General of Mallorca. I normally gave the briefing using 35 millimeter color slides but this time decided to use an easel and butcher paper with specially made cartoons for better effect. If the admiral liked the presentation it was my intention to transfer the butcher paper cartoons to 35 millimeter slides.

There was an enlisted man on my staff who happened to be a talented illustrator and who did a masterful job on the butcher paper graphics. On the day of the practice briefing I slipped the poster of the Norwegian Lady into the butcher paper pad at the very end of the briefing. My peroration stated that if we didn't maintain our fighting skills while deployed our combat readiness would "go down in flames"! While I was saying this I raised the last page of the briefing showing the Norwegian Lady. I watched carefully the expression on the faces of the admiral and his chief of staff.

It was truly a magic moment! There was a sharp in-taking of breath from the chief of staff as he waited for an explosion from the admiral but none came, just a very pregnant silence. Then the admiral smiled beatifically. Obviously, I had turned what he had expected to be a "ho hum" presentation into a startling experience.

About a week later a messenger from the admiral's staff came to my stateroom and asked to borrow the poster so that his boss could use it in a briefing. It was with some reluctance that I took it off the wall, fearing that I might never see it again. I must had said words to that effect to the messenger because he returned with the art work several days later along with a 35 millimeter color slide as well as an 8" by 10" glossy print of the Norse beauty. The slide became the final slide in my command presentation and was seen by an ever-widening audience as the deployment wore on.

At the end of my tour of duty as CAG 3, I made a big fuss over the turnover of the Norwegian Lady poster to my relief who in turn repeated the gesture at his own tour end. I really hated to part with the poster but it wasn't the sort of thing one took home from the ship.

Now, 32 years later, a Navy awash in political correctness and moral rectitude would never countenance such a suggestive visual aid being used in an official briefing. So my Norwegian Lady slide now molders in a cigar box full of miscellaneous slides. I suppose I should destroy it but I can't. Nor can I help but wonder where the original poster might be. It is inconceivable that anyone could have destroyed such a mesmerizingly beautiful picture.

Maybe the admiral has it!

THE CORNWELL AFFAIR

usn

"Victory is not won in miles but in inches,
win a little now, hold your ground,
and later win a little more."
Louis Lamour

The system whereby the U.S. Navy promotes its officers has been criticized over the years by many of us for a number of reasons, some of them valid others with not much substance. But, for all of its warts it is, in my opinion, still the best promotion system of all of the services. Navy personnel deserve a promotion system which rewards effort, integrity and commitment. They also deserve a system which keeps faith with the principles stipulated in their service contracts. This is a story about how the system maintained its integrity.

At exactly 0730 on 18 October 1983, I convened the Aviation Commander Command Screen Board at the Bureau of Naval Personnel in Washington, D.C. This is the body which annually meets to choose those fortunate young men and women to command aircraft squadrons and carrier air wings. These chosen few will ultimately become the future leaders of the Navy.

As the two-star president of the board, I called a meeting in the "tank" (the voting room) to introduce the board members to the staff assigned to assist them in their important work, to swear them all in and to make an important decision.

The tank is a large room with five rows of eight seats arranged on an incline facing a concave wall onto which are projected three large screens. Behind the top row of seats is a fairly sophisticated, well-equipped projection booth manned by several talented projectionists. The right arm rest on each seat is equipped with a signaling keyboard which permits the occupant to vote secretly with his fingers. There are five keys which permit graduated scoring. The left hand key, if depressed, registers a "no" or zero vote. The second key from the left produces a 25% confidence vote. The third key 50%, the fourth 75% and the right hand key equates to a 100% or "yes" vote. During voting the lights are turned down partially to permit better viewing of the screens but also to enhance voting discretion.

The board is not a statutory board and therefore is not bound by any particular set of operating rules. This meant that I could run it anyway I desired. However, it is such an important body in developing the future leadership of the Navy that I proposed that we operate by the rules which govern the deliberations of statutory boards such as promotion boards.

Promotion boards are guided by the Defense Officer Personnel Management Act (DOPMA), an act of congress and therefore the law of the land. We decided in a completely democratic manner.

We voted by secret ballot. I was pleased to note that we made a unanimous decision to abide by statutory promotion board rules and procedures.

As an additional task for that first meeting, we identified that portion of the candidates under consideration who would be ruled out by virtue of a combined numerical grade score based solely upon their fitness reports.

This is a standard first step on all selection boards on which I have served. We were very conservative in screening out a certain bottom percentage of officers well below that which represented the total number of officers to be selected.

This would be a purely numerical first screening and I returned to my temporary office to conduct some business.

Much to my surprise, I was approached by my administrative Assistant (assigned by the Bureau of Personnel), Captain McWhinney, who handed me a yellow telephone ticket. There was a knowing look in his eyes (which escaped me at the moment) when he handed me the paper. It simply stated that the Secretary of the Navy wanted to see me in his office at 0830. More curious than anything, I went over (it was a short ten minute walk) and reported to the secretary's executive assistant.

To my surprise, I was let into the inner office immediately and (even more sinister) the executive assistant didn't follow me in to take notes, which was his usual modus operandi.

The office was empty except for the secretary who walked over to the door and closed it saying, as it closed, "This is a non-conversation." I nodded my understanding and we both sat down at the coffee table in the center of the office.

"You probably don't know Lieutenant Commander Larry Cornwell, do you?" was the Secretary's opening statement.

"As a matter of fact, Mister Secretary, I do know him," I replied, explaining that Larry had been sent up to represent COMNAVAIRLANT in a study group I had convened (as OP-50 a few months earlier). "He seems to be a pretty good guy," I added, "But, I don't know him professionally as an aviator."

The Secretary went on to explain that Larry was not appreciated for his talents and was not in particular favor within his own community, pointing out that people, like Capt. Bruce Bremner (the AIRLANT heavy attack community representative on the board,) and Capt. Jim McKenzie (his West Coast counterpart) were simply not in his corner. Therefore, Larry's chances of being selected for command of a fleet squadron were slim.

It was obvious that the Secretary knew the board membership, as well as being personally acquainted with those board members from the A-6 community (Bremner and McKenzie).

The Secretary made no bones about the fact that he wanted Larry Cornwell to be screened for a fleet squadron and that I was the person who was going to see that it happened.

Not knowing Larry's operational reputation, I felt comfortable assuring the secretary that Larry's record would receive very close scrutiny, and that he would get every chance to be properly represented. There was a very good chance, I felt, that screening Larry would not be a problem. Little did I know what was in store for me!

It was perhaps half an hour later that I re-entered the board office and was greeted with quizzical stares from the several people in the office. There were knowing smiles when I asked for Lieutenant Commander Cornwell's service record.

Captain McWhinney was not one to mince words and approached me while Cornwell's service jacket was being retrieved from the main boardroom.

"Admiral, I think you ought to know that Lieutenant Commander Cornwell's record has already been screened out by the numerical cut." I was horrified!

"What? Was he that bad?" McWhinney's nod told me the worst.

"Please ask Bruce Bremner to step in here," I asked with a dry taste in my mouth and an empty, leaden feeling in my stomach. Captain Bruce Bremner walked in with a wry grin on his face. I think I understood its implications before I even began to speak.

"Bruce, do me a favor," I asked. "Please take a look at Larry Cornwell's record and get right back to me about what you think his chances are." The expression on Bruce's face was a study as he walked out. An hour later he reported back to me with the bad news.

Bruce shook his head and said, simply, "No dice, Admiral." My heart sank.

"Here, give it to me," I said, reaching for the file Bruce carried. "I'll review it myself."

The plain brown manila file contained an envelope with a few dozen microfiche files. Throwing them onto my microfiche viewer, I went through the official service record file on Lieutenant Commander Lawrence Cornwell, U.S. Navy (Reserve).

It was not good. Larry was definitely not what we would call in the trade, "a water-walker." There were too many Bs and even a few Cs on his record of fitness reports. Many of them contained recommendations for promotion "when eligible." One of the accepted requirements, for anyone wanting to screen for command, was promotion recommendations "ahead of his peers" or as they are called, "accelerated." I was now feeling even more uncomfortable, and called for Captain McKenzie.

Jim walked in a few minutes later with that knowing expression on his face which I was beginning to resent. I gave Jim the same spiel, handed him the now infamous file and watched him walk back to his desk. The same sinking feeling in the pit of my stomach returned. I knew what Jim's answer would be. When Jim returned an hour later he gave me the same verdict I had gotten from Bremner, "No way."

This was now serious, really serious! The Secretary of the Navy clearly wanted me to screen Larry Cornwell for command of a fleet A-6 squadron. It was also within my power, with a simple word, to direct that Larry Cornwell's name be put on the command list. But, there was a problem...me!

I really did not want to roll over under pressure from the Secretary. Furthermore, I had already seen some damned fine naval aviator's miss the cut simply because of the competition. This particular year, 1983, the competition was stiff. To arbitrarily elevate Larry Cornwell above so many other names whose records were far better rankled me. It would mean that one fine officer would fail to command a fleet squadron because it had been given to Larry Cornwell. It just wasn't right.

I believe I must have gone into denial for the rest of the week. We labored at the tedious process of screening out, officer by officer, those individuals who, for whatever reason, didn't quite meet the standards. After twenty years I do not recall losing any sleep that week but I'm sure I must have.

At any rate, we finished up and all signed the list of those highly qualified individuals to whom the system would bestow its highest honor - command of a fleet squadron.

Lieutenant Commander Lawrence Cornwell's name was not on the list!

On Saturday morning the screening board met for the last time to settle some administrative matters and disband. Then, with a dry mouth, I drove back to the Pentagon and walked the long walk from my regular office down to the Office of the Secretary of the Navy. This was not going to be a pleasant meeting, I knew. I had called the Secretary's executive assistant and asked to speak to his boss. He suggested that I come on over and he would try to fit me in to the several visitors that were lined up to see the secretary that Saturday morning.

Having been in the executive assistant's position in a previous Pentagon tour, I knew the routine. There were no formal visits or meetings on the weekends. The people who simply had to see the secretary just showed up and waited for an opportunity. My discomfort grew as I waited...and waited...and waited. After three hours of watching people go in and out of the Secretary's door, it became apparent to me that the Secretary already knew the results of the board and knew therefore, that Larry Cornwell was not on the list. It also meant that Larry, having had his last "look" would never command a fleet squadron.

It also became apparent to me that I was not going to get in to see the Secretary. So, I leaned over and tore off a sheet from the executive assistant's desk note pad. He watched me as I scribbled the following note:

"Mr. Secretary, we did our best but Larry Cornwell's record was simply not good enough to make the cut. This was a very competitive year for all prospective command candidates, especially for those in the medium attack community (Larry's and the Secretary's community). I am sorry, but it just wasn't in the books for Larry. Very respecfully. Paul Gillcrist."

The executive assistant watched me intently as I wrote the note and I sensed he was reading it (upside down). When I finished, I handed the note to the executive assistant, walked out the door and took the long hike down the E-ring to my office. I didn't know then that I had just committed career suicide.

It was years later that one my close friends, a Captain in the Navy told me that Larry Cornwell was "an old drinking buddy" of the secretary's who, himself a reserve officer, flew as a bombardier navigator in A-6s! The Captain also told me that everyone in naval aviation was watching to see if the Secretary would "roll me over"!

Perhaps it was better that I didn't know all of this at the time. Although I am certain that I would not have done it any differently!

On that sunny day in Washington, D.C. so many years ago the squadron command selection system was working the way it was intended to work. Thank God for that!

HO, HO, HO, MERRY CHRISTMAS

usn

"That's enough for any man, to keep a cool head."
Conrad

From the time our children were old enough to understand Christmas until the youngest was old enough to know better, my wife and I would follow the same routine on the morning of the 25th. We would complete the wrapping of gifts we had left unfinished the night before, set them around the tree and finally decide we were ready.

Then, I would take a small set of bells and, bending over to stay out of sight, run around the outside of the house shouting, in a loud voice, "Ho, ho, ho, Merry Christmas" several times. By this time I was back at the front door and I would slam it loudly. Then I would run around to the rear door and let myself in quietly and, picking up my cup of coffee, walk into the living room, sit down and watch the opening of gifts by a squealing foursome of excited children.

It was great fun and always seemed to work smoothly until the Christmas of 1958 when I tried the routine on a particularly cold morning in inappropriate attire. The reason for the glitch in our routine was that Nancy and I had over-slept a little. The kids were awakening and Nancy went down the hallway to keep them in their bedrooms until I had time to do my thing. There wasn't time, I had decided, to dress so I foolishly decided to do it in my underwear and without shoes. There was about six inches of snow on the ground and the temperature was somewhere in the low teens…definitely not the kind of weather to be running around outside undressed and unshod. But, what the hell I thought. I will only be for a minute or two. What could go wrong?

Quietly slipping out the front door of our single-dwelling brick home I made the circuit of the house, passing by each bedroom window making with the bells and "Ho, ho, hos." Then I went to the back door and tried to let myself in unobtrusively. It was locked, and Nancy was by now in the living room watching the children's antics! I knocked quietly and called her name. No luck. I tried it again a little louder. Surely, I thought, Nancy will wonder where I am and come out to the kitchen and let me in. Still no luck. By now I was cold standing there in my underwear and my bare feet were absolutely frozen. I was still reluctant to pound on the door for fear that the children would catch on to our little ruse and the wonder of Christmas and Santa Claus would be over forever.

It was at this moment that I became aware of someone watching me. Looking across the back yard to the house in the next row of brick homes, I saw our neighbor, Ellie Blaschka watching me intently through her kitchen window! The distance was no more than sixty feet or so and I could clearly see the expression on her face. Her face was inscrutable as she must have wondered what, in the world her neighbor was doing standing out in the freezing weather barefoot and in his underwear. It was one of those classic moments we never forget.

THREE IS A CROWD"

usn

"Luck is like a sum of gold, to be spent."
Allenby

Like most other landing signal officers of the era, "Moon" Vance was a legend unto himself. A big, burly man with the unerring eye of the skilled LSO, he commanded respect wherever he was assigned to guide Navy pilots back to a safe carrier arrested landing. A few years ago, when Moon died of cancer, I went to the effort to fly from San Diego to Washington, D.C. to attend his funeral and interment in Arlington National Cemetery. The Chief of Naval Operations, himself, insisted on rendering the eulogy in which he extolled the many unusual characteristics of the legend we all knew as Moon Vance. In attendance were hundreds of people, many of them old friends and shipmates whom I hadn't seen in ages. The small chapel at Fort Myers was filled to over-flowing. The side aisles were full and all space against the walls was occupied with standees. There was even a small crowd of Moon Vance admirers gathered out on the front steps of the chapel for lack of space inside. I recall thinking, frankly, that I'll be lucky to draw a fraction of this crowd when I check out.

Moon was an informal man, who readily disavowed most of the pomp and circumstance associated with a life and career in the military. His whole approach to living was laid back. But, when it came to his profession, he was intensely passionate and colorful. As an example, Moon loved the rumpled, casual look of the U.S. Navy fore and aft uniform cap, otherwise called the garrison cap, which was available only in the khaki color of the summer service khaki uniform. In those days naval aviators referred to the garrison cap as a "piss cutter." It could be folded and slipped into the pocket of a flight suit when flying and put on at the end of a flight while still sitting in the cockpit after removing ones helmet. As a counter obsession, he hated the standard Navy bridge cap which was specified for all Navy uniforms, whether blue, white or khaki (or even green). Changing the cap cover to fit the uniform was always a pain in the neck since it required disassembling the contraption whenever it needed to be either cleaned or changed.

So, when Moon was relieved of command of the N.A.S. Point Mugu-based Test and Evaluation Squadron FOUR (VX-4) in 1987, he did it with the typical Moon Vance flourish and *panache*. It was a combined change of command and retirement ceremony. The legend, known as Moon was leaving the service as a Navy Captain, after spending twenty-six years on the wind-swept LSO platforms of nearly every aircraft carrier in the U.S. Navy.

The specified uniform, that time of year, for official ceremonies such as changes of command, was summer dress whites, the fancy uniform with the stiff, choker, white collar. This was a non-negotiable U.S. Navy regulation adhered to with all the rigidity of the once-commonplace practice of keel-hauling. On a steaming, hot summer day at Point Mugu one might actually prefer keel-hauling to being choked by that damnable stiff collar. So, Moon, ever the maverick, decided to ignore the rules and conduct his change of command ceremony in the much more comfortable summer service white uniform with the short sleeved, open collar white shirt with epaulets. After all, he must have reasoned, it was his change of command and he was also retiring after a distinguished career!

But, it was not enough that Moon flaunted the uniform regulations in this manner. To add insult to injury, Moon created his own special alteration to existing uniform regulations. He went to a local tailor and had the man create a piss cutter made out of the same white polyester material as the summer service blouse. Now, this really took *chutzpah!*

I received an engraved invitation to the event and, as the former naval district commandant of that area, knew that the time of year for the promulgation of the change from winter to summer uniforms (and vice versa) had already occurred.

Knowing Moon for the maverick he was, I accepted the invitation with a nagging apprehension in the back of my mind. The man was certain to pull some stunt but what would it be, I wondered?

The day came for the auspicious event and I flew from Washington, DC, to be the guest speaker for the occasion. I knew from the invitation that the ceremony would be conducted in the non-regulation summer service white uniform and had chosen not to allow my aide to call and challenge Moon on the issue. After all, I rationalized, who else would be there? Who would put me on report in that tiny, out-o-the-way air station an hour north of Los Angeles? Despite exhortations from my aide that these things have a way of getting back to higher authority I let it go and flew to the affair in the illicit uniform hoping against hope that it would not get back to my boss. However, I did not own one of the illegal piss cutters, nor would I be caught dead wearing one. After all, I had to put my foot down somewhere in this whole process. So I appeared wearing the correct bridge cap with white cover.

An official sedan met me at the airplane and whisked me to the site of the ceremony on the aircraft parking ramp behind the VX-4 hangar. The spectator seating had been set out behind the hangar in a fan-shaped arrangement with a huge American flag draped on the hangar doors as a backdrop for the podium. I walked the dozen or so paces to where the side boys had been arranged flanking a length of red carpet and stiffened for the formal honors arrival ceremony. The side boys came to a salute, a boatswain's mate piped me aboard and the band struck up the familiar ruffles and flourishes (two repetitions for a two-star Admiral). During the ruffles and flourishes I watched in utter astonishment at the entire complement of the squadron drawn up in ranks with the officers in the front row all resplendent in snow white piss cutters. I distinctly recall further rationalizing the fact that they didn't look half bad. It was vintage Moon Vance and the expression on his face told the story. It was a peculiar combination of impishness, chutzpah, pride and rebellion. What a guy!

Then, I walked through the flanking side boys and went over to shake Moon's extended hand. The moment was golden!

For reasons I cannot explain, I do not recall anything particularly eventful about the ceremony or about the content of his farewell address. But I do recall watching him as he spoke and trying to imagine the scene for which Moon Vance will always remain vivid in my memory.

The setting for that event was the landing signal officer's platform on an east coast carrier, several years earlier, conducting night fleet refresher training carrier landing qualifications in the operating area off the coast of Jacksonville, Florida. Moon was "waving" an A3J-1, *Vigilante* (RA-5) whose pilot had just reported an engine problem which would require an immediate landing. Now the "Viggie" was a new airplane then, and a huge one. It was a twin seat supersonic attack airplane originally designed to deliver nuclear weapons at high altitude (70,000 feet) and high speed (mach 3.0). It grossed out at over 70,000 pounds and was the largest carrier airplane in existence. Since the airplane had its history of carrier landing problems, Moon did the prudent thing and cleared the platform leaving only him and his writer assistant LSO.

The Viggie came around the closed night pattern and approached the ramp reporting power fluctuations in the port engine. Moon decided to treat the airplane with great care and was judicious in his calls for power adjustments and glide slope changes. At the very last moment, just before the airplane crossed the ramp Moon's practiced ear heard the ominous sound of engines unwinding and at the same time noted the airplane begin to settle. He instantly called for power, power, POWER! When he heard no change in engine sound and saw the settling continue he did the only thing appropriate at that point and screamed for the aircrew to eject, eject, EJECT! At the same time, Moon squeezed the "dead man's" trigger on the optical landing system control "pickle" in his right hand, dropped it and dove for the safety net.

The dead man's circuit began sending a continual flashing signal to the optical landing system red lights as it lay on the now empty landing signal officer's platform. The other man on the platform was quick as a flash and beat Moon's considerable bulk into the safety net. The net deflected the assistant downward and onto the steel deck directly beneath the LSO's platform. It was not a gentle escape route but it was designed, however roughly, to save the LSOs lives from burning fuel and flying debris. Bruises, skinned elbows, knees and shins as well as contusions were an accepted occupational hazard of those who have taken that rigorous escape route. Moon's young assistant rolled out onto the steel deck and, scrambling to his feet, dove through the hatch located just inboard of the catwalk, burning fuel being still primary in his list of personal threats.

Once inside the dark compartment there was nothing else to do but make his way to the ready room. The flight deck was a screaming bedlam of fire trucks, medics, fog foam jets everywhere and a roaring maelstrom of still burning fuel. It was definitely not a place for a gawking by-stander.

The plane guard helicopter, which had moved in from its station on the carrier's starboard quarter, saw the ramp strike as well as the upward trajectories from the two rocket-propelled ejection seats and moved into the ship's wake to effect a pick-up of the aircrewmen, turning on it's spotlight as it did so. It searched the ship's wake for signs of the aircrew, found them, lowered its rescue sling and successfully affected the pick ups.

Up to this point, the whole unfortunate evolution had reached a happy conclusion with the ship's flight deck crew working in total unison to save lives. Miraculously no one had been injured by flying debris or burning fuel. The plane guard helicopter broke the deadly silence on the radio circuit with its report for which everyone waited with bated breath. But it was couched in the form of an amazing question.

"Tower, this is Angel Two Four. I got 'em and they're okay. But, how many crewmen are there in a Viggie? "

The air boss' response virtually dripped with sarcasm. After all how could the helicopter pilot not know that the Vigilante carried a two man crew? "Two, Angel, just two."

"That's what I thought, Tower. But, I just picked up three people!" The air boss was dumbfounded.

It is worth noting that the elapsed time between Moon's last transmission to the Viggie and the helicopter pilot's stunning announcement was probably not more than five minutes. The assistant LSO had not yet even made it back to the ready room and had not looked back over his shoulder in the dark to see how far behind him was his mentor, Moon Vance. It was a frenetic few minutes full of the sound and fury of sirens, explosions, the air boss' bull horn, flying debris and the shouts of fire fighters. Only one person knew what had really happened, and he was lying on his back on the floor of the helicopter in stunned silence.

What had really happened when Moon dove for the net directly behind his assistant was that he missed! His body cleared the top of the net and, unbeknownst to the world, Moon tumbled end over end the equivalent of a seven story fall into the dark sea below. To this day I do not understand how Moon survived the impact alone but survive he did to be picked up by the Angel. He must also have been extremely concerned that the rescue helicopter would only be looking for two survivors, not three. Unless he caught their attention early on, the Angel might just leave him alone in the wake of the ship.

At the Arlington National Cemetery interment the funeral detail, including the horse-drawn caisson and the Army riflemen, clopped along the macadam road to the gravesite with Moon's friends following along behind. Through it all I kept seeing the image in my mind of Moon's impish expression topped by the snow white piss cutter!

In Delicto Flagrante

usn

"Single men in barracks don't grow into plaster saints."
Kipling

On a visit by U.S.S. *Shangri La* to the beautiful port of Palma de Mallorca in the Balearic Islands of the western Mediterranean in 1964, I volunteered to serve as interpreter to the Governor-general and his party during an official visit by him to our ship. At the time, I was operations officer of VF-62, a fighter squadron in Air Wing TEN. I was enjoying the opportunity to practice my Spanish and also the fact that the captain of the ship had offered me unrestricted use of his personal gig to go fetch the official party and to deliver them back to shore after their visit. The party consisted of the Governor-general, his wife and half a dozen others who were probably relatives, friends and staff.

I had spent an hour or so the evening before running through my Naval Academy technical Spanish dictionary for such not-so-frequently used words as arresting gear, catapults, taxiing, jet fighter planes, aircraft elevators etc.

We toured most of the ship for a period of almost three hours including a respite in our squadron ready room where cookies, coffee and tea were offered to the members of the party. During the ready room stint I presented a PLAT tape presentation on the television mounted in the overhead which showed flight deck operations, catapults and arrested landings.

At one point in the tour of the hangar bay I climbed a ladder onto the gallery deck of hangar bay three and opened the door into a new electronics repair shop. The lights were out in the room, but

165

enough illumination poured in from the open door to reveal, much to my horror, a sailor having his way with a young lady on one of those narrow benches one often finds in work places!

The two lovers were, of course, naked and so deeply engrossed in their activities that, for a brief moment they kept at it until it became suddenly clear to the sailor that he had been *busted.* The door had not been open for more than one or two seconds before I slammed it fairly hard and turned to see if the Governor-general of Palma de Mallorca and his wife had seen anything. From the shocked looks on their faces I knew that they had seen it all. Speaking for my own central nervous system, it felt like a bucket of ice water had just been thrown over me.

There was a marine enlisted escort from the Marine Corps detachment trailing us around. I whispered to him in a voice that could probably be heard by our distinguished visitors, "Get the name of that son-of-a-bitch *and his girl friend.* " My recollection of how we got the party back to the hangar deck and what I said to them is fairly vague because I was probably in a greater state of shock than was the visiting party or even the miscreant sailor and his girl friend. Nor do I remember much of what was said for the rest of the visit. Everything I had told them, in my rusty Castilian, about United States Navy aircraft carrier operations was now totally forgotten. All the party would remember would be the U.S. Navy's own version of Venus and Adonis squirming on a wooden bench no wider than ten inches in the darkness of an electronics repair shop.

On the return trip to the shore, I spoke briefly to the Governor-general and his wife and apologized for the unacceptable behavior of one of our sailors. Then on the return trip to the ship I rehearsed my speech to the Captain of U.S.S. *Shangri La.*

It just so happened that the evening before entering port the captain had gotten on the ships 1MC public address system about how we were all ambassadors of good will for the United States and how our behavior would be our lasting first impression for many Mallorcans.

SHEEEEESSSSSH!

PART VI

THE WRITTEN WORD

usmc

Many years ago, it was suggested that I attend writer's workshops in order to improve my skills and to "Keep my hand in." Over the next ten years, I attended several different workshops and found it an interesting experience. The writers were a colorful group. They each had an agenda, such as the old fellow whose sole purpose was "to blow the lid off of the automobile upholstery business."

The real value of those workshops was the need each week, to complete the assigned task. Those tasks were so diverse. One assignment was to write a love story. The women all rejoiced, while the guys all complained, "We don' do no stinking love stories."

However, with regularity, the assignment would force us to dig deep for a story and sometimes we would surprise ourselves with a personal revelation. To quote Flannery, "The writer should be the person who is most surprised by her story. If the writer isn't more surprised than the reader, then the story isn't any good." - Flannery O'Connor. How true!

For example, one assignment was to write about the Persona that some individuals create for themselves. As I read my piece the following week, the whole group looked at me and told me that I had hidden a separate story within the assigned piece. Sure enough, as I scanned my story, the subconscious second story jumped out at me. It was a piece entitled, *Boots*.

I'll finish by quoting another writer, close to my heart, "I write from personal experience, whether I've had them or not." - Ron Carlson.

The following group of stories is a sampling of workshop assignments.

THE LAST DRACHMA

usmc

"Easy come, easy goes."
– Anon

"This is the ditches," Gaius complained to his buddy, Fabius, as they leaned on their scotums (shields), looking at the bleak, frozen Danube, from atop the defensive rampart and ditch.

"In the Third Cohort, we call it the pits, not the ditches," Fabius volunteered, trying to be helpful with the Third Roman cohort's newest recruit.

Gaius retorted hotly, "I don't give a shit what you call it. Ya know, you veterans make me sick, sometimes. Just because you have twenty-seven years on your military obligation and are a short timer, you lord it over us newbies. Ya realize I won't get out until I'm forty-six years old? That's a long time to march around Northern Gaul in a copper hat, carrying a scotum weighing as much as a kid goat. It's the ditches, like I said."

"The Pits, for Zeus' sake. You got a lot to learn kid," Fabius persisted, adding, "try to follow my lead and you'll stay out a' trouble."

"Yeah, yeah, here we are in winter quarters in Carnuntum, standing watch every night and up to our ass in snow, foraging for firewood all day, so the Centurion can take a steam in the baths and all the while, the barbarians are sitting in warm huts across the Danube, eating honey and gruel and chasing camp followers. It just ain't fair is all I'm saying," Gaius grumbled on.

Hoping to change the subject, Fabius whispered with a conspiratorial gleam in his eyes, "Hey kid, what say we duck in out of the weather and shoot some craps? They won't be around to check on us until the fourth watch."

"Not fer nothin', Fabius, but you always seem to win," Gaius snorted. "Besides, I only got one drachma left 'till payday," Gaius added, waving the lone drachma in the air as proof.

"You accusin' me of cheating," Fabius shouted, pumping up his chest. *I don't get no respect, and me, a seasoned veteran of the Gallic Wars,* he swore to himself. Then he exploded with anger at this sniveling recruit, swinging his scotum at Gaius, knocking him clear of the rampart. Gaius landed in the frozen ditch with a dull thud and the lone drachma spun off into the night and the snow, lost forever.

• • •

Homer was sitting by the Danube, back against a tree, enjoying the warm, August sun, looking at the river traffic and at Slovakia on the far side of the river. Today had been a blast. Only a week ago, Jimbo, had called home to say, "Come to Vienna. This is your last chance, brother. I've decided to retire next month."

With that incentive, Homer called the airlines and hopped a flight out of Little Rock. Now, Jimbo was showing him the Vienna tourists never see. Jimbo had been living in Vienna for the last twenty years and knew his way around. *Today is a special treat though,* Homer reminded himself. They were exploring the ruins of Carnuntum on the Danube, the site of the Roman Legions camp, from 15BC to 400AD.

After hours of exploring, the brothers had decided to stop for a break on the bank of the Danube. As they sat resting and chatting, an Austrian happened by, carrying a metal detector under his arm. Homer, ever curious and feeling expansive called out, "Hey partner, did you find anything with that detector?"

Jost, who was a lawyer from Vienna, grinned and came over to introduce himself and chat with the two Americans. "I always find somting here at Carnuntum," Jost replied, sitting down with the brothers, anxious to talk about his exciting hobby.

"You actually find two-thousand-year-old Roman stuff," Homer asked excitedly?

"Noting with da detector today, but I findt chards uf pottery unt blown glass over by da amphitheatre. You see, last night da heavy rains com, un't caused part of da vall to collopse, so I look behind da wall and find deese." With that, Jost held out his hand to show them the pieces of glass and pottery he found.

"Those are neat Jost. Imagine some Roman soldier throwing those bits of trash behind the stone wall as they built the amphitheatre," Homer visualized. Then he asked, "Do you ever find anything with the metal detector, Jost?"

"Ya. I haf room full of gold, silver un't bronze coins un't ring keys too at my home," Jost boasted proudly, "Dose are tings I find vit da detector. Each zummer, I take dem to Spanien on holiday un't restore da coins," he volunteered.

With that, Jost stood and turned on the metal detector, saying, "Kommun ze here. I show you how to use da detector, but iss nothing here, da actuol encompment iss a mila (1000 paces) back from da river. Heer iss verr da defensive rampart un't ditch vas. Da only place verr I find artifacts iss in da encompment."

At that moment, the detector beeped and Jost laughed, saying, "Ach iss your lucky day, Homer."

The three men immediately knelt and began lifting the sod, searching for the artifact. Homer was lackadaisical, thinking; *it's probably only a beer bottle cap*. However, Jost knew what to look for and soon picked up a black, lumpy pebble, handing it to Homer with a grin. Then, Jost proceeded to explain about restoring coins and incidentally, the destructive effects of modern-day fertilizers on the artifacts.

"It von't be long, before da artifacts are finish," Jost added wistfully.

Meanwhile, Homer sat holding a two-thousand-year-old Roman coin in his hand, like a communion host, stunned that a stranger would give him an ancient Roman coin without a thought of compensation. In that moment, Homer resolved to be as generous with Jost, inviting him to join them for lunch at a nearby wine cellar, warning Jost, "It's my treat, and pick out a case of good wine while we are there."

With the bargain sealed by a handshake, the three friends drove out of Carnuntum, bumping over the grave road. The road so called, because the Legions carved a stone sarcophagus for every fallen soldier, and then laid each sarcophagus crosswise under the road, to provide a firm foundation. After four hundred years, there were thousands of soldiers lined up in their stone coffins under the road. The sarcophogi went on for miles.

As they drove along, Homer looked out the car window, thinking, *there is nobody around. This is just a deserted section of farmland. With a come-along and my pickup truck, I could easily slip one a' them babies in back, an' take 'er home. Probably look pretty good out by the mailbox.*

As luck would have it, the car eventually bumped over Gaius' sarcophagus, rousing his spirit and Gaius, still in a foul mood, fumed, *well, there goes my last drachma!*

ROSETTA STONE AND OTHER STUFF

usmc

"To be a well-favored man is the gift of fortune; but to read and write comes by nature."
– Shakespeare

A few years ago, a notable and colorful politician from New York was sitting in his favorite pub in Washington, DC. He was slit-eyed and shifty after a few scoops of his usual draft and was looking for trouble. Then Rosetta Stone strutted by his table and hesitated, forlornly looking about for a table. His eyes lit up, along with his testosterone and he suggested she join him.

After one last look about the restaurant, Rosetta demurely sat next to the rake and managed to press her knee against his. Our man knew in that instant, that this would be a memorable evening. So with a regal wave, he summonsed his waiter and smoothly asked Rosetta if she had time for a cocktail. Then he wiggled an eyebrow as tangled as the Mato Grosso, which sent the waiter scurrying off for the lady's cocktail. "Heavy on the gin and make it a double," said Mato Grosso.

It was then that Rosetta introduced herself and confessed that she had spotted the great man and fanaticized about spending time with someone of his lofty stature. With that, the great man, secure in the knowledge that he was a singular gift to mankind, unwound like a broken clock and spilled enough dirt for a month's copy under her byline, which incidentally was not Rosetta Stone.

I warmed to Rosetta immediately upon hearing the story from an insider, but the story of *The Rosetta Stone* leaves me cold. I like things less complicated than a piece of rock that befuddled academicians for centuries. Having said that, I will admit there is also something to be said for durability of writing. God knows we have all written great works, capable of meteoric launchings of our careers, only to forget to stroke the save button. And then, there are all those inspired 3am stories that we promise to write as soon as the coffee perks in the morning.

Writing's a tough business. First, you have to have something called talent, which eliminates some of us. Then, you need to be savvy enough to avoid the tech traps of innovations in computers, like 3-inch floppies, which make years of work on 5-inch floppies useless. And there are the zip discs, the CDs, and the small CDs (I have stuff on all of the above) and who knows what's next. The stuff that slips through the crack with all these new formats is enough to make me weep.

Well, enough of self-pity. Who said life was fair? I looked at this week's assignment last night and was sufficiently inspired to do a little something about durability in writing. After a long search, I recovered a Journal about a young man's saga during the Gold Rush to the Klondike. It is a 50-page document written in 1898. Next, I spent hours gingerly scanning the yellowed and brittle pages, using OCR to convert it into a durable Microsoft Word document.

That done I sat back self-satisfied, and poured myself a thimble of Bushmills, while I wrestled with the class assignment for today. It always helps me think, does Bushmills. It clarifies stuff. Arcane issues become as clear as day. After a time and another thimble or two, I experienced an epiphany. I was so surprised that I fell out of my chair. I suddenly realized I shared the same sage view as a great man of letters, that durability in writing is a crock. As proof of this, I'd like to share with you his slant on durability in writing, paraphrasing his words a little in the process: "We profit, who **burn** in the morning, the writing we do late at night."

THE LANGUAGE OF THE SEAS

usmc

"He that will learn to pray, let him go to sea."
- Herbert

The Arctic Sea is as frigid as an old nun, who true to her vows, is silent and impoverished. The Sea, beset by frightening, seasonal fits of icy tumult, freezes solid. Then, after the winds begin to push the endless miles of ice, it shatters and scatters, thundering and rumbling, like an angry god, shoving massive mountains of ice about. The Sea then pushes the mountains south, petulantly blockading harbors, and sinking ships, crushing them in its jaws, slavering and slathering, despoiling all in its way as it creeps into the North Atlantic.

The North Atlantic Sea is stormy and violent, murderously taking toll of the crafty fishermen from Portugal, Korea and Japan, crossing its borders seeking to spoil and loot. This sea is a titan that can toss Aircraft Carriers about like toys, in seas impossible to imagine, or even describe to insouciant sailors from the waters of the Caribbean.

The Caribbean Sea is exotic and garrulous like the inhabitants, playful, except when night draws a veil over it. Then, the slaughter of the innocent begins. The hordes burst through the gaps in the reefs, plundering and gorging on small fry with abandon.

There is a hint of muskiness in the Sea too. It is a piquant perfume, a compound of sun, vegetation and animal life, gently stirred by the trade winds. It is a fusion of odors, of land crab burrows and breadfruit, of dead coral drying in the surf and climbing hibiscus, and sugar cane and charcoal, all drifting on the Trade Winds. There is also a subliminal odor, left on the surface of the sea by the life hidden in the depths below, combined with the Islands effluents, of things like precious, punky, sump water captured by tile roofs and stored in secure dark cisterns like gold doubloons. It is a melding of scents: its musk.

The Carib has many surprises, like the flickering of flying fish, sprouting from the surface beneath brutish bow plates, like apparitions, pectoral fins blossoming like hibiscus as the flyers glide for hundreds of yards, dipping into the sea in a blink, playing with the eye. It is durable gift, a souvenir— the flying fish, the peaceful silence before dawn, the balmy trade winds and the whisper of the tropical Sea, as it greets intruders from the north. To its south is the troublesome, South Atlantic.

The South Atlantic has oily swells and sargasso, and seasonal fits and birthings of unwanted tempests, which hatch far to the east, near the Mediterranean. These tempests are maliciously bundled and left on the doorstep of the Caribbean each fall.

The distant Mediterranean Sea is jaded and sophisticated, dissipated and desiccated, like a rich, old man, who hides his treasures cunningly, while he indulges in questionable diversions. In the fall, Africa devils The Med with its deserts, and taunts the sea with siroccos, soiling the azure waters with Africa's murk and musk.

Away to the east of Africa, *where the wind is in the palm trees and the temple bells ring,* lays the ancient China Sea. The China Sea is like an inner city recluse, keeping arcane pets: aggressive, venomous, sea snakes, surfacing from the ancient Sea by the dozens, a nightmare, as they raise their scaly heads above the sea and look their prey in the eye.

For centuries, the China Sea has acted like a receiver of taxes, patiently awaiting its due from the surrounding lands: a tax paid in souls, delivered, slowly, reluctantly, by perfumed rivers.

MOTHER TONGUE

usmc

"The artillery of words."
– Swift

Looking at the problem simplistically, children learn their mother tongue from their mothers. All it takes is a stroll through New York City to hear the variety of mother tongues. Aside from the murky notion of genetic memory, what stimuli influence our individual brand of mother tongue?

My conviction is the process begins in the home. For example, my mother was a teacher. Every day, she taught us the nuances of language. She couldn't help herself. Etymology was one of her favorite subjects. Soon after we settled in our home, she had my dad erect a blackboard in the kitchen. In those days, we only used the dining room on Sunday, so the kitchen became a classroom. It is a wonder we did not pledge allegiance to the Flag before dinner.

Perhaps, because my place as the second youngest sibling put me in the position of "Seen, but not heard," I was better able to observe and learn: to store the memories, while my older brothers and sisters were voicing opinions, and story-telling at the dinner table. They were also at risk. The reason was that it was a right of any sibling to challenge another's use of language during the dinner hour. If challenged, the miscreant was obliged to leave the dinner table at once and look up his choice of words in the dictionary or encyclopedia, because my dad would smile and say, "Get the dictionary."

Then, we would all listen to the victim's reading of definitions, hoping to catch them in the misuse of language. Let me hasten to add that language extended to all the languages we studied in school, not just English. In those days, we all studied Latin for three years, in addition to modern languages. Well, after sorting out things, the victim would write the correct word, pronunciation and definition on the blackboard and the meal would resume. My combined age, educational level and intellect did not augur well for any unsolicited comment, so I kept my mouth shut and observed. It was a good policy, when living in a family of overachieving elders, but what a learning environment it was.

I have since learned that in the Communist world the same technique is used for those prisoners in *Reeducation Programs*. "Not another bite of food, Comrade, until you digest and memorize the latest Pravda slogan." Do you suppose they found out about the technique from my mom?

That blackboard was like my soul in a way. Many concepts were impressed on it in those formative years. Life's environment has since erased much, but like an old blackboard, if you look carefully, there are ingrained, shadowy and sometimes elusive images that cannot be erased.

My mom knew that the logical extension of language was literature. "Read a good book," she would caution us when she found us idle. My dad reinforced the love of reading by reading to us every night. He made it seem real; modulating his voice and assuming accents like an actor changes costume. His reading selections fired our young imaginations. That fire still burns bright.

The influence of language was not entirely parental. No. On any given night, as the nine of us noisily did our homework. You could expect to hear, "Hey, what's the French word for butter?"

"Mantequilla."

"No, dumm kopf, beurre.

"Entschuldigung."

"Por nada."

"Silencio!"

My dad took a hand in educating us too. He was an uneducated farm boy, but he discovered language as a doughboy in France during WWI. For the rest of his life, we could expect to hear his endless collection of Gallicisms at any moment. He also saw a need to educate himself in order to keep up with his children, so he read and read. In later years, he'd finish the Sunday Times crossword before the sun set.

Another element in our love of language was the treasure trove of a journal my two great uncles wrote during their Gold Rush days in the Klondike. That journal was a lesson for all of us. Perhaps that stimulated our own inclinations to write. My three brothers are authors, and one of my sisters, an award winning editor.

My Gold Rush uncles set an example for us. After reading their journal, I began writing. My intended readership was to be the fifty nieces and nephews, and their offspring. My stories are about another place, another time, about the river of family evolution and about life's brief flight, of winging through time. My writing is intended to give the next generation the same glimpse of history and appreciation of mother tongue that my great uncles' offering gave my generation. Perhaps it will. Either way, it has been worth the trip.

The Magic Pen

usmc

"The pen is the tongue of the mind."
- Cervantes

Early morning is the best time for me. In the evening, I'm tired, combative, and suspicious, so I find a seat on the Long Island Railroad, open my laptop and scan the scribbling I wrought during my morning commute like an unemployed critic. That is all I'm good for when tired.

For years, I'd climb aboard the six-eleven out of Northport, look for a seat on the south side of the New York bound commuter train and try for a window seat in order to gain free rein for my left-handed, single finger typing. Then, the imagination of a well- rested mind would bound away like a Whippet after a hare.

Sometimes I am jarred awake in the dark hours by an odd sound. In those moments, I am wide awake; as I listen to make sure all is well. Once I convince myself that there is no threat, I try to relax and my mind shifts to other venues, such as my latest writing project, or one of those nagging files in my Unfinished Business folder: the folder that carries the bones of so many stories that I'd like to write.

Laying abed in the dark, with my mind booted up, I sometimes begin to write with what I call my magic pen. With it I've written stories so vivid, that in the cold light of dawn, I awake and search frantically, hoping to find them on my laptop. I'm still convinced that they are there somewhere.

It's odd, but once I've written stories with my magic pen I am released. I no longer have any driving need to develop those files. I never again open the files, or edit them…well not often. Only then, can I actually open my Unfinished Business folder and scratch those files off the list. Maybe it's better that way.

At other times as I lay in the dark, I develop the bones of a story and even scribble a shorthand reminder to prompt my memory in the morning. Those scribbled notes are as frustrating as the Rosetta Stone to decipher as I sit with a mug of coffee at dawn.

Then, there are the projects I wrote after forcing my body out of my warm bed. I shuffle into my little cell, quietly shut the door, turn on the PC and begin writing. Those stories survive 'till morning…most of the time, but even those are not the same as the magic pen stories.

Once, while recovering from surgery, I was relaxing in a recliner at home and wrote a story, which was later described by another writer as lyrical. I was on painkillers at the time. I wonder if that had anything to do with it.

On yet another occasion, I was sipping Bushmills, "To get the dust out of me throat," as I finished a piece for Writer's Space. I was forcing the piece because I was behind schedule. I finally decided the story was finished, when I fell out of my chair. The piece was entitled Rosetta Stone. Hummmm?

Perhaps someday, a story will make The New York Times Best Seller List, but none will ever match the magic pen stories. Those babies are my best work.

PART VII

HARD HATS, HARD HEADS

usmc

When I marched out the gate of the Brooklyn Navy Yard, after completing my hitch in the Marines, I had a sea bag on my shoulder, about ten bucks in my pocket, and no prospects, so I headed for my parents home. What else was there to do?

After some fits and starts, I got a job as a Mason's Tender alongside my brother Dan. Mason's Tender, (aka hod carrier) was a fancy name for laborer. The job was to bring the bricks, blocks, mortar and heavy things like fire escape platforms to the bricklayers, as we built the apartment buildings of the City.

That job was the genesis of my career in the construction business. There followed a path of surveyor, inspector, designer, estimator, general superintendent, and so on. All those years were spent with a select community of individuals, all of whom shared the same characteristics: long muscular arms, a shuffling gait, massive bone growth over the brow, no forehead at all, and very hard heads. It took a Herculean effort the get any one of them to change the way they had been doing things.

"You talkin' ta' me? I been doin' it this way for eighteen f...ing years!"

Marrone! I could tell you such stories!

183

THE CRACK OF DOOM

usmc

"There is no ghost so difficult to lay as the ghost of an injury."
– Smith

It happened as the two of them leaned against a full pallet of nine-inch concrete block, trying to catch their breath. Laborers didn't take breaks on the job normally, but this was an exception. The ironworkers were behind schedule, slowing down everyone else, and the mason tenders were ordered to move a big pile of steel beams in order to help the ironworkers catch up. Steel beams always seemed to be glued to the deck when you tried to pick them up, and worst, they didn't give. If you dropped one end and caught your hand under the beam, your hand was what gave, not one of those beams.

Well, as the two leaned on the pallet of concrete blocks, the smaller laborer shifted his weight and a block fell off the pallet and landed on his foot, breaking it with a crisp snap, the crack of doom. The bigger laborer looked up and saw tears course down the dark cheeks of his friend, and he knew! Those were not tears of pain. No, they were tears of frustration and despair. In that moment, the delicate economic balance that makes it possible to pay the bills and feed the family ended. His friend was out of work. There was no assistance for him. He was done. They never saw him again.

It was a go-go job, and it was understood that you took your break after 4:30p.m. There was none of that business of drifting down through the floors of the building to wash up before quitting time. That was out! The foreman would lose you as soon as he noticed any slacking off during the day.

185

All the mason tenders pushed as hard as they could until the shop steward blew his whistle. Then, there was a mad scramble to get down to the street level. Most of the laborers were big, strong young men and they would jump off the top floor onto the chain link mesh that covered the material hoist and climb down all the way to the city streets clinging to the wire mesh like monkeys. Nowadays that would be ground for a safety violation. Much has changed in the industry over the year, but not the laborers. They are still society's underachievers, its' disadvantaged.

The crew was a mixed one with its share of characters. There was Beal, who the rest of us called Bill. He pronounced it Beal, but who knows. Beal's body was magnificent. He could walk on stage and win any bodybuilding competition. Beal liked to complain about society and the problems of the blacks. To listen to him, you'd think that Beal was ready to pillage and burn. He mouthed the politics of the Black Panthers, of which he was a member, making the crew uncomfortable, but in his heart, he was just a man trying to break out of the cage. When the going got tough, the real Beal surfaced and that was the Beal the crew liked.

Tom was the oldest and the biggest. Over the lunch break one hot summer day, as they sat in the only shade the laborers would enjoy all day, Tom told of working as a stevedore on the docks of London for four straight years during the Second World War. The stevedores were an all black Army battalion of laborers. The workday was sometimes double the length of the crew's ordinary workday. The stevedores worked six and seven day weeks. They never rotated home. There was little time off. It was what the Marines called *Day on and stay on,* for the duration. Tom rarely shared such intimate thoughts with anyone. Tom wasn't a racist, but when some new laborer showed up, who wasn't black, Tom became suspicious and judgmental.

If over the course of the project, you hustled enough to beat Tom to the next buggy of mortar that came up on the hoist, or grab the next fire escape platform and muscle it into place for the bricklayers, day after day, he would change his mind. The big white laborer found that out one day. He had been pushing, because he never wanted it said that he didn't do his share and more. He grabbed the next buggy of mortar as it came off the hoist, and a bigger hand clamped down on the buggy, pulling it away form him unexpectedly. Tom was acknowledging that the white guy could work as hard as he could. When lunchtime arrived, Tom finally sat down next to the white guy, and they developed a habit of chatting about life's twists and turns. That was when Tom spoke of the London docks. He didn't complain about it, he simple shared a story.

The labor foreman was a lean, Italian guy with a loud voice. His name was Salvotore. He was the Labor Foreman for Perri Construction, the Builder. Sal subscribed to the theory that if some laborer didn't understand him, then he'd talk louder. It never occurred to Sal that being more explicit might work better. He'd talk louder and louder, until the laborer figured it out or the two of them came to blows. Sal seemed to carry a sea bag full of complaints around all day. Sal felt the world was unfair. He was right, but for the wrong reasons.

Thirty years later at a wake for someone from the old days on the construction sites, Sal and the big white laborer met again. The first words out of Sal's mouth were "That wasn't nice of you to give me the finger as you drove off, the last day of that project in Forest Hills." The big laborer was stopped for a minute, then grinned and decided they were getting too old to start throwing punches again, and at a wake for Christ sake, so he said, It's good to see you too, Sal."

The black guy, who was injured while leaning on the pallet of concrete block, was the smallest of the laborers. He was strong and fast though and pulled his weight. His name was Willie. He frequently worked in the street in front of the building project, mixing the mortar for the laborers to deliver to the bricklayers. He'd stand there swing a broad shovel all day, loading the mixer. Three parts of sand to one part of mortar cement, add a bucket of water, mix the lot while the lime spattered on his clothes, eating up his boots, clothing and hands.

One day, some of the crew passed an accident on the Cross Island Parkway. There was Willie sitting in his Cadillac, covered with mortar. Willie had mixed an extra load of mortar at the end of the day and filled his car with spackle buckets of mortar. Willie was obviously planning to do a little moonlighting after work and was rushing to his part time job with 1000 pounds of wet mortar in spackle buckets, jammed into every corner of his car. Taillights went on up ahead and when Willie slammed on the brakes, the car couldn't stop in time, because of the extra weight. The mortar exploded on impact, coating the interior of his Cadillac with cloth-eating lime. The car didn't look so good any more, and Willie didn't look too good either.

The laborers were a rough-hewn lot, but it was mostly façade. An example of their hidden sensitivity was displayed when those who rode the subway to work brought fresh clothing, so they could change into something clean and inoffensive before making the subway trip home after a hot sweaty day on the job.

THE RIVER

Usmc

"This body is not a home, but an inn; and that only for a short time."
— Seneca

The River is implacable. It answers to no man, although, from time to time, man makes Homeric efforts to dissuade the River. It is not a big or broad or deep river, like the Orinoco or Amazon, but like a productive ball player, its statistics are impressive.

Statistics might be too scientific a term. Perhaps local knowledge would be more appropriate. We all know that within the river's scoured trench, sleeping with the fishes in concrete shoes, are a legion of the City's underworld citizens. They stand erect, swaying in the current like subway riders at a local stop, swaying in the eddy of the fast moving express, waiting for the local to Judgment Day. Together they formed an impotent constituency that the Princes of the City are well aware of.

The River's many tributaries are the hiding places for more stolen vehicles than the whole of the Russian Army, all manner and make of vehicles, even one fully loaded ready-mix concrete truck. The concrete truck was not stolen; it was just an object lesson for a smaller firm. The truck's driver was given three seconds to exit the truck before it was driven off the end of the Thirty-Eighth Street pier. It was ample time for the driver.

There was once a flotilla of river barges that carried on deck, a complete Pennsylvania Railroad freight train. The watchman assigned to tend the dock lines decided to warm up in the nearest bar and forgot to adjust the dock lines as the moon tide lowered the river. The lower

189

the river, the more the barges tilted, until the complete freight train rolled into the murky depths. There was a ripple in the River, then the calm steady flow resumed.

Along the River's banks, living under abandoned, rotted-out timber piers lived some of the City's disenfranchised, existing and breeding like rats, coming out after dark, moving silently through the alleyways and shadows of the City; foraging.

Down at the Battery, at the confluence of the East and North Rivers, the traffic is heavy. There are frenetic little ferries, tooting about, and ocean going vessels sailing to and from Marseilles and Murmansk, from Hamburg and Haiti, from Biloxi and Bilbao and Pago Pago too.

The River carries both commerce and casualties in its current. One day a barge-load of Brazilian coffee was cut loose by errant schoolboys. Millions in coffee and a man's career too, were swallowed up by the River that day. It was unmoved.

The River gives the impression of placid benevolence, but like the keeper at the zoo said, "Keep your eyes open at all times." It is one thing to grind coffee beans in your ship's screws. It is another matter entirely to try to grind an overturned barge-load of eighty-foot timber piles.

In winter, the River carries along in its current, endless sheets of thick, jagged ice. These sheets of ice cut through the shore side structures and piling like a giant saw blade. The river pilots know and the insurance companies know too.

The River passes through the City every day and all night without once turning its head to admire the skyline. It is not impressed. The River has been making the journey for a million years, long before the city was even born.

The River's beginnings were in the mountains to the north. Every trickle and rivulet contributed to its life. In the beginning, it was clear and bubbling with vitality. As the River progresses on its journey to the sea, it becomes somehow sullied and less spirited. Its vitality diminishes. Something has gone, perhaps its innocence.

The Journey's end is at the sea, a place for another beginning. It is there, that the impediments, needs, desires, the baggage of life were left behind. Discarded, forming a kind of delta of cravings. A delta made up of all the things that the River accumulated during its journey. Things that it turns out were not very important after all.

Things are not a measure of the Journey.

COCOON

usmc

"Like the winds of sea are the ways of fate, As we voyage along through life:
'Tis the set of the soul that decides its goal
And not the calm or the strife."
- Wilcox

He awoke with a start. The ships clock told him it was five in the morning. The sun was just a Seville-orange glow in the east. Later, he would never be sure if he really heard them, but in that subliminal moment on the edge of consciousness, he knew fish were feeding inches away from his bunk, just beyond the hull of *Cocoon*. In that instant in time, he envisioned the small fry screaming in terror, as large, predatory, snaggletoothed maws swept through the dark school of fry, swallowing the hopeless remains of the school. It was disturbing. It always would be. Nevertheless, he unzipped his own cocoon of nylon and down, and hopped out in his skivvies. He grabbed the fishing rod and scrambled up on deck to try to catch breakfast, joining the other predators in the feeding frenzy.

With the first cast, he hooked one of the other predators and fought it alongside, where he pulled in a beautiful iridescent weakfish. With a winch handle, he clobbered it, filleted it and put it in the fry pan on the stove. He did it without a thought, and yet his own voyage dealt with these same issues: life and death, survival of the fittest, the order of nature, life's lack of fairness, the food chain, chance and fate, love and hate. Heady stuff.

Next, he started the alcohol stove with a hiss and put on a pot of coffee. *Nothin' beats hot, black coffee for creating a contemplative mood,* he reminded himself. He had some hard thinking to do as he took a seat in the cockpit. By chance, he noticed a buck leisurely strolling along the beach as was its due, accepting life, keeping its dignity despite the lack of a Constitution, Bill of Rights, lawyers, food stamps, etcetera. *Why am I having so much trouble dealing with things beyond my control? That buck appears to be doing a better job of maintaining his equilibrium, than I am,* he mused.

Two weeks ago he had set sail, because he felt compelled to get away from all distractions and reorganize his life. His goal was to try to untangle the *Gordian knot* of obligations, circumstance, commitments, vows, and even his choice of a profession. It was imperative to prioritize these interconnecting elements. He should have done it long ago, but time flies when you are young and bullet proof. Now, middle-age had struck.

For example, he had to decide just how important his career was. Was it more important than his marriage? The job offer of a promotion, and relocation to the main office in Houston was definitely important to his career. On a more fundamental level, he needed to examine his approach to life.

We know life is not fair. We all have friends who sail on a broad reach throughout their lives, never once encountering so much as a squall. Why am I stuck with the burdens of family illnesses, deaths, elderly concerns, interfamily conflicts, envy, money problems, homeowner questions, tax increases, four burglaries, and so on? I'll go crazy, he worried, and so he decided to go for a sail and try to make sense of his lot, to alter his attitude and to approach problems differently. *Just sail and think,* he reasoned. *That's all, no distractions, no newspapers or commercial radio.*

However, sailing is not fair either as he found out, so he decided to approach sailing differently as well. Just yesterday, he made a very difficult passage from Prickly Pear. It was blowing a gale, right on his nose and the 35 miles turned into 53 miles with all the tacking. By the time he reached his destination, his foul weather gear was sparkling with salt crystals, and he was exhausted. Strewn about the cabin were the contents of the drawers and shelves. Everything had been dumped in the violence of sailing through the gale. It took over ten hours of tacking, close-hauled to reach the lee of Seal Dogs. An hour before he reached Seal Dogs, the main halyard broke, causing the main sail to drop on deck. Without the main, he was in trouble, so he ducked into the shelter of Tampion Cove and dropped the anchor with a splash and a sigh. Then he went below to clean up the mess, change into dry cloths and have a jar of whiskey.

Tampion Cove was a desolate place, looking like Scotland's coast. A lump of granite poking up out of the sea, covered with rock outcroppings and low wind-pruned pines. There was also a sprinkling of sheep, white specks against the green of the land; soothing to a sailor's eyes. Tampion Cove was sheltered by a rocky promontory jutted into the channel. On the promontory an ancient, stone lighthouse stood eternal vigil. It was a favorite anchorage for *Cocoon.*

Cocoon's cabin had narrow bunks, and a galley containing a gimbaled stove, icebox, sink and table. The warm wood-clad bulkheads held swinging gear nets and bookshelves of current charts, pilot guides, tide tables, guidebooks on birds, fish, tidal pools and an assortment of poetry, mythology and mystery novels. There was a small shelf with wood spindles holding brandy and Bushmills. A gimbaled oil lamp gave the cabin a snug, warm, scented glow.

His bunk was by the companionway hatch, giving him a view of the night sky. The location of the bunk also gave him a sense of changing wind direction and changes in sea conditions, foretold by a distant bell buoy and the lighthouse foghorn. Throughout the night, the rigging thrummed in the dying winds. High overhead geese were flying through the night, calling encouragement to each other, as they made their spring passage, accepting their lot in life with uncommon grace.

The scent of the coffee wafted up the companionway telling him it was ready and the middle-aged man sat in the cockpit sipping and thinking. He turned on the weather radio and heard a forecast for a southerly wind for tomorrow. That translated into a smooth, beam reach all the way to Green Cay, if he delayed until tomorrow. *Now that's better than trying to make the passage today, and getting beat-up again,* he decided as he looked at the sky, adding, *it will give me a chance to fix the main halyard as well. First problem solved,* he boasted. *Ya know,* he philosophized, *life is a lot like sailing. Don't sail too close to the wind or you'll end-up in irons.*

Continuing in that vein, he made other decisions. He vowed to stop pushing so hard on the job, to curtail criticism, to stop and smell the roses, to be more considerate, to give his wife more time and attention, to learn to accept things as they are, to look at the bright side, and to turn down the Houston offer.

Screw the company! So I don't get the promotion or the pension! The big companies are all reneging on things like that nowadays anyway. Some companies value their employee's quality of work life. Get a job with one of those companies. Make the house livable for the wife. Remodel the kitchen as she asked. Fix the car and keep it another year. Start an IRA. Life is short. I'm on a roll now, he smiled.

He spent the rest of the day, while *Cocoon* gently rocked in the cove, listening to the musical slapping of the halyards and the gulls cries, making decisions and taking notes. The final decision he made was to get to a phone when he reached Green Cay, and call home.

THE SINKING FUND

Usmc

"Easy come, easy goes."

Paddy's Day had come and gone and the flounder-fishing season was in full swing. The weather did what it always did at that time of year. It promised, but did not produce better weather: those halcyon days of spring we all dream of during the stark cold winter. Those days of sun and blue skies, of warmth and the fellowship of flounder fishing, rarely materialized. More often than not, the three middle-age construction workers ended up fishing in a cold, damp wind under a murky sky.

Gil continued to go fishing with the other two despite the weather, because as soon as the three men stepped aboard the boat, they always assumed distinct roles. They were instigator, foil and victim. The roles rotated, based on the consumption of Johnny Red, the day, the weather and the unfolding of events. Vince and Hank drew trouble to themselves like a magnet and Gil was rarely disappointed with the day's bizarre events, as the sea hare episode gave witness.

Hank was staring at the end of his fishing line, a frown creasing his weathered brow. He was befuddled. The early morning Johnny Red and Bud chasers did little to help the situation. He was sure there was a hook on the line when he lowered it into the waters of their secret flounder-fishing hole in the marshlands. Now, there was this tennis ball like thing enclosing the end of the line. The skin of the ball was tough and non-responsive. Hank poked it again, while Vince and Gil made fun of him.

"First fish means just that Hank," Vince reiterated with a sly grin. "That tennis ball thing does not constitute a fish, so kiss the five-dollar bet 'Goodbye,' pal."

Hank always pulled in the first fish and won the five-dollar pool. Vince and Gil were convinced Hank cheated, but could not figure out how he did it so consistently. On this occasion, they were delighted to see a tennis ball, instead of the first flounder on the end of Hank's fishing line. Even better, with his line in his hand, instead of in the water, the likelihood of Hank catching first fish was growing more remote by the minute. Hank stood transfixed, staring at the ball, his mind racing. *If only I could identify this thing as a fish, I would win the pool,* he was thinking.

Finally, with genuine curiosity, Gil hazarded a guess. "Hank, I think you just caught a sea hare. It's a guess, because I've never seen them turn into a tennis ball before, but I think that is what it is."

"Yeah? then it's a fish and I get the money," Hank reasoned gruffly.

"No!" Gil lied," a sea hare is a small mammal that crawls around, holding its breath and feeding on the bottom. If you were on the very bottom, you would actually see it hopping around, Hank. That's why it is called a hare." Gil was watching Hank's eyes as he slathered on the bullshit, but Hank was distracted. He was truly amazed. This was something new to Hank and he swallowed Gil's story, hook, line and sinker.

"Give it to Helen," Vince suggested, feigning helpfulness. "She can make Sea Hare Parmesan for ya. You've never tasted a real treat until you've had Sea Hare Parmesan, Hank," Vince added with a Budweiser burp. *Keep distracting him,* Vince reasoned, *As long as Hank's line is out of the water, he won't collect the bet for first fish.*

Hank was quick with his wits, but also with his fists. When Gil met him, he thought that the quick fists were the reason why Hank was once a union enforcer. Later, when Gil knew him better, other influences, namely the Mob, seemed a likely explanation for the enforcer job. Hank was stocky, with a disarmingly innocent, round face. He had the complexion, eyes and nose that marked him as a *Mick.* Hank's accent was *East Side.* When Gil fished with him, Hank was the General Superintendent for one of the biggest sheet metal contractors in New York.

Vince had the face and build of an oversized fireplug, with the same coloring. His skin was as impervious to the slings and arrows of life, as was the cast iron of a fireplug. He would have been a very successful pirate if he had only been born a century earlier. In this century, he was a general contractor. There is little difference between the two job descriptions. Vince was bigger than Hank, his complexion a darker shade of red. Vince had worked his way up from laborer, his face and hands attesting to the fact. Vince came from the same neighborhood as Hank did.

On the fateful day of The Sinking Fund episode, Vince was doing his normal forty knots, conning *Strap Hanger* across the bay on the way to the fishing grounds. It was sunrise. Hank was leaning with his butt against the gunwale, arms crossed, absorbing the impacts with his butt, as the boat skipping over the low, bay chop. This jarring motion caused his money roll to slowly creep out of his hip pocket, unnoticed.

Now Hank, as part of his job, needed several thousand dollars available to make the necessary payoffs. "It takes two hands to butter a slice of bread," he would remind his pals, whenever he discussed a payoff.

The first indication that the money roll had slid out of Hank's pocket was an explosive cloud of familiar looking green paper streaming behind the boat in the forty-knot breeze. Vince was mesmerized by the scream of the engines and the violent motion. Hank and Gil turned to look idly at this green cloud: puzzled.

Then, realization hit Hank like a sledgehammer. "Stop the boat," he screamed. Gil had to shake Vince to bring him back to earth, and the boat covered an additional hundred yards before Vince was able to turn and retrace his course to look for Hank's money roll.

Gil quickly grabbed a boarding net and started scooping up *twenties* and *fifties*. Hank stood transfixed, shouting warnings of dire punishment to the fisherman excitedly converging on the fortune strewn in the wake of *Straight Arrow*. In desperation, Hank started shying one-ounce lead sinkers at anyone closing in on the precious flotsam, threatening to remove their innards by reaching down their throats. Meanwhile, Vince continued maneuvering the boat, while Gil scooped up the soggy greenbacks. Vince was torn between moving the boat too quickly and risking swamping the floating bills and moving too slowly and risking the certainty that the bills would absorb enough water to sink of their own accord.

Eventually, Hank sat on the deck, legs splayed, chastened, spreading, drying and counting the soggy greenbacks Gil dumped in his lap. After several more passes over the area without finding any more bills, Vince asked Hank what the damages were. Hank was glum. He was short $800.

"You guys aren't holding out on me are you" he asked with a piercing stare? When there was no reply, Hank threatened a strip search back at the dock.

Then, looking him right in the eye, Gil asked with his brow cocked, "What kind of guys would hold out on a fishing buddy who always seemed to win the first-fish pool?"

Hank looked at Gil as his mind calculated how many times he had stung his pals over the years. Vince chuckled aloud. He was enjoying the exchange, but seeing the steely looks in both their eyes, Vince started passing the Johnny Red around for another hit, soothing ruffled nerves thus ending another typical day in the warmth and fellowship of flounder-fishing.

PART VIII

THE ELDER YEARS

usn

The expression, "Elder Years" mean different things to different people. Since each of us retired more than once, the expression probably should mean that point after which permanent work ended.

THE ABYSS

usn

"Danger, the spur of all great minds."
- Chapman

One of my friends once told me, "Everything in the Gillcrist family is a contest."

He was right. One of my children decided to have a contest with his cousins in the swimming pool at our home in Los Angeles. My son, Peter, took a heavy metal artifact, used to tether horses, into the pool to invent yet another contest. It was a heavy metal block of iron with a ring in the top of it through which one could pass the reins of a horse to keep him put temporarily. Of course, any horse could have dragged the weight easily, but I guess they didn't even try for some reason. Nancy had bought the tethering device from an antique store and it graced our patio near the pool. Peter took the device into the pool and walked the length of the bottom of the pool holding onto the block as a way of keeping him on the bottom. That proved to be easy. But, when he next tried to walk the entire perimeter of the pool bottom it proved to be much more difficult and challenging. That became the challenge he dropped on his cousins one summer day.

There was much fun, shouting, daring and laughter as they pursued this game for an hour or so. Finally, the inevitable occurred; and one of them dropped the device onto the pool drain cover breaking it. I will give them credit for not knowing they had done the damage, but the pool cleaner, on his weekly visit, pointed it out to me; explaining how much it would cost to replace it. The expense horrified me until he explained how he would have to rent an underwater breathing device that would enable him to go to the bottom of the pool at a depth of 12 feet and do the replacement. Two lousy dollars for a replacement drain and 150 dollars to effect the replacement! Now, I was irate.

That evening in my Jacuzzi I decided that any red-blooded 63-year-old Gillcrist male could hold his breath long enough to unscrew two lousy Phillips-head screws, replace the broken plastic device and screw in the new one. Sheeesh!

After many trips down to the bottom of the pool the next day (while Nancy was out shopping) I learned that the problem was not lung capacity but buoyancy. The solution was found in the offending device that had created the problem in the first place. After an hour of experimenting, I found that by tying the weight to my waist with a three foot tether I could do the job, suspended inverted three feet off the bottom of the pool held down by the device as it rested on the bottom. Naturally, the hazards of this approach occurred to me. Also, the thought of Nancy finding me there, in that awkward position, dead of a heart attack gave me some pause. But, I concluded it was do-able and simple as long as I tethered myself with a knot that was easily releasable with one yank on the bitter end of the tether.

During my maiden voyage to the bottom of the pool I got the cover off but dropped one screw and it quickly disappeared down the drain. Aborting that attempt, I had to go to the garage to find a replacement sheet-metal screw of the right dimensions. Back into the pool I went realizing that I now had the additional constraint of time. Nancy was due back from shopping soon so I had to get the job done quickly. I carried additional screws in case I dropped any more. Where to carry them, I wondered? You guessed it, I finally ended up by putting them in my mouth. This made access easy but blowing out any air had now to be done through my nose. The sheer idiocy of all of this was gradually seeping into my mind, so I said a silent prayer to Saint Anthony as I began my next descent into my own abyss. If they did an autopsy on me and found six sheet-metal screws in my sinuses what, I wondered, would the coroner conclude?

Of course, prior to each descent I hyper-ventilated; a trick I had learned years earlier at, you guessed it, The Three Sisters Islands. Long story short, I had just completed the replacement when Nancy returned. Thankfully, I had the native intelligence not to mention the entire silly affair.

Nagging Nag's Head

usmc

Love the sea? I dote upon it... from the beach.
- Jerrold

It was October and for several days, there had been a gale blowing out of the northeast. Because of the gale, the ocean was piling up on the shore, furious that it couldn't erode the entire Outer Banks away, once and for all. The only witnesses to this power play were retirees who enjoyed the relative solitude and reduced rates of the fall season.

The couples' room was on the top floor, ocean side. Marie would have left the door to the balcony open all night, if only the weather had cooperated. The pounding of the surf and the woofing of the air against the glass picture window were Marie's secret pleasures. The indelible marks of years of rising before daylight, years of drudgery and fatigue, all of life's weathering washed away by something as natural as an ocean breeze and some salt spray. Both readily available at reduced rates and applied before going to bed.

A simple pleasure of Jim's was to sit on the balcony with a mug of hot black coffee and let the elements mesmerize him. In some civilizations, it was necessary to fast for days and chew on herbs to enter a trance. All Jim ever needed was a mug of coffee and an early morning ocean view.

On those occasions when Marie ran off to one of the many shopping outlets, Jim would move onto the balcony and subconsciously fall into the work habit of his youth, he would watch the surfers for telltale signs. And from time to time Jim would pick a good wave and surf it in his mind as he surfed his memories.

Everyone has some private memory, a recollection of a special summer, a kiss, a first car, or a season with an abundance of camaraderie and good health. One of Jim's memories has been of those meager few seasons of life guarding at Jones Beach.

Quitzau, Manheim, McGroaty, Barr, and all the other boys of summer would bring a reflexive childlike grin at the memory of the endless antics of body surfing, beach parties, and boat races. Watching the surfers was the only serious part of the guard job, that and the rescue. The rest was pure fun.

Jim was a tall, 60-year-old whose body showed all the signs of the three-and-a-half-hour daily commute to New York City. Long gone was that fitness he enjoyed as a young lifeguard. He was balding and gray, with a face lined by the stress of too many construction projects in New York, the toughest town in the universe. Marie was a lively, loving, woman who had recently retired after thirty-two years as a high school teacher. They made a perfect pair of occupational bookends.

Sitting on the balcony at Nags Head 40 years later, the habit of guarding the surfers was still ingrained. The need to watch the surfers was enhanced, by the absence of lifeguards this late in the season. The gale had tapered off, but the surf was slow to settle down. "Watch those two little, tousle-headed children collecting pails of seawater. If the undertow plucked those tiny souls into the deep, could I run down five flights, through the hotel and on to the beach in time?" he mused.

He wasn't really too concerned, just speculating idle subconscious ruminations. Many other thoughts crowded Jim's mind, such as the construction projects back in New York and whether a move to North Carolina would be best for Marie.

There was a tattooed surfer on the beach below the balcony, who looked something like Charles Manson. He was frolicking in the surf with an overweight woman. They didn't look like they could take care of themselves, but they stayed in knee-deep water. The next day Fate would whisper in Mr. Manson's ear and Jim would meet him.

The following day, their last day on The Outer Banks, dawned with a nature show in the surf below Marie and Jim's room. The porpoises were everywhere, feeding and cavorting. At one point, a pair jumped clear of the sea in a delightful ballet, true free spirits. Marie and Jim watched for hours, delighted, recording a video for a quiet, snowy winter's night.

The sun finally broke through around noon. The wind eased further. The air became balmy, and the beach beckoned. And, as always, the sea was waiting.

Marie and Jim grabbed the beach bag and the sand chair and headed for their favorite spot. The pair had noticed a part of the beach where the erosion hadn't altered the bottom. They decided it was safe enough to enjoy a little careful body surfing together. A quarter hour was enough. Then Marie sat back in her beach chair to read, and Jim took up his post, watching the surf.

A young couple came down the wood stairs from the hotel, a burly fellow, his wife and their three-year-old daughter. The husband dutifully laid the blanket and set up the umbrella. Some comment passed between them and then, as though unleashed, he bounded off towards the surf, powerful legs pumping. With a final leap, he punched into a "coamer" and stroked straight out to sea.

Jim was wearing Polaroid sunglasses as he watched the young man. With the glasses, it was easy to see those spots where the undertow was active. Those danger spots were usually a sandy color, the result of fast moving water lifting and carrying the sand. In his youth, the lifeguards called the phenomenon a *sea puss*.

The burly young man was unaware of the danger of the *sea puss*. As Jim watched intently, the young man began to realize that he was being drawn farther offshore. His stroke was powerful and confident as he turned towards the beach. A dozen strong strokes and the young man's head came up to check his progress. There was none. If anything, the young man was farther still from the safety of the shore.

The moment the realization came to the young man that he was both mortal and in mortal danger, Jim knew. After years of life guarding, the signs of panic are clear. *If only they could stay calm,* Jim mused; *it would be a cinch.* Everyone knows that if challenged, they can relax and float in their backyard pool, nose barely above water, breathing, for many hours. What does swimmers in, is the notion of mortality. God will come and take all of us away one day. We know that! But, that fateful day will certainly be many years from now. Not now, no!

But when the Sea wraps its icy fingers around a frightened swimmer's ankle, a rictus state overcomes him. Oxygen, blood sugar, coordination, and learned skills all desert him. Drowning follows after a fierce struggle to stay on this Earth.

In that moment, Jim said, "Ah shit" to the sky and Marie, threw off his sun glasses and shirt, and sprinted for the surf.

"Help me, help!" the young man gargled, frantically. The retirees including Charles Manson gathered on shore, and stood watching with Oriental acceptance. Charles had been a guard in the Rockaways for many a summer, but he made no move to help the drowning young man, because he knew how dangerous it was. The retirees reminded Jim of a distant memory, of a group of Vietnamese, gathered to watch an execution.

Porpoising out through the surf was an old skill. The knowledge that no other lifeguards would come out to help was enough to keep Jim out of the young man's reach. The young man looked at Jim, expecting him to do something.

"Swim parallel to the beach" Jim called out. "We will swim out of the *puss* together," he added. For a time the youngster tried to follow Jim's example, but he lost faith too soon to escape the *puss*. Then the young man discharged Jim, and turned towards the beach again, still in the grip of the undertow.

There was nothing, Jim could do. To wrestle with the drowning man was worth his own life. So, the old man swam next to the young man, but out of reach, waiting for him to slide under. The young man slid under shortly, struggling back to the surface, vomiting. His eyes were white, bulging. He gargled, "Help!" It was finally the time, for the old man to grab him under the arm and pull the young man towards the shore.

The *sea puss* had them both now: the old man and the young man too.

Jim's breathing was ragged. Fatigue had its arms wrapped around his neck, hanging on, pulling him under. At that moment, Jim realized with a jolt, that they were both going to die.

"I've made one too many rescues." Jim thought to himself, "Either the young man will pull me under or I will drown from exhaustion." It was a shock for Jim to be reminded of his own mortality.

Panic erupted. In his soul, he decided to let the young man slip under with the young man's wife and daughter standing on shore, just a few scant feet away. The young man turned to the old man and screamed. He knew!

Then, he grunted in despair one last time and slid under. Jim lunged for him and put his arm around him, pulling him close. The two spent swimmers looked into each other's eyes and Jim told him, "We will make it to the beach together."

The rest was shear concentrated effort, with no relief: just one more stroke. God was good and sent two huge waves crashing down on them, pushing the pair towards shore. The old man's foot brushed the turbulent, sandy bottom. Another wave and he was dragging his young brother through the frothy surf.

Marie had organized some support. She had sent a retiree to the hotel pool for the life-ring. The retirees still stood staunchly, united and not volunteering to help. Marie was just heading out through the surging, ankle grasping surf, struggling to bring her husband the life-ring.

Utterly exhausted, Jim roughly ordered four of the retirees into the knee-deep surf to carry the young man up the beach. As Jim climbed the storm eroded sand shelf, he tripped and fell on his face.

A hand hovered before his sand-filled eyes. He accepted the helpful hand gratefully, and was pulled to his feet, trembling.

Jim took a quick look over his shoulder to make sure that the young man was being carried up the beach to aid and then trudged wearily toward his own blanket with his arm around Marie.

For years after, Jim was troubled. He kept asking himself, "If there was another spent swimmer, would I help, or would I stand safely on the beach and watch, while a soul cried out for help?"

A Trip Down Memory Lane

usn

*"Those who do not do battle for their country, do not understand
with what ease they accept their citizenship in America."*
- Dean Brelis

It all began rather innocently while I was home in La Jolla checking my
e-mail. A message came in on the Crusader internet circuit announcing
that a Kevin Costner movie was in the making titled, "Thirteen Days,"
about the Cuban Missile Crisis. The author of the message, someone
named Stu Neuman, asked for a volunteer former F8 driver to serve
as a technical advisor. I responded just for laughs and was asked to
submit details of my qualifications in a fax message to an office in
Glendale, California. I sent in my dossier with a little bit of Hollywood
bulls--t thrown in for good measure, and a week or so later received a
telephone call from someone who identified himself as Peter Almond,
the Producer.

Peter asked me to come up to the studio in Glendale to interview
for the job. He, of course, never used the word "interview" but that's
what it was. Two days later I walked onto the Whitehouse set at the
Glendale studio of Barwick Independent Studios replete in what I call
my "sincere outfit." Gray wool slacks, blue sports jacket, blue striped,
button down shirt and brightly colored red tie. I was the picture of a
technical advisor, or so I thought.

The sign on the side of the huge building said Barwick Independent
Studios. The "Thirteen Days" production company was named Mutually
Assured Productions, and the umbrella production company is called
Beacon Communications. For the purpose of funding the enterprise

Beacon allied themselves with another studio called New Line. I do not want anyone to even try to explain the complicated wiring diagram of all this to me. It took me thirty years to learn the complex structure of the United States Defense Department. There aren't enough years left for me to do it again in the entertainment industry.

The reason for the Crusader credentials was that the movie depicts Commander Bill Ecker, commanding officer of the Navy's east coast Light Photographic Reconnaissance Squadron (VFP-62) when he flew photo reconnaissance missions over Cuba in October 1962. On one of Bill's photo missions the now famous pictures of the theatre ballistic missile site at San Cristobal were taken. The incontrovertible photographic evidence of Soviet adventurism in the western hemisphere was used very theatrically by U.N. Ambassador Adlai Stevenson to embarrass a glowering Soviet Ambassador Dobrynin live on television on the floor of the U.N. security council. It was indeed a rare moment in American history. Although never a fan of mine, Adlai Stevenson endeared himself to me forever and made himself famous beyond his wildest dreams. With his pointer Stevenson indicated the blown-up aerial photos of Russian missiles at San Cristobal and Sagua La Grande and asked Dobrynin if he still denied their existence. There was a pregnant pause after which a red-faced Dobrynin said he would need a moment to confer with his aides before he responded. Stevenson seized the moment with the now historic riposte, "Sir, I am prepared to wait until hell freezes over!" That was real "theatre."

There was a miniature version of the White House constructed inside a very large warehouse-like studio building! No kidding! As I strode purposefully up the front steps of the White House I stumbled over a bundle of electrical wires which were strewn like spaghetti all over the place. Luckily, I took two or three quick steps and barely kept from falling flat on my face. They were "shooting" at the moment and I thought nobody on the set took notice. This little near-pratfall did not go unnoticed by the troops. One of the dolly grips later told me that he and his henchmen, watching from the sidelines, got an enormous bang out of my Hollywood two-step. But, it was nevertheless a "grand entrance" any way you cut it. Here was this pompous, seventy-year-old "techy" walking on to the set trying to look as though he owned it and got his come-uppance from a bundle of extension wires. What a way to begin!

As soon as they finished shooting the scene, Peter Almond walked over, introduced himself and then took me over to meet the cast, director, executive producer, production designer, first assistant director, second assistant director, cinematographer, key grip, dolly grip, gaffer, best boy, art department director, production safety officer and so forth down the pecking order of the entertainment industry. After a few more minutes of moving things around the set, they were ready to shoot another scene. It became obvious that I was in the way, so I made my exit with the tenuous understanding that I was hired. As she said goodbye, the executive producer, Ilona Herzberg, told me they would fax me a contract that afternoon. I was in another world!

As I drove off the studio lot a few minutes later the gate guard waved me through as though he knew me. That did it! Pulling over to the side of the road, I put the convertible's top down, turned the sound system up to a high decibel level, selected a CD titled "In The Navy" by the Village People, lit a cigar and drove south on Interstate 5 feeling as though I owned the world! In a way, I guess I did!

The last week in January was spent, fourteen hours a day, shooting scenes in Glendale using mock-ups of the Crusader and the U2, preparatory to the move to the location site in the Philippines. That Friday, we all went home to pack for the trip to the Far East. Sunday night about thirty of us flew from LAX to Manila. Arriving at 0400 after a grueling 12 hour flight, we checked in to our hotels, unpacked and went directly to the location sight for what is known as a "scout."

The two shooting locations in the Philippines were the former Clark Air Force Base, about two hours northwest of Manila and Pagsanjan, Lagunas, about the same driving time to the south. The scenes to be shot at Clark were to simulate flight operations at three bases in Florida, Naval Air Stations, Cecil Field and Key West and Homestead Air Force Base. The scenes to be shot at Pagsanjan were to simulate a Russian medium range ballistic missile site in Cuba.

The portions of the film to be shot at Clark all dealt with reconnaissance flights out of the Florida NASs and strike preparations at Homestead. Again, we worked a twelve hour day at least and meals were catered in the one of the hangars. My fondest recollection of the "shoots" at Clark was what I call the "bad hair day." One scene was shot in the simulated VFP-62 ready room and it included a gathering of simulated photo reconnaissance pilots. There must have been at least ten actors dressed in flight suits, posing as pilots. My first glance took in some pretty scruffy haircuts, at least for Navy photo pilots, and I made a comment to that effect which, of course, was overheard by the director. He instantly jumped on it and asked me to identify the offending haircuts. I walked around the room, with great delight and pointed my finger at four or five pilots each of whom sported $75 dollar Hollywood haircuts. To my surprise, they had a barber in the hangar somewhere. The pilots I "fingered" were whisked away to the barber and properly shorn in accordance with Navy regulations circa 1962. I felt like a Marine staff sergeant at boot camp.

The weather on Monday was brutally hot and humid and the poor pilots, Chris Lawford and David O'Donnell, our two simulated F8 pilots, were practically parboiled by the end of the day. But we stuck fairly much to schedule that day. My feet, knees and hips were killing me when I rolled in to the bunk that night at the Clark Field Holiday Inn.

Just to set the historical record straight, in 1977 the Philippine Air Force bought twenty-six F8 Crusaders from the US.

They had been stored at the Defense Aircraft Recovery Facility at Davis-Monthan Air Force Base. The contractor, Chance-Vought Aircraft, agreed to refurbish the airplanes. Twenty-five of them were reasonably late model F8Es. The twenty-sixth airplane was what we called the "Twosader," a tandem two-seater version. I never got to fly the two-seater, nor did I ever want to do so. The reason is that part of the mystique of being a Crusader pilot is the fact that when we climbed into our first Crusader each of us did so with the full knowledge that we were strictly on our own for the next hour and one half, live or die. There would be no instructor in the back seat to save our asses if we screwed up.

The Philippine Air Force (PAF) began flying their newly re-furbished Crusaders in 1979 and finally put them out of commission in 1989. I believe that the principal reason for the stand-down was the fact that the airplane was simply too hard to operate safely. One of the starkest statistics of the Crusader's history is that 1,245 were built and there were 1156 major accidents, not counting the PAF experience!

When the "Thirteen Days"" preparation crew arrived at the Crusader storage facility at Basa (halfway between Clark and Manila) they found only twelve hulks left. They were not flyable, their engines would never run. This would imply that the PAF destroyed fourteen of the airplanes in the ten years they were in service. The set production crew picked the best ten and transported them to Clark for the filming. Surprisingly, the PAF had never even removed their engines. Some utility company has made a bid on the twelve engines to generate electrical power.

The airplanes, in their new U.S. Navy markings (circa 1962, of course) looked fairly authentic. They were not "taxiable" so a triple towbar rig was configured allowing us to simulate taxiing while towing them with a tractor that could remain off camera. Later, during the editing process the cinematic magicians would electronically erase the towbars and dub in afterburners etc. Thursday, February 11th, the shooting unit moved south to Pagsanjan (the missile site) and I headed home.

The shooting of the movie was completed and scheduled to air on December 20th, 2000. After making a dozen telephone calls to friends in Washington I concluded that DoD was reluctant to cooperate because the screenplay depicts General Lemay as sort of a war-monger (which I think he probably was). The production company, Mutually Assured Productions, had already moved out of the Barwick facility and relocated to office space in Santa Monica.

On the long flight from Manila back to LA, I had plenty of time to contemplate my good fortune at having survived my 2,000 plus hours of flight time, 167 combat missions and 500 plus carrier landings in the Crusader. Out of all that Crusader experience I only had to jump out of one of them! For a brief moment in time I was able to re-live some of those memories, it was fun! I wish you could have been there!

WEIGHING THE CALF

usmc

"Men think God is destroying them because he is tuning them.
The violinist screws up the key till the tense cord sounds the concert pitch;
but it is not to break it, but to use it tunefully, that he stretches the string."
- Beecher

Marsha was a vivacious, indomitable, woman with artistic talent that no one even glimpsed during the years that she lived in the village. Through all the years of cocktail parties and backyard barbecues, of casual meetings on the street and in the supermarkets, we saw no outward signs of the artist hidden within.

When she and Paul, her professional husband, moved into their new home, we were glad to have such a genteel couple complement the village. They were educated, well traveled, and financially secure. They had not a care, other than the raising of the children, and their offspring soon moved on with their own lives, flying the nest. The timing was perfect, because Paul's aging father moved into one of those vacated bedrooms.

Then one day the unthinkable happened. It did not at first manifest itself as a calamity. It was something that almost went unnoticed. Paul's longtime friend and professional partner saw an error in Paul's work. The two partners had always spot-checked each other's work as a precaution against just such an event. The partner showed him the error and no more was said, but the partner lay awake that night, preoccupied with the error. It disturbed his rest. Something indiscernible bothered him about the nature of that error.

In the following months there were more errors. Those casual discussions that followed the crosschecks became difficult and combative for the partners. Something was wrong with Paul and his partner now saw the professional partnership at risk of a devastating lawsuit if even one of Paul's errors went undetected. More to the point, Paul saw no error or denied having made them. The situation was impossible, the lawyers were called and the partnership dissolved.

Paul displayed no anger at the loss of his livelihood. He simply sat at home, strangely calm. Marsha, in desperation, sought medical assistance for Paul and the nightmare, the unthinkable finally had a name. Paul had Alzheimer's.

During the next few years, Marsha assumed the role of caregiver for both Paul and his aging father. "What else can I do," she would ask?

Her days began to blend into a never-ending task. The physical struggle to maneuver and care for two males who outweighed her by 50 pounds was exhausting. The demands on Marsha's time, to feed the hungry and cleanse the incontinent became endless.

Marsha grieved for the lost companionship and sharing of the good and bad that bound her to Paul as one through all the years. Her grief gnawed away at her being. She was desolate, but she was also fiercely independent and determined to do the right thing and not to draw friends into her private vortex.

Then one day, while her son was visiting and she had a few hours of grace, Marsha went to the local spring art festival. As Marsha wandered alone among the exhibition booths, chatting with the artists, she sensed how they all reveled in the pleasure of self-expression.

That night, after she put her charges to bed, Marsha dragged her wooden art case out of a musty corner of the cellar, where it had lay unused since her university days. On the kitchen table, Marsha opened the case to find dried out brushes and hardened tubes of titian red, titanium white and tungsten blue and one sealed tube of yellow ocher. She broke the seal and swirled the oil about on her palette.

The movement of the knife in the oil, the texture of the oil itself, and its scent mesmerized Marsha. She felt as though she had surfaced after a deep dive. She sat at the table breathing deeply and then excitedly began scribbling a long list of fresh art supplies. Marsha had found an outlet for the suffocating need for expression and stress relief.

Thereafter, when the men were napping or in bed for the night, Marsha would open her case and spread her wings. If anyone had observed Marsha during those stolen moments, they would have noticed the hint of a smile as she worked like a demon. "There is no frigate like a book to take us lands away." Emily Dickinson said. Emily, in her poem, could easily have exchanged "palette knife" for "book." In the days ahead, Marsha found herself subconsciously planning her next art project as she cared for her charges. Marsha became conscious of the sound of the mail carrier's truck and would almost run to the mailbox out at the road to search for art catalogues and newsletters of art events in the area.

It was as if she had discovered a secret room hidden beyond all the other rooms of her mind, rooms that she had sadly closed off and sealed forever. Her newly discovered room grew bigger each time she entered, and sunnier too. Marsha would sneak off to that secret place whenever there was a spare moment. One of the mysteries of artistic creativity is the relationship between the artist's ability to express herself and the level of human emotional turmoil in the artist's own life. The mystery is that the quality of the artist's work is enhanced as life's burdens bear down. Marsha's work blossomed.

In idle moments, Marsha would examine her commitment to her patients, knowing that there was no chance of remission or recovery. She could not look far enough down the road to see Life's next crossroad. It was as far away as eternity.

One day Marsha found herself comparing their circumstance to a contest her father once spoke of. The contest was called *weighing the calf*. As a boy on the farm, her father and his brothers would pick a newborn calf each spring. The contest was to see which brother could *weigh the Calf* one last time as the calf grew. The idea was for the brothers to lift the calf each day. The calf grew heavier every day, reaching a weight of 1000 pounds in time, so the boys knew it was inevitable that a day would arrive on which they could no longer weigh the calf. It was a part of natural law.

Caring for her ill and elderly was like weighing that calf. Each day the calf grew, with the inevitable outcome. The day will surely arrive when she could no longer pick up the calf.

For Marsha that day was the day her father-in-law shuffled through the television room as his son sat consumed by the colors of flowing motion and the sound propagating from the set. A curled edge of carpet caught the old man's slipper and he hit the stone floor with a sickening crack. The old man regained his senses long enough to feebly attempt to get his son's attention. His son only sat a few feet away, but Paul was as far away as the moon.

Marsha discovered the tableau an hour later when she returned from the laundry room. By that time, the father had gone into shock and then, had quietly stolen away. His son sat by his side entranced by the swirling movements on the screen, a faint smile on his face.

Marsha stood for a moment, in the midst of the Dantesque scene as a fusion of exquisite sadness and relief flowed through her body. Then, she slowly walked to the telephone.

Marsha could no longer weigh the calf.

DIRTY HARRY

usn

"You people need a new sheriff"
- Clint Eastwood "For a Few Dollars More."

Each time I see a replay of the Dirty Harry movie where, at the very end, Clint Eastwood points his .44 Magnum revolver at the perpetrator and announces, "…this is the most powerful handgun in the world," I am reminded of a scene in my back yard in which I did somewhat the same thing.

Many years earlier, about 1956, I had purchased, from a mail order house a used .455 caliber Webley British army issue revolver. It was as old as the hills and is the kind we used to see the movie RCMP officers wearing holstered and with a lanyard around the neck as they "got their man." As a matter of point, my Webley had a bore that was fifteen thousandths of an inch larger than Dirty Harry's cannon.

As a result of an earlier intruder incident I had changed my evening ritual in two ways; I now wore a bathing suit and resting in a carrying case at the jacuzzi's edge was my Webley, loaded with an empty chamber under the firing pin.

As luck would have it, about a year after the first intrusion, I was lying in my jacuzzi, puffing on a cheroot when I heard the rolling gate at my garage rattle followed by distinct sound of two pairs of feet striking the pavement in front of my garage door. Reacting instantly, I slipped out of the jacuzzi, whipped on the bathrobe, picked up the Webley and walked over to the walkway leading fifty feet or so to my garage. Even though it was dark, I could make out the silhouettes of two people standing there motionless.

"Freeze," I called out in my best Clint Eastwood voice. "I am holding the largest handgun in the world and it is aimed right at you. Get on the ground face down right now or I will shoot." In actual fact I had the gun pointed down at the ground for fear that it might go off and I didn't want that enormous slug to hit anyone at this juncture.

The two figures instantly flung themselves to the pavement, and I approached admonishing them not to move a muscle. At this point I was surprised to hear Nancy's voice calling to me from the upstairs bedroom window asking what was going on. I told her to call 911 and tell the police that I had apprehended some intruders. She did this and added the one bit of information guaranteed to get the police moving, "my husband has a gun!"

The prone figures, it turned out, were two terrified neighborhood kids. By the time I had marched the two boys to the back patio there were two police helicopters circling over the house in a figure eight pattern each with a powerful searchlight illuminating me and the perpetrators. By now the two boys had identified themselves to me and explained that they had scaled my rolling gate in trying to elude members of a street gang who were pursuing them. I put the revolver down and asked Nancy to open the front door.

She had barely done so when four police ran through the door, guns drawn and yelling at all of us to freeze. It was almost like a bad comedy. One officer asked me brusquely where the gun was. I pointed to it and he picked it up examining it for a safety catch. Of course, Webleys had no safeties. Instead they had a spring lever which held the firing pin away from the face of the bullet. That same lever was used to unlock the revolver break mechanism causing the barrel to be rotated 90 degrees downward for reloading. The officer was completely mystified, never having seen such a relic before. When I offered to unload it he jumped away and told me not to reach for the gun again. Finally, after another 30 seconds of fumbling, he allowed me to unload it and stood there marveling at the empty weapon.

After a few more minutes of clarifying everything the helicopters flew away and I assured the policemen that I did not want to prefer any charges against the kids and asked them to deliver the boys to the front doors of their respective homes down the block. Before I did this, however, I had watched the police cuff the boys. It was an experience they needed to have. I felt sure that their parents would be more than happy to "take care of their sons". I knew both parents and felt certain there would be serious retribution for the kids. When they left, the policeman who had been unable to unload the Webley handed it to me, still in the broken open configuration, with the comment, "Sir, take my advice. Get rid of this thing and get yourself a good gun."

The story didn't end there. Next morning I went out to the garage and there, underneath my car I found a paintball gun. All the lights went on in my head. The kids have been shooting the paintball gun, probably at passing cars and had gotten their come-uppance. They had obviously ditched it when Dirty Harry showed up. I took the paintball gun to one of the neighbor's houses and gave it to the father explaining how dangerous it would be if a policeman saw that thing in the dark in his son's hand. He was guardedly grateful. There were no more intruders at 300 South Lucerne Boulevard.

NIGHT INTRUDER

usn

"Don't tread on me."
Motto on the American Rattlesnake Flag- 1776

Our home in Los Angeles was 76 years old but in remarkably good condition for a Norfolk style frame house. Our neighborhood, called Hancock Park, was a large tract of gracious houses which had been the home of the early movie colony before Beverly Hills was built. Our house featured what was called a California basement, a small space large enough for the furnace and hot water heater, with a building block wall that only rose about six feet above the cellar floor. Above the wall was access to the crawl space throughout the underside of the house. A series of screened air apertures vented the crawl space to the outside of the house. Not all of the screens were secure.

One morning Nancy's mother noticed what seemed to be a small pile of short gray hairs on the floor around the opening in the kitchen counter into which the dishwasher had been installed. The opening was probably 1 1/5 inches wide and partially guarded with metal flashing where the installer had not done a perfect tailoring job. Thinking I might have a mouse or two to deal with, and remembering Nancy's aversion to them, I waited until she went to bed before setting a few mouse traps on the kitchen floor around the opening. I remember falling asleep thinking about those gray hairs.

I woke up around 4:00 am, went to the bathroom to do my ablutions and, remembering the traps, went downstairs to the kitchen to see if I had caught anything. What I saw when I peeked around the corner into the kitchen nearly turned my stomach. Both mouse traps had been sprung but empty and the rear end of a huge Norway rat could be seen as he tried desperately to squeeze back through the space at the bottom of the dishwasher cabinet. He must have heard me but couldn't squeeze back through the hole because the thin metal flashing around the appliance wouldn't flex inward. I grabbed the broom and lunged at him with it managing to pin him down under the straw end of the broom. He squirmed out and I chased him across the kitchen floor toward the pantry pinning him down again and holding him down as hard as I could push against the broom handle. He was frantically squirming and gradually wiggling free from the broom. I knew if he got free and made it into the pantry with all of its hiding places there would be hell to pay.

Standing there in my underwear and bare feet I wracked my brain for an immediate solution. Holding onto the broom handle and watching the rat work himself free I knew what I had to do and it curdled the juices in my stomach. Picking up my left foot I stomped hard on the brooms straw sweeps from under which the squirming upper half of the rat was now emerging. I nearly threw up!

It took me half an hour of scrubbing the tile floor and my foot with heavy-duty detergent before I dared go upstairs and then stood in the shower for a long time before I felt clean enough to get back into bed. Nancy was snoring away, blissfully unaware of the carnage wrought in her pristine kitchen. The next day, armed with a new roll of heavy-duty screening material, I crawled around in the bushes surrounding the house, sealing off every conceivable opening to the crawl space. Then I stuffed steel wool (recommended by the animal control people) around all pipe openings through the floor of the house. The experts explained that the rats would attempt to chew through the steel wool, swallow some of it in the process and it would kill them…yuck! I never ventured back into the crawl space again. Now I know why a career in plumbing never appealed to me.

INCOMING

usn

"Weigh the situation, then move."
Sun Tzu

Recently I attended a two-hour long marathon Holy Saturday Easter vigil service at our church in La Jolla. The celebrant was doing the blessing of the congregation with holy water when I experienced a vivid flash-back to an earlier time in my life during the same ceremony. The celebrant in the earlier episode stood in the center aisle abreast of the first row of pews, dipped the instrument for dispensing holy water into a basin held by an altar boy. Then he raised it shoulder-high and, with a powerful fore-and-aft motion, began sprinkling the audience with droplets of holy water, all the while mumbling in Latin.

I cannot remember the name of the device, but it was about two and one half inch brass sphere mounted on an eight inch wooden handle. The sphere had openings all around its perimeter which permitted it to retain a fair amount of water each time it was dipped. The celebrant swung left and right several times like a harvester of souls seeking to get a few droplets of salvation onto each of us in the congregation.

At some point in this anointing process I watched the brass sphere detach itself from the handle just at the peak force of the priest's forward motion. I knew, before the sphere had gone six inches, that it was headed for me. Spewing droplets of holy water much like Haley's Comet spews streaks of celestial debris, the sphere began it's long, majestic upward parabola. There was an audible gasp from the congregation as it watched the missile arc high above the pews, headed my way. The apex of its voyage must have been at least fifteen feet above the congregation.

Then it began its dramatic downward return to planet earth. People in front of me and on either side ducked down as if it were some deadly Scud missile. Reaching out, I caught the sphere in my right hand and was rewarded for my effort by a wholesome dollop of water in my face. Out of the corner of my eye I saw the altar boy scurrying in my direction at the orders of the celebrant obviously to retrieve the sphere.

When I handed it to him he scurried back and returned it to the celebrant, who like some faithful believer, screwed it back onto the wooden shaft and began to dip it into the basin. When he lifted it to resume the sprinkling I heard myself call out involuntarily, "NOOOO." Undeterred, the priest renewed the flailing motion whereupon the part of the congregation toward which he was gesturing began to weave and bob almost in unison like waves of grain in a wheat field.

Fortunately, the sphere remained in its post and there were no further demonstrations of Gallileo's Laws of Motion. Ever since that event so many years ago I never fail to watch the celebrant's hand and the sphere...waiting for the inevitable.

NEAR MISS

usn

"Danger gleams like sunshine to a brave man's eyes."
Euripides

It was the 6th of May 2004, and I was doing my daily half-mile in the La Jolla YMCA pool. The life guards had gotten into the habit of putting in a lane divider at the side of the pool allowing me to do laps while the remainder of the pool was kept available for the 30 or so ladies (including Nancy) who were engaged in something called water jazzerobics. Each woman wore a flotation belt, webbed gloves and booties and was protected from the sun by some outlandish head covering. Nancy's choice was a baseball cap. They moved their arms and legs to the cadence from a loud voiced female trainer and a boom box which was playing, at the moment, "The Girl From Impanema. "

My swimming goggles gave me an underwater view of the torsos of thirty senior women kicking and waving in unison…I guess you had to be there to appreciate the exquisite irony of the sight. On one of my laps past the group I notice two of the torsos detach themselves from the others and drift toward the lane divider. Just as I passed them, close aboard, I rolled my head to take a breath and was rewarded by a small sheet of water splashed in my face causing me to cough and lose rhythm. Choking, I continued to the end of the pool and made my turn, during which I looked back to see; that Nancy was one of the two women near the lane divider and that they were both laughing at me. I was not amused.

Now, anyone who swims laps knows that the key to success is to maintain a rhythm. Nothing is allowed to break that state of **nirvana** into which the swimmer must settle if he is going to swim any serious distance. The two perpetrators had violated my "space" and I was determined to exact retribution.

On my next trip down the lap lane I approached the pair of torsos still alongside the lane divider and saw that I was in position to strike back. I also took notice, for the first time, that the two ladies were wearing nearly identical one-piece bathing suits with a blue and white floral design. I reached under the divider and stretched out my hand to pinch Nancy sharply on the ass. When my hand was inches away from the syncopating target, the good Lord must have been perched on my shoulder because a small voice whispered in my ear, "Don't do it!"

The temptation was terrible but caution prevailed and I swam on. When I made the turn at the end of the pool I was horrified to note that the two women had inadvertently switched relative positions; and I had almost pinched the wrong woman on the bottom.

For the rest of the half-mile, a series of horrifying images flashed across my mind of banner headlines in tomorrow's morning edition of the local newspaper reading "PERVERT APPREHENDED AT LOCAL SWIMMING POOL. TURNS OUT TO BE A LOCAL RETIRED FLAG OFFICER!!! ARRAIGNMENT SCHEDULED FOR THURSDAY."

Odyssey

usn

*"A ship is always referred to as 'she' because
it costs so much to keep her in paint and powder."*
Fleet Admiral C.W. Nimitz

Sometime back in 2004, I forget exactly when, Nancy and I decided to celebrate our 50th wedding anniversary in a unique way. First of all, neither of us is much interested in making a big deal over our anniversary; we are private people in that regard. But we knew that our children would attempt to do something. Therefore, in order to preempt an elaborate exercise, we decided to invite our four children and their spouses on a cruise to Alaska.

We did this in an interesting way, by sending each of them an e-mail containing a scrambled puzzle. The puzzle unscrambled said: "Cruise to Alaska in 2005 50th Anniversary." The puzzle idea was a failure. No one could unscramble it without repeated clues.

On July 22nd, 2005, Jim and Kathy, Tom and Terese; and Mary all met at our home in La Jolla at 7:15 a.m. for a limousine ride to the airport and the beginning of the odyssey. In typical fashion, our son Tom's vehicle developed a flat tire while parked in our front driveway. So, while the limousine waited, he and his brother, Jim, did a pit stop routine on the car. The incident set the mood for what was to be an adventure full of surprises.

Nevertheless, we made it to the airplane, and Mary, Tom, his wife Terese; Jim and his wife, Kathy and Nancy and I arrived in Vancouver in time to rendezvous with Peter and his wife, Amie and Sarah

231

Hammann, a friend of Mary's who would be her room mate for the cruise. The ten of us stayed in the Marriott Hotel in Vancouver the night of July 23rd. We had a nice, if pricey, dinner at a place called "The Bridges." It was 10:30 p.m. before we got out of the place but it was a memorable evening.

The next morning was "natural rising." Nancy and I breakfasted at the hotel's buffet. We were joined by Kathy and Jim and the four of us took a cab to the ship, MS ZAANDAM, Holland America Lines. Once at the dock, it took almost two hours of winding our way through endless, serpentine cattle chutes before we finally made it aboard.

THE SHIP

I believe a few words about our cruise ship might help the reader to understand what follows. MS ZAANDAM is 780 feet long, with a beam of 106 feet. It displaces 63,000 tons (about the size of the U.S.S. ORISKANY fully loaded) and has a top speed of 23 knots. The crew numbers 647 and the passenger accommodations can handle 1,440. It is powered by five diesel engines, is driven by two screws which deliver a total of 45,200 horsepower. The total distance cruised was 1,813 nautical miles.

DAY NUMBER ONE

Our first official act after we crossed the gangway was to eat. A sumptuous luncheon buffet was underway in the Lido Room. Kathy, Jim, Nancy and I enjoyed our first meal courtesy of Holland America Lines. Amie and Peter were the next to show up, followed by Tom and Terese and finally Mary and her friend, Sarah. What a relief it was to collapse in our stateroom! We had made it!

We got, underway about 4:00 p.m. on Saturday July23rd. We had hardly cleared the harbor before an "abandon ship" drill was called. This is an international requirement for all passenger ships. It took the better part of an hour to count heads; with much ribaldry and joking by the passengers as they milled about in their life vests at their various lifeboat mustering points. Underlying it all, however, was the understanding among most of us that when the real thing happens in the middle of the night; we will be eternally grateful that we had gone through the motions of a drill.

We all ate a late meal in the sumptuous main dining room; and it was after 10:00 p.m. before we retired to our rooms. We all slept well on our first evening at sea.

DAY NUMBER TWO

Since it was Sunday, July 24th, we went to mass. It was celebrated by three priests, no less, from something called the Ministry at Sea, or words to that effect. I had to remind myself that these are priests who manage to make trips like this, free of charge, in exchange for saying mass for Catholic passengers. I remember my uncle Dan, a Dominican priest, used to do this every once in a while on Caribbean Cruises, pretty soft!

After mass we all got together in the Lido Deck dining facility, went through a sumptuous breakfast buffet line, then lingered over coffee with a great deal of "laughing and scratching. " The rest of the afternoon was spent on various activities around the ship including Jim and Peter trying their hand at the gaming tables in the casino. Peter even went to the trouble of taking a quick course on how to play the various gambling games such as blackjack, roulette and craps. Jim entered a contest at one of the gambling venues and found himself entered in the semi-finals of one of the slot machine contests.

One of the downers of the trip was not being able to sit at a ten person table. So, we ended up with a four and a six person table arrangement. Then, as if to rub salt into the wound, the maitre d' failed to locate the two tables in close proximity. But, as it turned out it wasn't a problem, after all. The plan we evolved was to rotate all of us between the two tables over the course of the cruise. Nancy and I shared the four person table with Jim and Kathy for the first evening. One of the benefits of the four seat table was that it was next to a port side window. This was where we were delighted by the sight of a school of half a dozen porpoises cavorting close alongside the ship right outside our window. They kept at it for half an hour. For the second evening we sat at the six person table with Peter and Amie, and Mary and Sarah and so on. Near the end of the meal the maitre d' showed up with a 50th anniversary celebration cake with one candle burning brightly.

Everyone at the surrounding tables and many of the waiters joined in a Happy Anniversary song in our honor. It was a touching moment.

That evening we all went to the theatre to watch a most enjoyable musical production which contained many golden oldies like "Moon River" and "Love Me Tender." Nancy and I retired to our state room, rolling in at midnight; leaving the others to participate in a kareoke contest. The clocks were set back that evening and the additional hour was a godsend for all of us. Sometime during the night ZAANDAM entered the approaches to a scenic fjord called Tracy Arm.

DAY NUMBER THREE

We rolled out of bed in time to have a sit-down breakfast before we moved up to the aft observation deck (6th deck) where we were afforded a spectacular morning of scenic views as the ship maneuvered deep into the Tracy Arm where the ship slowly threaded it's way in between the towering walls of the fjord to the point where the ship had to come to almost a complete halt. Then, with minimum way on, ZAANDAM backed her port screw, went ahead on the starboard screw and swung around amongst floes of blue ice. There were only two sightings of seals on floes and one whale. We made our way back out of Tracy Arm and proceeded to a 2:30 p.m. entrance into the port of Juneau where we were scheduled for an eight hour port visit. Mary, Tom, Terese, Peter, Jim, Kathy and Amie went on a white water adventure. Sarah opted for a hiking trip, Nancy opted for a shopping trip and I remained aboard ship.

As was our intention, everybody was supposed to do what they damned well pleased. Considering that it had begun to drizzle, I believe my choice was not a bad one. We all agreed on one thing; liberty terminated at 10:00 p.m. but most of us decided we wanted to be back for the evening meal at 8:15 p.m. It was another wonderful dinner and we stayed on in the dining room until the help asked us to leave. Our entire group wanted to see the 11:00 p.m. floor show, except for Nancy and me. We opted to go to bed.

DAY NUMBER FOUR

ZAANDAM was tied up in the port of Skagway. This was a "sleep-in" morning, so Nancy and I slept until 7:00 a.m. We enjoyed a leisurely breakfast in the main dining room. Amie and Peter went for a morning run and then we all took off around noon to take a train ride to the top of White Pass. Nancy and I rode our train round trip and we enjoyed a spectacular 3-4 hour ride. The others rode a different train which went up to the summit from whence they bicycled down. It was a pleasant tour for all of us. The *piece de resistance* of the day was a delightful informal dinner in the main dining room. We sat at the six-man table with Peter and Amie; and Tom and Terese. Kathy and Jim; and Mary and Sarah sat at the smaller table. The cuisine was excellent. About half way into the dinner the ship pulled out of Skagway and headed for Glacier Bay. We all went to the evening show which was based on past Broadway Hits, put on by our ship's entertainment ensemble, four men and five women. Nancy and I rolled in at 11:30 p.m. It's hard to understand being tired on a cruise but we were tired.

DAY NUMBER FIVE

We woke at 5:30 a.m., looked out the window at what appeared to be a foggy open ocean and rolled over. We woke a second time at 8:30 a.m. and could see that we were running north at a fairly good speed in Glacier Bay. There are six glaciers all running into Glacier Bay. We reached the northernmost arm of Glacier Bay which marks the entry point of Margerie Glacier. It is less than half a mile from the Canadian Border. This was truly spectacular. The ship came to "all engines stopped" and we drifted along parallel to the face of the glacier. I was startled to note that the ship was no more than about 200 yards from the face of the glacier. It was cold and drizzling light rain, but the railings were lined with people who seemed to be waiting for the glacier to "calve" an iceberg. There were all sorts of cracking sounds, as sharp as rifle shots. A few spots at the very base of the glacier seemed to be gushing melted ice water in small cascades. The sea was filled with small ice floes. Twice I heard a loud report and a few very small chunks of ice broke away from the glacier and crashed into the ocean. Inside some of the larger cracks on the face of the glacier could be seen a beautiful shade of light blue, deepening in tone toward the interior of each crack. We stayed just off Margerie Glacier for the better part of an hour.

We finally steamed south in Glacier Bay to where it empties into Icy Strait; thence southeast to Chatham Strait. Where Chatham Strait intersected Summer Strait we turned east and continued on to Clarence Strait then almost due south to Ketchikan.

We all enjoyed one anothers' company at a delicious dinner that evening as we continued the long trip to Ketchikan. The after-dinner floor show featured an act by two brothers, Brits, who sang a number of the Beatles' hits. They were only "so-so" in the talent category but the tunes, at least the ones I remembered, had a pleasant ring of nostalgia to them. It was 11:30 p.m. when Nancy turned out the bedside lamp.

DAY NUMBER SIX

We had agreed the evening before to meet for breakfast in the main dining room at 8:30 a.m. Mary and Sarah joined Nancy and me. The view out the window showed we were steaming south at, at least 20 knots with land no more than a few miles to the east. We were due to make port in Ketchikan at 2:00 p.m. All of us are becoming more and more aware of the fact that our voyage is coming to an end. The ship remained tied up at the pier in Ketchikan for six hours. Nancy and I went ashore and split up. She went window-shopping; I found a nice viewing spot on the sea wall where I was able to smoke one of the cigars which Amie and Peter had given me a few nights earlier. For an hour or so I watched the take-offs and landings of the many sea planes which came from, and went to, many spots in the hinterlands. For many destinations in this neck of the woods, the sea plane is the ideal (and some times the only) form of transportation. While Nancy and I were so occupied, Sarah went on a snorkeling expedition dressed in a fairly heavy gauge wet suit which kept her remarkably insulated from the cold water. Jim, Kathy, Mary, Tom, Terese, Peter and Amie went on a trip by electric-powered, four-wheeled vehicles exploring a local rain forest which apparently was great fun.

The ship sailed on schedule at 8:00 p.m. headed south for Vancouver. The evening floor show, "H20" featured many oldie but goodie broadway tunes which were cleverly delivered by the ships entertainment ensemble in a series of entertaining skits. It was 11:30 p.m. when the show ended and, as we retired to our staterooms, we were reminded to set our clocks ahead one hour to coincide with the Vancouver time zone. Nancy and I slept well that night.

DAY NUMBER SEVEN

At about 3:30 I woke and noticed that the ship was booming along in what looked like "pea soup" fog. I found myself wondering whatever happened to the time-honored sea-faring tradition of slowing down in foggy weather. I guess, nowadays the combination of surface-search radar and global-positioning systems renders such prudent niceties irrelevant. I felt sorry for the poor seaman whose small wooden vessel offers no radar return. He would be dead meat for the 60,000 ton ZAANDAM, stooging blithely along at 20 knots in zero visibility fog and while we are at it what ever happened to fog horns? We got up at 8:30, had breakfast in the dining room and attended a debarkation lecture. After that the high point of the entire cruise occurred. A group of passengers gave a skit and I found myself in stitches, again and again. Jim and Kathy; Peter and Amie; Tom and Terese; and Nancy and Mary all had parts.

The "Splish, Splash" skit involved Mary, Nancy, Kathy, Terese and Amie, dressed in white terrycloth bathrobes and was hilarious. At one point Nancy flashed the audience and brought the house down. (She wore a bathing suit under the bathrobe.)

Peter and Amie did a "Sonny and Cher" routine that had tears rolling down my face. Then Jim did a solo skit about Elvis Presley. He wore a wig and an Elvis costume and lip-synched one of his songs; gyrating just like Elvis during the music. Tom and Terese participated in a skit about some rock singer. I sat next to Sarah in the audience and she tried valiantly to catch it all on a video camera which someone handed to her at the very last minute with absolutely no instruction. I could have missed every other thing on the cruise.but to have missed this would have been a crime.

As if this weren't enough, we went to the lounge late that evening to watch a karaoke contest complete with judges. Ordinarily I don't bother watching stuff like that but this evening it was different. Tom and Peter were scheduled to do a duet. Their number was, "That's

Amore" and it was truly hilarious. In the middle of their delivery, as if on cue, they put down their microphones and stepped across the small space between the bandstand and the audience; and Peter swept Nancy up into a lively dance routine. Tom did the same to a lady, a total stranger, who was also sitting in the front row and was about Nancy's vintage. After a few turns they deposited their dance partners and returned to the bandstand, picked up their microphones and finished off their number. It brought the house down. They should have won the contest. It was a great way to finish off the last evening at sea.

We are steaming south toward Vancouver at about 20 knots and are scheduled to arrive there tomorrow morning. All in all, it has been a wonderful experience for all of us and a memory which our children and their spouses will carry with them forever.

FINALE

The arrival at Vancouver involved the usual unending sinuous passage through cattle chutes to customs. Amie and Peter; and Sarah split off from the rest of us for their flights to San Jose and San Francisco respectively. The plane trip for the rest of us, to San Diego International airport went without incident. There was one last customs "stork dance" at the airport and before we knew it we were lining up for taxis to our home in La Jolla, where we experienced one finale act. Tom's car wouldn't start. It was reminiscent of the inauspicious beginning of the odyssey. We rallied around Tom's car, hooked up the jumper cables and, 'lo it started on the first attempt. Tom was not amused when I suggested he sell his car. If we were to sum it all up; I'd have to say it was a roaring success; and an experience which all of our children and their spouses will be talking about for the next fifty years! Maybe next year we'll try a cruise to Tahiti!

POSSE COMITATUS, MY ASS

usn

"Remember, gentlemen, an order that can be misunderstood,
will be misunderstood"
- Helmut von Moltke

On the several occasions when called upon to counsel young military officers, I have always issued the following warning:

"There will probably come a time in your career, particularly a 'defining moment,' when you will be asked to make a difficult decision. As luck usually has it, there will not be time for the careful weighing of the pros and cons or consulting with wiser heads. More often than not the decision will have to be made in seconds. Under those circumstances, call it the best way you can and acknowledge your willingness to live with the consequences, good or bad. "

I am sorry to observe that a few of those young officers never had that decision thrust upon them. What a pity! I am also sorry to observe that many of those who were faced with such decisions, pushed them aside and chose to let the moment pass. thereby becoming a tragic footnote in a story that future generations will be embarrassed to read. There are also those who made the wrong decision (for perhaps even the right reasons) and lived to pay the consequences. Finally, there are those precious few who made the right decision and came away in the final analysis, "smelling like a rose." This is about one of those fortunate people.

Lieutenant Colonel Charles H. Pitman, USMC, returned from his third combat tour in Vietnam having been wounded on his last flight. Once out of the hospital, his new orders as Commanding Officer of the Marine Air Reserve Training Detachment (MARTD) at Naval Air Station, New Orleans, Louisiana, should have provided time for recuperation. It was intended to be a low stress assignment that would give the colonel the opportunity to get himself "back in the saddle" regarding helicopter flying while supervising the flight operations of two reserve CH-46 helicopter squadrons. Little did the Marine Corps envision the maelstrom into which Pitman was being sent.

All hell broke loose on the morning of January 7th 1973, when an unknown number of snipers began firing on police, firemen and innocent civilians from the upper floors of the Howard Johnston's Hotel in downtown New Orleans. The weather that morning was below flight minimums so Pitman had gone out to exercise. Upon his return, his staff showed him the television broadcast as the drama was unfolding. Firemen and police had already taken several casualties. The police, armed only with handguns and shotguns, were firing toward the upper floors of the hotel with no effect Meanwhile the sniper or snipers had started a number of fires in various rooms of the hotel. So the first consideration was rescue by helicopter of any guests that might have gone to the roof.

As a result of a high-rise fire a few years earlier, in which a number of lives had been lost, the Coast Guard and MARTD had done some contingency planning to coordinate how they would work together in the event of another high-rise disaster. It was decided that the Coast Guard would be "first responder" since they were fully equipped for rescue. So, at about 12:30 PM, Pitman sent two of his Marine marksmen over to the Coast Guard to provide protection during any rescue attempt. He then continued to follow the action on television. After about two hours, his marksmen returned. The Coast Guard had decided not to launch because the weather was below approach minimums, there were high winds and the freezing level was at 1,000 feet.

Realizing that the police were in serious trouble and out-gunned, Pitman had his staff call the police to see if the Marines could help. The answer was. "Wait, out." About an hour later, now about 4:15 p.m., the police called to say they would like the Marines to come down. The weather was still a major factor with visibility 1/4 mile, ceiling indefinite and icing at 1,000 feet. So, Pitman and his crew launched after dark (about 5:15 p.m.) and air-taxied a mile or two to the Mississippi River.

There, they headed north toward the city hovering below the level of the ships anchored in the stream, under the power lines and toward the famous Mississippi River Bridge.

Seeing the bridge in the fog overhead, Pitman flew his helicopter up alongside and headed north along the freeway taking the second turn-off to the City Hall parking lot. There, he was met by a policeman who told him to report to the Chief in the Command Post, which had been hastily established on the main floor of the besieged hotel. As might be suspected, when the Colonel arrived he found mass confusion. Firemen lying around in the dark, resting and waiting to return to their trucks; guests in the cafeteria in pajamas, being interrogated and policemen in the lobby shooting up the elevator shaft. In the command center itself, there were about 40 armed officers and senior officials from the New Orleans Police Department, several local sheriffs' offices, Louisiana National Guard, State Police, the mayor's office and, of course, the New Orleans Chief of Police. This was the man running the show, for better or worse.

The hotel command center was a scene of chaos. This was in the era before SWAT teams. There was no specially trained or equipped group of police officers to deal with a "terrorist" type threat. The first shooting had begun before 11:00 a.m., but it was almost 7:00 p.m. before Pitman, Major Wimmler (copilot), two crewmen and four New Orleans police, armed with shotguns, AR-15 assault rifles and other assorted firearms, was able to launch. Flying along the streets because the taller buildings were in the clouds, they lined up on the hotel and ascended to a position just above the roof of the 18-story building. Their first mission was to shoot the steel reinforced fire door on the east roof access off its hinges. It was believed that the snipers had sought refuge inside the rooftop door and were hiding in the stairwell between the 18th floor and the roof exit. The last police officer killed was the Vice Chief of Police, who was shot from that doorway several hours before.

Chuck Pitman had communications only with his copilot and two crewmen, who would then relay information to the police sharpshooters who were armed to the teeth in the rear of the helicopter. But, he had no contact with the rest of the police operation or any other agency. This lack of communication presented additional risk, given the various forces involved and live firing in the middle of downtown New Orleans.

Pitman was aware that groups of police were located inside guarding the doors to the stairwells leading to the roof on both ends of the building. The exact location and the number of the snipers were unknown. This, of course, added to the danger of the operation. Pitman and his team landed several times to re-arm and to get the latest intelligence, then flew back up and down the streets to return to the roof.

On the fifth pass and after the fusillade of weaponry at the door had partially dislodged it, a single man ran out of the surrounding cubical and onto the roof in full view of Col. Pitman. As he swung his searchlight around to illuminate the man so that his sharpshooters could see him, the sniper aimed a .44 Magnum rifle at the helicopter and fired. It was extremely close range for such a powerful gun. Pitman could see the jet of fire emanating from the barrel of the gun as he watched the single round come at him, passing a few feet above his head. The round ripped through the forward transmission housing. Fortunately, the rugged helicopter kept on running.

As the searchlight's beam reached him, the sniper ran back into his concrete reinforced hideout. But, before he could reach safety, shrapnel from a shotgun slug hit the wall behind him and ricocheted wounding him. Then, most likely seeing the end, he came out to shoot again. What followed was a fusillade of fire from the helicopter and from police snipers located in and on surrounding buildings. In all, the shooter and his weapon were hit by over two hundred rounds and he fell dead. As far as anybody knew, that left an unknown number of other shooters still at large somewhere in the building and still extremely dangerous.

Pitman pulled away because he was receiving friendly ricochets and had seen no other snipers in the cubical area. He returned to the City Hall parking lot to report to the chief on what had happened. The Chief thanked him for his efforts and said that the colonel's adjutant had called. He called Captain Judy to find that the National Military Command Center (NMCC) had called with an order to, "Return to Base. " Pitman said okay, but he would need fuel to be able to return to the base due to the terrible weather. Judy agreed, alerted the refueler and hung up.

When the refueler arrived, it was escorted by Navy Shore Patrol and the Commanding Officer of the Naval Air Station, one of Pitman's bosses. The Captain suggested that there was still more to be done and that Pitman should call the NMCC in the Pentagon to advise them of the situation. Pitman sprinted, half bent over, through the freezing rain to the telephone booth, which stood within full view of any of the remaining rooftop snipers.

In the relative shelter of the phone booth, Pitman dropped a nickel into the slot, and asked the operator to place a collect call to the National Military Command Center (NMCC) in Washington, D.C. After what seemed like an eternity, Pitman spoke to a colonel who passed him to another colonel who passed him to yet another who finally approved the collect call. He explained the current situation and added that the Lieutenant Governor, Adjutant General of the National Guard, New Orleans Mayor and Chief of Police were all here and had asked him to continue his support. The colonel at NMCC asked for the number of the phone booth and said that he would call back. Pitman waited for what seemed forever and finally the phone rang. The Colonel said that Pitman was cleared to continue to provide support. He explained the principle of "posse comitatus," a post Civil War federal statute, which forbade the military from assisting in civil law enforcement.

Sprinting back through the freezing rain, Pitman scrambled back aboard his helicopter and launched again with his posse. They arrived back at the rooftop site and attempted to put the sniper's rifle out of commission with gunfire. They had also had reports that another sniper had been seen near the roof access cubical at the other end of the building, where the Vice Chief had been killed earlier. As luck would have it, the rifle the Vice Chief carried became wedged in the door opening. They had recovered his body, but the weapon still protruded from the door, which had been secured by rope to the stairwell railing. The police in the stairwell had been waiting for hours to kill whoever opened that door. As the helicopter, with its searchlight, hovered near the door, the rifle stuck in the door jam began to move. Seeing this, one of the police aboard the helicopter, thought it was a sniper and fired through the steel door wounding one of the police waiting in the stairwell.

Then, seeing the door move and having been shot at, the police in the stairwell opened fire through the door. As a result, two of Pitman's aircrew received minor injuries and the aircraft took several hits before Pitman could pull away. All of this occurred early in the morning on the 8th. As daylight arrived, the weather improved and the National Guard and State Police helicopters showed up, but the CH-46 was still the most capable air platform. The entire day (Monday) was spent firing tear gas into various openings in the building and searching the area.

Late the night of the second day, police and federal agents cleared the building and concluded that there had been only one sniper after all, a man named Mark Essex. Essex, armed with a semi-automatic rifle, some firecrackers and about fifty rounds of ammunition had held the city hostage for more than 30 hours.

In the aftermath, somewhere in the chain of command, someone concluded that Pitman had possibly violated federal law ("Posse Comitatus") and recommended that steps be taken for an Article 32 investigation and subsequently, if warranted, a court martial,

The wily Congressman from Louisiana and resident of New Orleans, Eddie Hebert, serving as Chairman of the House Armed Services Committee, got wind of this latest development. He contacted the Secretary of Defense and they were able to put the investigation to rest. Subsequently, the Navy League selected Pitman for the John Paul Jones award for inspirational leadership in 1973. Later, he received a single mission air medal for his actions. Certainly, this beats a court martial. What would you do?

As a footnote, Pitman continued his career and was eventually promoted to Lieutenant General. He retired in August 1990 from his position as Deputy Chief of Staff for Marine Corps Aviation. On January 7th 2003, the City of New Orleans held a thirtieth anniversary ceremony of the historic event dedicating an Eternal Flame Memorial to honor those police and firemen killed in action. During the ceremony, Pitman was designated an Honorary Captain of Police for the City of New Orleans and presented with another plaque to commemorate his participation at the Howard Johnson's. What a fascinating ending to an incident which will forever remain as one of General Pitman's most interesting combat mission!

THE INTRUDER

usn

"He that is too secure is not safe."
Old English proverb

The back yard of our house in Los Angeles was surrounded by a seven foot wall covered with ivy which provided a deceptive sensation of security and privacy. It became a routine for me every night just before bed time to sit in my poolside jacuzzi, smoke a cigar, gaze at the stars and think profound thoughts.

One night my attention skyward was interrupted by a shadow of a person passing the jacuzzi. Since the walkway the person was using passed only ten feet from the jacuzzi, I got a good look at the dim figure of a male adult with shoulder-length hair walking in a leisurely manner toward the French doors which led into my dining room. The bedroom light was on upstairs leading me to conclude that my wife, Nancy, was still in bed reading. Before I could think of what to do the intruder opened the French doors and entered the house. That sent me out of the jacuzzi like a Trident missile. Grabbing one of those four-foot long sprinkler head adjusters I sprinted toward the French doors (a distance of about fifty feet), shouting in a loud voice as I ran, "Hey, you! Get the hell out of my house!"

At that point I saw that the intruder was in the kitchen and when he heard me he turned and ran for the French doors emerging on a dead run as I approached. He saw me perhaps ten feet away, running at full tilt, buck naked and dripping water as I swung the long metal rod over my head. Quick as a flash the intruder spun to his right and ran toward the rear corner of house and toward the gate which led into

245

the front lawn. Aha, I thought, I've got you, since I knew the gate was locked. I raised the metal rod high and swung with all my might at the top of his head. The force of the intended blow was calculated to stove in the skull.

But with all the quickness and grace of a Nadia Comaneci, the intruder vaulted over the gate, my weapon missing him by but a few inches and clanging on the top of the door. The thought of giving chase passed through my mind but was dismissed instantly as I wondered what I would say to the police if they happened upon me sprinting south on Lucerne Blvd. stark naked. Besides, he was younger and faster than I.

THE IRON MAN

usn

"He conquers who endures."
Persius 34 A.D.

The purpose of this essay is to give the man on the street some idea of what exactly is involved in the extreme racing event known as the Ironman.

On August 23rd, 2003 my son, Peter, completed the Vineman Run at Winston, California, having swum 2.4 miles in the Russian River, bicycled 124 miles from the river through two loops to Winston High School and then run 26.2 miles in a double loop from Winston and back all in thirteen hours and forty-two minutes!

When I first learned of Peter's plan to compete I told him he was too old, at age 40, to be doing that kind of crazy stuff. But recently, when he told me of the impending date of the event, I volunteered, albeit with some misgivings, to be his support team of one. This is the story of what will forever remain in my mind as a vivid reminder of the power of the human spirit.

As a prologue, it needs to be said that we made many mistakes before Peter raced into the Russian River and began his journey. But once the journey began Peter performed like a champion. Our first mistake was to get caught up in unanticipated traffic on the narrow road in the pre-dawn darkness that led to the river venue. This led to our having to hike a fair distance in the darkness after having successfully assembled his $2,000 dollar racing bike on the side of the road more or less by feel. Time was running out so Peter dashed off in the darkness with his bike and I limped along behind him, some support team! The urgency was that Peter had to register his bike in the holding area on the banks of the river where the swimmers would run out of the water, change clothes and jump on to their machines. By the time I arrived the four waves of swimmers (numbering maybe 300 men and women), had already assembled at the water's edge. That was when Peter informed me that the computer chip which he was supposed to wear on a wrist band during the race was in the trunk of the car a good country mile away. So much for race validation.

At 7:45 the first wave of swimmers (men under 39 years of age) and wearing green bathing caps, barreled into the water amid much shouting and spirited invective. It was a moment filled with excitement and anticipation. The second wave, Peter's wave, (men over 39), wearing blue caps took off at 7:50 and I found myself yelling at the top of my lungs for my youngest son. I also found myself wondering what I was doing on the banks of the Russian River at such an ungodly hour. Then it dawned on me that this was the Army-Navy game!

But, back to how did I get here? On Thursday, August 21st, I drove from La Jolla to Los Gatos and spent the night in Peter's home. The following morning we drove north, across the Golden Gate Bridge and up into the beautiful wine country of Napa Valley. After "casing" the bicycle and running routes, we checked into a small hotel in Santa Rosa, ate a high carbohydrate dinner at the local Acapulco's and turned in early.

The alarm went off at 0400 and we rolled out like soldiers and headed for the local Denny's for a big breakfast with several cups of coffee, whose purpose, in addition to fuel, was to get Peter's lower digestive system functioning before he entered the Russian River. He was successful in that regard and was now ready for the ultimate assault on his body.

The Russian River venue was a course upstream 0.6 miles to a buoy, then back to the starting buoy then up and back one more time for a total of 2.4 miles. The water temperature was not too cold but the ambient temperature was 53 creating a warm-up difficulty for the bicyclers in the early part of the race. To our surprise, Peter climbed out of the water in one hour and eight minutes; well ahead of his best time ever in practice. As he scrambled into his biking gear I began to realize just how important a part adrenaline plays in this ordeal.

Hiking back to the car with a plastic bag containing Peter's swimming gear I drove carefully along the narrow road. The first part of the bicycle tour shared the narrow, two-lane road with regular traffic! When I got to Winston High School I parked the car and made my way to the road in front of the school where Peter would pass by on the first loop of the bicycle course three hours later. Amie showed up with the children and we settled down on the grass in plastic lawn chairs in the shade of a tree with all the trimmings of a picnic to await Daddy's passage. At this juncture plans seemed to be neatly falling into place. At the estimated hour, based upon Peter's previous times in the event, we started watching for Peter to appear. He didn't! We waited until almost three o'clock with increasing concern felt for Peter. Where was he? Had he had an accident? Without his computer chip there was no way of tracking his whereabouts!

Finally, Amie made a terrific assessment. She assumed Peter had passed without any of us noticing. This meant that he might have completed the second loop of the bicycle race and was already in the marshalling area where bikes were to be guarded during the marathon.

That is exactly where she found him suiting up for the final leg of the triathlon, the 26.2 mile run. That was the good part. The bad part was the terrible way Peter looked as he was making his way out of the starting chute and onto the open road. It only took one glance for me to conclude that Peter would never make it through the next 26 miles in this terrible burning sun, never! But a minor miracle occurred before my eyes!

He was mincing along at a painfully slow trot when he glanced up at Amie and the four children. A huge grin spread across his face and he stopped and gave each one of the children a big hug, then one for Amie. There was a small crowd watching this and Peter got a standing ovation as he headed down the road at a more purposeful, and respectable trot. It was now time for Amie to start the long drive home. I don't believe she realized how much of a boost her appearance with the children gave to her husband. The time was about 3:10 p.m.

The long vigil in the stands at the finish line began as the afternoon wore on and darkness fell. As reassuring as it might be to see the tremendous organization of the event, the way stations, medical facilities, the energy gel packets, water and power bars being dispensed to the racers along the way, I was not at all assured that my son would ever cross the finish line on his own two feet. Our calculations were that Peter could finish the marathon in five and one half or maybe six hours. As the time clock moved past 8:00 pm my worry increased.

There was a huge bank of flood lights at the finish line directed down the dark road. Runners would hove into view about a quarter mile away and be indistinguishable except for gender for the next two minutes. The painful progress of each figure was mute testimony to the ravages inflicted upon the bodies of each contestant by the preceding twelve hours of intense effort.

The small grandstands were full of people who vigorously cheered on each finisher. Many of the contestants responded with a wave of the hand or a wan smile. But there were many racers for whom a simple smile or hand wave was just too much effort. The eyes of each contestant were fixed on the yellow tape where a photographer waited to make the racer's accomplishment "official."

Then the miracle happened! A figure appeared in view of the flood lights that was unmistakably Peter's. He later told me that he started the marathon "well-throttled back" for fear that an attack of leg cramps would make finishing impossible. But when he made it past mile 22 he knew he had it made and opened up the throttle. The figure I was fixated on had all the vigor of a Kipchoge Keno as he whipped across the finish line.

By the time I reached him and gave him a big hug, a race official had already hung a bronze shield on a colored ribbon around his neck. Inscribed on the shield was a single word that said it all, "FINISHER."

Epilogue: The word Ironman is not used anywhere in any of the venues. That is because the term is legally protected against infringement by an organization of that name. So the race was called Vineman for the fact that it occurred in Napa Valley. But, let there be no question about the distances and events and the professionalism surrounding both the conduct of the race and the valor of the racers.

Peter and I retrieved his bike and went directly to the motel where he took a luxurious hot bath while his remaining enchilada from the previous evening dinner was being zapped in the microwave. Then we stretched out on our beds and watched "Dirty Harry" until about

11:00 p.m. Somewhere during the movie's finale Peter slipped off into a well-deserved sleep and didn't move until 7:00 a.m.

Just before dropping off to sleep myself I said a prayer of thanksgiving to the Good Lord for bringing my son safely through this and added a small request that He never allow this to happen again! Life is good!

THE LAST SYNAPSE

usn

"Maintaining situational awareness is the first rule of combat."
Lcol. Dotan, Israeli Air Force

The garage in our home in Los Angeles was my workshop. It was where my son, Peter, and I taught ourselves how to use my Total Shop Woodworking machine and also where we learned how to weld, silver-solder and braze. We also learned a little about electricity, perhaps more than we wanted to know.

The project on this particular day in 1995 was to complete the fabrication of a hotwire. This device is used to cut very accurate curved shapes through blocks of Styrofoam. When the hot wire was plugged in to house electrical power the wire, suspended tautly across two supports, heated up and, when hot enough, could be drawn easily through a block of Styrofoam creating a smooth cut to what ever shape your steady hand could describe.

Peter had entered a competition under his boss' auspices to design a radio-controlled glider and compete in an acrobatics contest. His competition was other young Lockheed design engineer colleagues. The hot wire would enable Peter to design his own airfoil for the competition. Peter had just finished building the hot wire and was in the process of attaching the electrical cord and cutting it to the desired length. For measurement purposes, Peter plugged the cord into the power source at the workbench then walked it across the garage to the place where he would be doing the cutting; a distance of maybe twenty feet. Holding the coil of electrical power cord in one hand he announced that, this should be about the right length whereupon he reached down with a pair of wire cutters and snipped the wire. Having no idea that he planned to cut the wire while it was still plugged in to house current, I didn't say anything until it was too late.

What followed was a huge white flash and Peter's body convulsed while he seemed to lift an inch or two off the garage floor as he dropped both wire and wire cutter to the ground. His back was toward me but I could tell he knew I was already in tears of laughter. Slowly he turned around with a look on his face that said quite eloquently, I can't believe what I just did! I remind you that Peter holds an engineering degree in mechanical engineering from the University of Virginia and my Annapolis diploma announces that I am an electrical engineer.

"I was instantly transported back to the Christmas of 1967 in our home in La Jolla when Peter, then age four, went behind the Christmas tree in our living room while we were decorating it on Christmas eve. I heard a clunk and saw that he was stretched out on his back and his body was convulsing. I reached over, touched his ankle and received an enormous jolt of electricity. Then, I noticed that the end of the electrical power cord was in his mouth. In an instant I made a decision that there wasn't time to crawl over to the wall socket to unplug the cord. In the few seconds that would take Peter would probably be dead. So, I snatched at the cord and yanked it out of his mouth. There was a small flash as it came out of his mouth then he began crying. The electrical arc burned a deep scar in his lower lip. But other than that he seemed to be alright. The doctor suggested that we give him a popsicle to suck on to relieve the swelling and pain in his mouth. When Peter and I discussed all of this in my garage in Los Angeles we examined the huge notch burned into the blade of the wire cutter and concluded that, between the two near-electrocutions, he had probably fried most of the synapses in his brain and that he might well be down to his "last synapse. "

THE OWENS VALLEY TRAIL

usn

Each of us, I'm sure, holds a special time and place, or perhaps a special event that is so poignant, so unforgettable, so moving an experience that it occupies a unique place in one's scrapbook of memories. One of mine is what I choose to call the Owens Valley Trail.

The experience occurred on September 7th,1995, the day I drove alone, to Reno, Nevada to take part in the 1995 Tailhook Reunion. The president of the Tailhook Association, an old friend, Lonnie McClung, had called me a month or so earlier to ask me to be the banquet speaker at the annual event being held, for the first time, in Reno. I accepted, and recall being worried afterward about messing the speech up.

As vintners are wont to say, '95 had not been a good year for me. The reasons had to do with health. In February, while cleaning out the rain gutters on my home in Los Angeles, I had an accident. It was like a bad Laurel and Hardy movie. The 26 foot extension ladder collapsed while I was at its very top and I fell to the sidewalk below, breaking my left arm and several ribs, dislocating both knees, ripping a large zigzag scar in my right temple and savaging my right shin so badly that it became infected (cellulitis) and put me in the hospital on IV for a week. The broken arm failed to heal properly and, after two frustrating months in a cast, the doctors came close to a decision to put in a metal plate. Luckily, at the last moment sufficient healing began, to convince us to let nature take its course after all.

But, that was not the whole story. During the bone-healing process, I began to experience increasingly severe sciatic pains coursing down both legs. The problem worsened and paralysis began to set in,

255

in the right leg. Finally, it got so bad that I went into the hospital to have portions of a lumbar disc removed from pressing on my spinal column. (The MRI showed that it had been squinched down to 20% of its normal diameter). Since then, relief has been almost immediate and spectacular. Life is truly good! '95 was also a bad year because my car was stolen. It was a relatively low-mileage Oldsmobile Cutlass. We turned that into a less unpleasant experience by indulging in my first convertible (at age 67). It is a slick looking black machine that I am enjoying immensely. Talk about a second childhood! Having indulged myself so thoroughly, I decided to go whole hog and get a set of personalized license plates. Now, that is something I never thought I would ever do. Dad would turn over in his grave!

My Navy call sign was GATOR, so nothing would do but GATOR license plates. Unfortunately, there were thirteen other GATORs in the state of California, numbered GATOR and GATOR1 through GATOR12. So, I had the lady at the DMV computer substitute the "A" in GATOR for a star and I came out a winner. It was unique and I received my new plates almost immediately. The car dealer explained that he could not easily swap the $1,000.00 compact disc stereo system in the car for a simple cassette player type and asked if I would accept the fancy sound system if he threw it in at no extra cost. I accepted and was now the proud owner of a really hot machine!

The day came for the trip to Reno and I had already decided to make it in my new car, despite the admonitions of my back surgeon against extended automobile trips, and of my wife to fly up there. She was away in Atlanta at the time, so it was easy.

Packing out early on one of those spectacular sunny southern California days at 7:00, I jumped on the freeway and got clear of the LA traffic before it got tight. The Antelope Valley Freeway (Highway 14) took me almost directly north across Antelope Valley past Palmdale, Lancaster, Edwards and Mojave to where it intersected Interstate 395 north of Ridgecrest and China Lake. The first surprise, (and it is always a surprise) were the windmills. Huge sixty foot steel towers sticking out of the desert floor with enormous two or three-bladed steel propellers mounted on them. When the wind blows in the San Bernardino Pass, which it usually does, the propeller blades turn and convert wind power into electric power. By California state law, the local electrical power companies are required to buy the kilowatts which they generate from the owners of the windmills, at the going rate. The first impression, when the first windmills appear on the horizon, is mild curiosity. Who, in his right mind, one is compelled to ask, would buy a windmill in this day and age? The answer is a whole lot of people. The second impression, as one heads north by northeast along Highway 14 is one of absolute astonishment as the immensity of the windmill farms begins to unfold. There are not just hundreds or even thousands. There are virtually hundreds of thousands! Windmills as far as the eye can see to the north from the highway. In my view they ought to be listed in the Seven Wonders of the World.

They turn lazily, but inexorably, around and around, row after row, field after fields as far as one can see. These things turn in the wind are a tribute to man's altruistic attempt to garner power from one of the last of God's free energy sources.

But, it isn't free. Nothing is free. If there are ever enough of them, they will extract so much kinetic energy from the wind that the weather patterns of southern California would change. No longer would the air masses move the wet polar air across southern California as easily, creating clouds and then rain, always cooling the surface of the terrain, making it suitable for the growing of grapes, carrots, lettuce, cotton and citrus groves. The resultant climatic warming will probably turn lush, productive Southern California eventually into a desert. Nevertheless, the sight of all those whirling blades simply boggles the mind!

Interstate 395 runs north-by-northwest straight up the Owens valley all 400 miles to Reno. It is a relatively quiet, almost lonely stretch of two-lane, blacktop highway flanked on either side by the raw, jagged mountains of the Sierra Nevada. The highway stair-steps up gradually, but in three general tiers. The climb is steady but still distinctive. The drab desert surrounding China Lake gradually turns to high desert, then to lush green prairies, then pine forests and finally the rugged beauty of the high mountain lakes country where the mountain tops are mostly bare and rocky and still covered with patches of pure white snow near their summits.

Antelope Valley at Mojave is only about 2,500 to 3,000 feet above sea level. Proceeding northeast past China Lake one becomes aware of a cooling sensation as the altitude passes 4,000 feet. There are strange and quaint names like Inyokern, Olancha, Cartago and Lone Pine with small clusters of houses, farms and ranches. Horses and cattle graze on the plentiful grass. Cartago is unusual because it takes its Spanish name from ancient Carthage. The roadside sign says "Pop. 75, Elev. 3,678 feet."

The highway passes the Owens Dry Lake to the west and one sees the unusual lava rock formations cut by the Owens River along the right side of the highway but there doesn't seem to be a western bank of the prehistoric river formation. The road climbs steeply for a few miles and, passing the small town of Independence, comes to the first tier of the mountains at Sherwin Summit. The roadside sign says "Elev. 7,000 feet." The roadside sign also points to Mt. Whitney to the west. With an elevation of 14,494 feet it is the highest point in California and a magnificent sight. It is a bold thrusting of sheer rock topped by some of last summer's vestiges of snow fields near its peak on the eastern slope. It is in Inyo National Forest, a major element of the Sierra Nevada mountain range.

The 24 valve motor of my new, black convertible was purring. The top, of course, was down and my stereo system was blasting away with CD albums called, "Hammered Dulcimer" and Aaron Copland's "Themes of the Common Man." My Snowy River hat was fluttering in the wind, and my heart was somehow startlingly full. The thought came to me that it just doesn't get any better than this!

A few miles past Mt. Whitney the road goes through Big Pine and another small cluster of sun-bleached, lonely buildings. The road passes through the small town of Bishop and Owens Valley widens out into the most beautiful landscape of green pastureland with small, scattered swatches of goldenrod flickering richly in the distance as the wind ruffles the surface of the tall grass. I imagine how content the cattle must be to call this their grazing land. Life is good, I think!

The road passes a cobalt blue Lake Crowley on the east side while stately Red State Mountain rises above the valley on its west wall over 11,000 feet. Farther away to the north "Devil's Postpile" National Monument is a ragged upthrusting of serrated rock peaks in a cluster. Just past a small group of buildings called Tom's Place, we come to the next gradation in the incline. It is called Deadman's Summit and the roadside sign reads "Elev. 8,036 feet." The air is so crystal clear now, that one feels as though he can recognize individual trees on mountain slopes over forty miles away. I also felt the temptation to breathe deeply of the clear air. It made my lungs feel good and purged them of smog and other man-made crap!

On the right, a few miles farther we come past Mono Lake, that briny ecological curiosity with monstrous stalagmites growing out of its bottom. Its shoreline shows that over the last few years the level of the lake has been gradually dropping. But, Mono Lake is just as clear and blue and as beautiful as its sister lakes along the way.

Just past Mono Lake the road comes to the third and final tier of the step ladder of the Sierras. It is called Conway Summit and the roadside sign says, simply, "Elev. 8,138 feet." We are now just at the rear side of Yosemite National Park and the small blue Bridgeport Reservoir is marked by a small town of the same name to the east while the "Devil's Gate" looms close aboard the highway on the west. The road now crosses Walker River (really a small creek at this point) and turns to the right to follow its course for several miles. My instincts tell me there are trout in it. How I wish I had a fishing rod! The road begins its gradual drop toward the Reno plateau and passes an exquisite Topaz Lake, as gemlike and beautifully blue as its name implies. The lake sits astride the California-Nevada border. I'm feeling a tremendous high. The hammered dulcimer is now playing "Oh, Dem Golden Slippers" and then the Irish Hornpipe dance and I feel like getting out of the car and giving it my best on the shoulder of the road. Surely, the highway patrol would haul me in!

I feel also as though all of my planets are in congruence, all of my bio-rhythms are peaking, all of my cylinders are firing and all of my worries about making a good speech in Reno have vaporized. The only thing that could make it any better would be if Nancy were sitting by my side!

Three days later I made the trip in reverse. I felt even better, (if that were possible) because the speech in Reno was a roaring success. The scenery was even better. The mood was even greater. The CDs were even prettier, the day was sunnier and the mountains more spectacular. I counted my blessings and made a vow that next year Nancy and I will make this same trip together!

ZONING OUT

usn

"After battle sleep is best."
Roden Noel

The 7th and 8th grade students in my creative writing class at All Hallows Academy often use the expression "zoning out" to describe a particular kind of mental activity in which they become transported to another planet; and I thought I understood what it meant until recently. But a little background is needed.

Several years ago, after I had begun a daily swimming exercise program, my son, Peter, sent me a swimming radio. It was about half the size of a pack of cigarettes and half as thick and contained a set of ear pieces, a trailing wire antenna and was powered by a small battery. The idea was to attach it to my head by slipping it underneath the goggles strap. It had a button which permitted the user to switch to several pre-set radio channels with the touch of a fingertip. The trailing wire antenna picked up the radio signals and the radio played the broadcast into my ears. Pretty slick!

I found that it permitted me to slip into a different mental level from the standardboredom of watching the slow passage of the bottom of the pool; replete with the standard parade of band-aids, bobby pins, dead worms and other detritus which one finds at the bottom of most swimming pools. The fact that I am not a good swimmer causes the passage of this assembly of such trash to be even slower and more boring than for those in adjacent lanes who pass me with frustrating frequency. The mental state that the music put me into depended, of course, upon the music being played. Furthermore, I found it virtually impossible to avoid adjusting the rate of my swimming to match that of the tempo of the music. It was unavoidable. I suspect this same phenomenon occurs to walkers who wear headsets.

Somehow, the music helped to pass the thirty-five minutes or so which it takes me to swim the requisite 36 lengths. Finally, the battery wore out and at least a month transpired before I could make it to the Speedo shop where replacement batteries could be purchased. With the new batteries installed I again reverted back to swimming in step to the music.

As I got more proficient at swimming over the ensuing years, I fell into an easier and less exhausting routine. As a consequence, I found myself adding a few laps to my regular routine, especially since the music would cause me to miss-count the laps-to-go to the end of my half-mile.

There was also the need to discipline myself so I didn't lose count. My solution to this problem was to associate a meaning to each successive number as I counted down from 36 to zero. For example, when I got to lap number 34-to-go, I would recall the hull number of the first carrier on which I deployed as a young lieutenant; U.S.S. *Oriskany* (CVA-34). There were other carriers in my career; *Bonhomme Richard* CVA-31, or *Monterey* CVS-26, *Hancock* (CVA-19), *Lexington* (CVS-16), *Ticonderoga* –14, *Essex* – 9 and so forth. Then, there were other numbers which I was able to conjure up for a change in pace like my age when I got married, the number of years I served in the Navy, etc. etc. and the list could go on forever. So, each successive lap brought up a recollection and my swimming regimen turned into a trip down memory lane.

The life guards in the pool became more accommodating in setting up my own swimming lane over the years and were particularly interested in why my swimming tempo would sometimes change dramatically from lap to lap. I never told them the reason; but the change from Willie Nelson's, "It Always Will Be, " to ABBA's "Take a Chance on Me" constituted a dramatic change of tempo.

Recently, my swimming had become so much more fluid and relaxed that when I got to lap number zero, I decided one day, purely on a whim, to double the distance and swim 72 laps rather than 36. This was when I inadvertently zoned out and slipped into something like what deep sea divers call rapture of the depths. *I was truly zoned out!* A series of Willie Nelson tunes was playing and I lost it completely.

When I got to lap zero the second time, I decided, what the hell, why not go for two miles? The pool wasn't busy and the life guards seemed to be so accommodating, so I pressed on feeling good about myself. I finally finished up the 144 lengths of the pool feeling like Johnny Weismuller.

That evening at the supper table, I sat across from Nancy thinking I was pretty hot stuff and enjoying the meal when, all of a sudden the sound of my fork falling on the table woke me. Startled, I came to the realization that I had fallen asleep sitting straight up in my chair. I looked up quickly across at Nancy to see if she had noticed. A look of incredulity was on her face as she looked at me. Yes, she had noticed my head drop down on my chest and my eyes close. This, I decided was carrying "zoning out" to a whole new level. My conclusion from this bizarre episode was that 7th and 8th graders may zone out, but 76 year-olds just fall asleep at the dinner table!

TWENTY-FOUR NOTES

usn

"Now here is peace for one who knew,
The secret heart of sound,
The ear so derlocate and true,
Is pressed to noiseless ground."
- Roethke

I couldn't begin to count how many times I have stood rigidly at attention; right hand over my heart, or fingertips touching the visor of my uniform cap, as a bugler played the haunting music of "Taps." Only twenty-four simple notes but it evokes more emotion than any other musical composition I have ever heard.

Most people don't even realize that "Taps" used to be played at U.S. military installations all over the world to signal the ending of the day. That was its original meaning, the end of the day. But, "Taps" was also mandated for use at military funerals by the U.S. Army Infantry Drill Regulations for 1891.

More and more these days, days of a brutal war on terrorism, Americans living rooms grow silent when the large screen television shows the military burial ceremonies of our finest young men killed in godforsaken places where madmen blow themselves to oblivion in grotesque attempts to show their hatred for us. In those living rooms millions of Americans watch in hushed silence as an honor guard fires three rifle volleys, twenty-one shots, followed by a single bugler playing "Taps." Two of the honor guard fold the American flag which covered the coffin. The final act of the drama is the flag's delivery, by the military escort, to the widow or mother of the fallen soldier. *This is heavy stuff for modern America.*

So, when I hear those twenty-four plaintive notes, a kaleidoscope of vivid images parades across my memory; each of them as fresh and crisp as though they had only happened yesterday.

There was the scene 36 years ago on a snow-covered hilltop cemetery in Cottonwood, Idaho when my best friend and Naval Academy classmate was buried. He was the first of the little town's losses in Vietnam. As my friend's escort, I presented the freshly-folded American flag to his young widow. Her tear-stained eyes were riveted on mine as I intoned the traditional, "*...on behalf of a grateful nation...*" speech.

In about 1985 a good friend and Pentagon co-worker, Rear Admiral Charlie Prindle passed away rather suddenly from cancer. An old friend of his and I, dressed in our blue service uniforms, marched behind the horse-drawn *caisson* carrying his coffin. It was an impromptu decision made by each of us separately. We were a sight to behold, the two of us limping along from leg injuries. The crowd of mourners following the procession opted, by tacit consent, to drop behind us. We ended up being a second honor guard determined to see this event through to the bitter end of the long procession from the Fort Myers chapel to the gravesite.

Then, most memorable of all the Arlington National Cemetery burials I have attended, there was the one when my older brother, John, a Navy Captain, was laid to rest. His eight siblings and their spouses marched along behind the *caisson* followed by a large number of nieces and nephews. Behind the immediate family members was an enormous number of friends, all of us marching to the beat of the drums of the military escort, each of us absorbed in our own private remembrances of "big John."

Today, Arlington National Cemetery averages 25 memorial interments each weekday. Arlington's west coast counterpart, Fort Rosecrans, was the scene of at least a dozen similar ceremonies with the additional ritual of the "fly-over" for a fallen aviator comrade. The formation of as many as eight *Crusaders* would circle at low altitude a few miles off the coast waiting for the signal over the radio that "Taps" was about to begin. It took exquisite timing on the part of the flight leader, under FAA control, to turn his flight inbound and roar directly over the gravesite while the last notes of "Taps" were still hanging in the air.

In those days, the missing man theme was still an Air Force twist. Our *Crusaders* maintained their tight formation as they passed overhead and then returned to Miramar.

Then there was the incredibly poignant burial at sea from the flight deck of U.S.S. *Shangri La* as she steamed slowly downwind on a gentle swell in the cobalt waters of the Aegean Sea. I cannot remember the details of how and why the burial at sea was approved; but it was. The squadron was formed up in their dress blues, the Marine detachment rendered the honors and four squadron officers lifted the inboard edge of the *catafalque* allowing the coffin to slide slowly out from under the draped American flag and fall into the ocean. Of course, flooding holes had been cut into the bottom of the casket and weights added so that it quickly disappeared from sight.

And, how could I forget the burial at sea where the casket refused to sink. After watching for 15 minutes, the frustrated ship's Commanding Officer, anxious to get on his way to an important operational commitment, ordered the honor guard to sink it by shooting holes in the casket with their M1 rifles. To his surprise, this extraordinary expedient didn't work. Finally, in total desperation, he ordered a ship's gunner to sink it with fire from a 20 millimeter machine gun. Unfortunately for the C.O., a crew member took still pictures of this *macabre* event which eventually ended up in the decedent's hometown newspaper. The furor raised by those images was unbelievable. The thoughtless and irresponsible Commanding Officer was summarily relieved of his command. It was shortly afterward that designated burials at sea were restricted to urns of ashes only.

Perhaps the most memorable burial at sea was the one for Lieutenant James Hise, U.S. Navy, in the turgid waters of the Tonkin Gulf on March 26th, 1967. He and his brother, George, also a lieutenant were both pilots in the same squadron, VF-53. Jim Hise was lost in a carrier landing mishap following a combat mission and his body was never recovered. His brother, launched on a combat mission just minutes before Jim's death, was unaware of what had happened until I informed him two hours later as he climbed down from the cockpit of his airplane. The ship conducted a memorial service at sea with the entire air wing and ship's company formed up on the flight deck. An empty flag-draped coffin, suitably weighted down, was symbolically dropped into the ocean in that desolate place.

On an average of three times a week, during the late 1970s, designated Atlantic Fleet ships were assigned the additional mission of burials at sea for qualified veterans who had requested this honor in their wills or by next of kin. I suspect similar burials were conducted in the Pacific Fleet as well. The implementing message order referred to the urn of ashes as "cremains." They were delivered to ships before they left port. Then, far out in the Atlantic operating areas, the combatant vessels would come to "all engines stopped" at the appointed hour, drift for long enough to conduct the ritual with great dignity and solemnity; then resume their assigned duties.

I have never understood what the attraction is for veterans to want their remains to be disposed of in this fashion. There is no gravesite which descendants can honor on Veteran's Day. There is no connection to a particular plot of ground, no matter how humble, to which loved ones can attach memorial significance. There is no gravesite, which loved ones can decorate with flowers, and trim the grass alongside the marker. There is no name, date and perhaps a verse engraved in stone for the ages. There is only the intense finality, the sense of total closure. In a way, cremation and burial at sea is a means of erasing ones name from the book of life. Nevertheless, it remains a popular choice for many veterans today.

The music of those twenty-four notes dates back to the Civil War when Union Army Captain Robert Ellicombe was with his men near Harrison's Landing in Virginia. He heard the moans of a wounded soldier in no-man's land between the opposing forces and crawled out to him during the night to bring him back for medical attention. When he got him to a medical facility he saw, to his horror that it was his own son. In his son's pocket were the musical notes of a piece he had composed. The grief-stricken Captain got permission to give the Confederate soldier a military burial. His commanding officer, General Daniel Butterfield, Third Brigade, First Division, Fifth Army Corps, Army of the Potomac, directed that it be written as a modification to an existing regulation U.S. Army bugle call.

There are even simple lyrics that go with the music. The first three stanzas of one version are as follows:

"Day is done, gone the sun,
From the hills, from the lake,
From the sky,
All is well, safely rest,
God is nigh.

Fading light, dims the sight,
And a star, gems the sky,
Gleaming bright,
From afar, drawing nigh,
Alls the night,

Thanks and praise, for our days,
Neath the sun, neath the stars
Neath the sky."
As we go, this we know,
God is nigh.

Unfortunately we don't hear the lyrics sung much anymore because they were written to symbolize the end of a day not of a life.

SEA LAWYERS

*"I know that you believe that you understand what
you think I said. But I am not sure you realize that
what you heard is not what I meant."*
Sign on a Pentagon office wall

It all began on a warm summer morning at my home in Los Angeles
in 1996, when the phone rang and a most interesting new chapter of
my life began. The caller identified himself as the location manager of
a television show called "JAG." Had I watched the show, was his first
question? Unperturbed by my denial, he pressed on, informing me that
he had gotten my name from the information operator after reading
a book I had written, in which the fly leaf mentioned that the author
resided in Los Angeles.

My caller went on to explain that after getting my number and
address, he realized that I lived only a few blocks from the set where
they were shooting a scene for an upcoming JAG episode. Would I be
interested, he asked, in coming on over to the set as his guest to watch
them shoot the scene? Not being involved in any pressing projects at
the moment, I accepted, told my wife where I was going and drove to
the address he had given me. He never told me it was a gay bar in West
Hollywood!

The establishment had a temporary chain link fence around it, and
the set people had removed all of the gay decorations from the walls
replacing them with the kind of stuff which one would find in a biker
bar like neon Budweiser signs and Harley-Davidson pictures. For the
moment the place had been transformed into a rough, tough, knock-

down-drag-out, kick-ass beer establishment in a rough, tough part of town.

The location manager, Tony, was a wealth of anecdotal information about the entertainment industry in which he had been working his whole life. A catering service arrived and set up harvest tables covered with a sumptuous buffet fit for a king. Time flew by and I finally made my good byes and returned home. My wife wanted to know where I had been for the last three hours and did a double take when I told her, matter-of-factly, that I had been in a gay bar in East Hollywood!

I had written the whole incident off as one of those odd experiences one often has in southern California when, a few days later, Tony called me again and asked if I would like to come to the Paramount lot to meet the show's creator, Don Bellisario. Again, I had some free time and again I drove off to Tinseltown. This time, I noticed in the rearview mirror, my wife watching curiously from the front doorway.

The meeting with Don Bellisario was pleasant and he seemed unperturbed when he inquired if I had seen the show and got a no, for my answer. He politely asked me why not and I told him that I had seen a "trailer" on the TV and thought the whole thing was "hokey"! There was a short moment of awkward silence as several of his staff shifted uncomfortably in their seats. From this I judged that Mr. Bellisario ran his organization with a firm hand.

Then Don asked me if I would like to help him make it less hokey, I told him I would be delighted to do so. There followed a series of visits to sets in the greater Los Angeles area; one where a Marine Corps rifle range was simulated, another where a grave side burial ceremony was re-created at the Los Angeles National Cemetery. I was invited to sit in the Director's folding chair and watch them shoot the scenes. A former Marine drill sergeant named Matt Sigloch was introduced to me as technical advisor. I also met "gaffers" and "grips" and "ADs" (assistant directors), make-up people, cinematographers and the myriad of technicians which it takes to produce a quality film. They were all extremely pleasant and helpful in explaining the intricacies of the business to this neophyte.

Shortly afterward I received a call inviting me to come over to the studio and meet the small staff of teleplay writers. I hit it off well with the writers and found myself reviewing proposed episodes and making technical comments in red ink. One episode, in particular received an inordinate amount of red ink and some of my marginal comments may have been a little caustic. I was asked to drop into Don's office to discuss my comments. When I told him how I felt about that particular teleplay he asked me if I thought I could do better myself. I imprudently said, yes; and he invited me to try writing my own episode.

Obtaining a copy of Syd Fields seminal book on how to write screenplays, I dove in. The staff of writers also jumped in and gave me an enormous amount of help. In the process of writing this teleplay, the writers demonstrated the patience of Job in helping this neophyte get his feet wet. I had selected, as a backdrop for the episode, the Ex-USS Oriskany, a rusting aircraft carrier hulk tied up at a pier in Vallejo awaiting the cutting torches of the demolition men. Oriskany had been the carrier on which I had made my first carrier deployment.

It was decided that several of us, a staff writer named, Steven Zito, the production manager, Jim Weatherill and the location manager, Paul Brinkman would travel to Vallejo to visit Oriskany and meet members of the Pegasus Corporation, the firm that had contracted to turn that wonderful ship into razor blades. Our rental car was turned away at the main gate when we mentioned the name Pegasus, by a visibly disturbed rent-a-cop. It seems that there had been a riot on the pier just the day before by the cutting torch men because the Pegasus Corporation had issued them bogus paychecks. It took a few minutes and a close scrutiny of my military identification card to get us on to the base. When we arrived pier side, we found the access gate to the pier swinging wide open, the padlock broken to the gate on the brow and the forlorn hulk of my old ship loosely tied to a single bollard. There was not a soul around. My three companions were reluctant to go aboard under those circumstances. After I made a quick scout of the hangar deck and flight deck I hailed them aboard from the flight deck pointing out the only route I had been able to find since the 0-1 level hatches had all been welded shut. We were able to get a good scout of the stateroom area on the main deck as well a tour of the flight deck and the superstructure locations where several sets were envisioned. In all, it was a very productive scout.

The group was enthusiastic as we headed for the airport and our return flight to Los Angeles. The show, "Ghost Ship" premiered the third season of JAG and received the highest Nielsen ratings the show had ever gotten up to that point. I need to point out that Don Bellisario, when he reviewed my first effort, found it necessary to re-write it and give it his unerring touch. As is done in such cases (I think) the two scripts, (his and mine) were submitted to the Writer's Guild of America (WGA) for arbitration to determine credits. I was given credit for the story line but was remunerated, as stipulated in the contract, for the writing of the script. This got me into the early stages of membership in the WGA.

Sometime during the fourth season, I received a call from casting asking me if I could appear at Whiteman Airport east of Los Angeles to play a small part in scenes for two episodes which were being shot there. There were only three simple lines for me to read, but I was accorded all of the trappings of stardom including a dressing trailer, a trip to the make-up man, a visit from the wardrobe department and another contract which put me into the early stages of membership in the Screen Actor's Guild. The contract lady knocked on the door of my trailer and asked me to sign the contract. Just below the signature line was a line marked, "Stage Name." I couldn't resist the temptation and, after thinking for a moment, wrote down, "Slade Klondike"!

I think I can say, with all candor, that I bombed! Despite the Herculean efforts of the Director, Terrence O'Hara, to get me to do my lines with feeling it just didn't go well. The kindest adjective my children could find to describe my performance was "wooden." Was it Andy Warhol who wrote about everybody's fifteen minutes of fame? Mine was more like fifteen seconds!

By the fifth season most of the work I did was either by telephone or over the internet. The studio had installed a software package on my laptop computer that allowed me to edit a script over the internet and return it electronically directly to the writers.

Working in Tinseltown can be occupationally hazardous. During my fourth season I parked my car on the lot and was walking to the Clara Bow building, a distance of maybe two hundred yards when I spied a starlet walking across the parking lot on a course that would cause her to pass close abeam. As the distance between us closed I could see that she was "drop dead" gorgeous. She was tall, blonde and willowy and walking with a seductive, slack-hipped movement which was going to be difficult to ignore.

I reminded myself that I was 71 years old, happily married and the grandfather of fifteen grandchildren and had no business staring at her when she passed. So, I stoically fixed my gaze on the Clara Bow building and continued on my present course. Unfortunately, I have extremely good peripheral vision and found myself anticipating the close encounter. I even picked up the scent of a seductive perfume. But, it turned out that my peripheral vision was not good enough. Just as she passed by me and out of my field of view I walked into a parking meter!

The very best and fondest memories I have of my connection to the show relate to our three day visit at sea aboard U.S.S. Stennis where we shot a great deal of shipboard footage and a number of scenes for two episodes. The reception by the Navy, from Rear Admiral "Rabbit" Campbell down to the seamen who stood in as extras for the flight deck scenes was heart-warming.

My connection with the cast has been minimal. Nonetheless, I found all of them, to be decent and considerate professionals who work very hard at their trade. My wife, Nancy, and I attended a "wrap" party at the end of the second season which was held at a Los Angeles restaurant. It was a pleasure to introduce her to all of these fascinating people; the technicians, cast, directors and producers. Nancy seemed particularly taken with what a genuinely classy lady the female lead, Catherine Bell, is.

In the eleven seasons that I have been involved with JAG, I have caught a great deal of "heat" from former shipmates who chide me about the central theme of the show. After all, they tell me, JAG lawyers don't run around West Hollywood kicking down doors of bars with guns drawn. Nor do they fly F-14s. We all know that. I keep reminding them that some of JAG's greatest enthusiasts are real JAG lawyers. I think they watch the episodes vicariously, wishing their lackluster daily duties could be anywhere near as exciting as they are portrayed on television.

One other point needs to be made. The Defense Department and the Department of the Navy were reluctant, at first, to cooperate with the show. I suppose that could have been understandable the first season or two. Certainly, the "hot button" issues of our society are also those which attract the interest of the JAG producers as well as the audience. Some of them make the military uncomfortable. That is also understandable. But, after watching eight seasons of JAG I should think that the powers that be in the Navy and Marine Corps would realize that in JAG episodes the good guys eventually win and the bad guys eventually are caught and punished. There are no hidden agendas, no sinister conspiracy to undermine the military, no effort to denigrate the servicemen and women of our military, no subliminal cynicism which so often emerges in the industry's pursuit of the all-important "ratings." It is fairly straightforward, honest entertainment.

I guess, in summary, I can say that the entertainment industry is an enormously complex business. The logistical effort involved in producing what is essentially a forty-four minute feature film every seven days for twenty-six weeks is incredibly demanding. I have met no "weirdos." Yes, there are colorful characters. Yes, there are a few large egos. Yes, the costs of carrying out the day-to-day business of film-making are mind-boggling. However, from my perspective all the stereotypes I have read and heard about Tinseltown and its denizens are grossly exaggerated. The only thing I found that is truly hard to fully comprehend is the simple fact that it is all make-believe! But, what the heck, that's show business!

"TINSELTOWN"

usn

"There are three kinds of men: the ones who learn by reading; the few who learn by observation; the rest of them have to pee on the electric fence for themselves."
- Will Rogers

Almost once a week, for the past eight seasons I have been making the long journey from my home in La Jolla to Hollywood and back...all in one day, to work on the television series, "JAG", as a technical advisor. It makes for a long day, but a fascinating one, nonetheless!

The network, ABC, decided not to renew the JAG contract after the first year but CBS picked it up and the trajectory of the show's Nielsen ratings has shown a steady upward march ever since. Somewhere about the fifth season the show's production department moved from the Paramount lot to Valencia and next season the headquarters of Belisarius Production moved from the Clara Bow building at the Paramount lot to Sunset-Gower Studios a mile north. In 2003, the network approved a JAG spin-off show called, "NCIS" which kicks-off in September. I am also a technical advisor for that show which is essentially a forensic spin-off from JAG.

The experience I have gathered over the past eight years in Tinseltown has been enormously instructive and most enjoyable!

A typical day begins with an early start at 0745 to get ahead of the morning traffic heading north on Interstate 5. Of course, the convertible top on the Oldsmobile comes down, the JAG ballcap is donned, a Willie Nelson CD is selected with the volume on high and I zone out for the next two hours. The histrionics are all set for the weekly Tinseltown experience.

The first of a day-long series of meetings with the staff writer's is scheduled for 1100 am. If the traffic is normal I usually get to the Larchmont area about 1030 and there is time for a quick cup of expresso at the *Coffee Bean & Tea Leaf* in the shopping center where I sit at a sidewalk table and watch the passing parade of filmdom's *wannabes* gearing up for another star-crossed day. The high-octane jolt is a good start to what is usually a frenetic day. At 1050 I head north for the short drive to the studio.

The rent-a-cops at the studio gate always provide a comic beginning to my Tinseltown experience and serve to set me in the proper mood for the rest of the day.

Most of them are former military policemen and they have grown to recognize the black convertible with the two-star decal on the windshield. When I pull to a stop at the gatehouse, one of them will call out in a loud voice, "Attention on deck!" Then the two stiffen to attention and salute; at which point I return the salute and shout, "Carry on" in an equally loud voice as the barrier rises for my entry. It is our private little joke and makes it great fun just getting onto the lot!

In the last several years my visits to the production studio or on location have been minimal. So, my contact with members of the cast is also nearly zero. My main occupation is reviewing scripts and interfacing with the writers to develop story lines and ideas for future episodes. It was in this capacity, nearing the end of the second season, that I got my first opportunity to contribute in writing. My editing notes on a particular script were sufficiently barbed as to offend the author. In short order I was called to the producer's office to explain my criticism. Then I was asked if I thought I could do a better job than the author. I rashly said, "yes", and got the assignment.

With a lot of help from the writers, I turned out a proposed teleplay which was ultimately re-written by the producer, premiered the third season and received the highest Neilsen's yet achieved by any JAG episode. My idea of using of a mothballed aircraft carrier as the set apparently appealed to both the producers and the audience. My part in this signal success ended up being minimal; but my contract to produce a script had been honored and I was appropriately compensated.

Opportunity knocked again in the fifth season when I was offered the opportunity to act in two episodes. It was a small part, just three lines; but the lessons learned were enormously useful. The first lesson is that acting is a difficult profession; the second is that I am a lousy actor. The kindest adjective my kids could find when they viewed my performance was, "wooden".

Most of the work I do now is either by telephone or over the internet. The studio has installed a software package on my laptop computer that allows me to edit a script over the internet and return it electronically directly to the writers.

Working in Tinseltown can be occupationally hazardous. During my fourth season I parked my car on the lot and was walking to the Clara Bow building…a distance of maybe two hundred yards when I spied a starlet walking across the parking lot on a course that would cause her to pass close abeam. As the distance between us closed I could see that she was "drop dead" gorgeous…tall, blonde, willowy and moved with a seductive, slack-hipped movement which was going to be difficult to ignore.

I reminded myself that I was 71 years old, happily married and the grandfather of fifteen grandchildren…and had no business staring at her when she passed. So, I stoically fixed my gaze on the Clara Bow building and continued on my present course. Unfortunately, I have extremely good peripheral vision and found myself anticipating the close encounter. I even picked up the scent of a seductive perfume. But, it turned out that my peripheral vision was not good enough. Just as she passed by me and out of my field of view I walked into a parking meter!

FEET OF CLAY

usn

"Oh, what a tangled web we weave, when first we practice to deceive."
-Anonymous

Almost 200 years ago a British man-of-war stopped and boarded a United States merchantman for the purpose of "impressing" a few seamen. It was a common practice in those days when the Royal Navy ruled the oceans of the world. Whenever one of their vessels became undermanned while at sea, it simply stopped a ship from another nation and shanghaied one or more members of its crew.

In this particular instance, the young seaman selected for impressment didn't want to go, for obvious reasons, and resisted this particularly high-handed example of maritime arrogance. In the scuffle that ensued, a saber was drawn and the young man was seriously injured. Of course, the newly established nation-state that called itself the United States of America, treated this incident as an act of maritime aggression, declared war on the British Empire and won! Later on, the history books would call it the War of 1812.

In much the same manner, the United States treated the Barbary Coast pirates to a touch of U.S. Navy retribution off the coast of Tripoli, on May 6th 1805, and for the same reasons. This was to convince the Barbary Coast pirates to leave our unarmed merchantmen alone as they plied the waters of the Mediterranean Sea off the coast of North Africa. The method of retribution was simple and direct. A squadron of American men-of-war sailed close-in off the coast of Tripoli and bombarded the city. And, more to the point, when the Barbary Coast pirates captured the American vessel, *Philadelphia,* Lieutenant Stephen

Decatur took a landing party on board while she was tied up at a pier, and set her afire rather than allow the pirates to use her. The message was clear- don't tread on me! The resultant diminution of piracy against American traders is proof that the pirates understood us and had begun to respect us. There are those in our country now who would argue that such a foreign policy wouldn't work in today's more complicated geo-political environment. I remind such nay sayers of President Reagan's gesture on December 4th 1983. In response to the killing of U.S. Marines in Beirut, an air strike against "enemy targets" in the Bekaa Valley was appropriate.

But much has changed in the way of retribution which was so poorly executed in the Bekaa Valley in 1983 and the way it was so handily done in Tripoli 178 years earlier. As all military people all over the world know, a certain readiness to wage war is required, nay demanded, for those forces at the "tip of the sword." The battle group on duty in the Sixth Fleet received word with tasking to deliver a blow at a prescribed hour; and the carrier's crew and embarked air wing began the preparation for the strike. There were aircrews to brief, airplanes to fuel, configure and arm, weapons to be brought up from the carrier's magazine. Aircraft had to be brought up from the hangar deck and re-spotted on the flight deck. All this effort was in preparation for a launch that would put the strike aircraft at the delivery point at the crack of dawn. They needed to take advantage of the sun angle on the targets for ideal approach routes, the element of surprise and had a host of other problems to work through. The air wing commander, an acquaintance of mine, knew the time would be tight; and he hurled his air wing into the task. The ship's captain also knew that the time would be tight and put the full effort of the 5,000 men on his ship to make the deadline. The embarked carrier group commander, a rear admiral, another friend of mine, also knew that the time would be tight and worried about the repercussions all the way up the chain of command should his aircrews fail to meet the target time. The careers of all three gentlemen were hanging in the balance because the orders had come all the way from the White House, through the Joint Chiefs of Staff, through the four-star U.S. commander in Germany, through his three-star naval component commander in London, through the three-star Sixth Fleet commander in the Mediterranean , through the two-star task force commander also afloat in the Mediterranean, to the two-star battle group commander embarked on the strike aircraft carrier. The last four of these gentlemen are close acquaintances. As the preparations proceeded apace it became apparent that they would probably not make the launch schedule.

It is impossible to know all of the off-line verbal exchanges which went on among the three commanders aboard the carrier; the admiral, the ship's captain and the air wing commander. I interviewed the wing commander and am, therefore, privy to much of it nevertheless. I know the ship's captain well. When the wing commander informed those in the chain of command above him on the carrier that they would probably not make launch time, they would hear none of even a suggestion to the powers further up the line that a delay in launch time would ensure a safer, more orderly and therefore, more effective strike. The carrier had a strike order, a readiness obligation, and career reputations were on the line. The strike would go as ordered or heads would roll. At some point, the trio lost track of their most important commitment second to following orders. That was the safety of their air crews.

We probably all know what happened. It was a fiasco. Airplanes were hurled into the pre-dawn sky incompletely configured (one drop tank as opposed to the two required for the wing commander who was leading the strike in an A7 Corsair II), other airplanes with only half a bomb load, yet others with improper external fuel loads. It was proper for the wing commander to inform his two superiors afloat, which he did. It could have been proper for the ship's captain to pass this information on to his superior afloat which he probably did. If he found the suggestion to delay the launch to be unacceptable to the admiral he could have done so with an official message, info to higher authority (a ballsy move, to be sure). Finally, the embarked admiral could have so informed his superior by the use of a much-used technique known as a "UNODIR" message.

In Navy message parlance, UNODIR is short for "unless otherwise directed." The message could have simply stated that because of short warning time and unexpected difficulties, the safety of the aircrews demanded that a thirty minute delay should be imposed on the target time. As a consequence the embarked carrier group commander would launch thirty minutes later than planned and the bombs would hit their targets thirty minutes later than directed by the National Command Authority (Pentagonese for the White House).

Of course, no one in the chain of command between the embarked carrier group commander and the NCA would have dared to send a countermanding message ordering that the original target time be adhered to; and the reasons are simple.

1. The sender of the UNODIR was closest to the scene of action and therefore knew the most about the situation.

2. The target time was not that important, anyway.

3. If things went badly, the sender of a countermanding message would take the fall, politically.

So, no message was sent, the launch time was adhered to and the raid predictably went badly. An A-6 Intruder was shot down, its pilot was killed and the bombardier/navigator, a black aviator, was captured. The wing commander was also shot down but he managed to get his stricken airplane to the relative safety of the Mediterranean Sea where he ejected and was rescued by helicopter. Much to the chagrin of the entire military establishment, Jesse Jackson interposed himself, went to Lebanon and brought home the captured airman. It was vintage Jesse Jackson!

The Secretary of the Navy was beside himself with embarrassment and initiated immediate changes to the way the Navy trains its airmen. The implied assumption was that it was a problem with training. Nothing could have been further from the truth. Out of this came the institution of an organization known as the Strike Warfare Center, not a bad thing in itself, and a few other reporting responsibility changes to the job of Carrier Air Wing Commander. The hue and cry in the U.S. media was awful to behold.

There is a long record of events in our nation's history that fall into the same category; an American vessel on the high seas (international waters) is threatened or harmed while innocently occupied in legal commerce. Always the United States has exacted retribution from those who would dispute our claim to freedom of the seas. This is based upon an accepted set of rules known as the "international law of the sea." Its basic tenet is that a U.S. ship occupied in legal activity in international waters is "sovereign territory." In other words, it is a "piece of the United States."

This same rule applies to airplanes. But, there is another aspect to this basic principle of freedom of the seas and airspace and it applies when the victim of the threat is a ship or airplane of the United States Navy. In that respect the ship's commanding officer or the airplane's pilot in command is required to take whatever steps are necessary to keep his command from falling into enemy hands. His naval mission is his first priority and the safety of his crew is his second.

The best example of this is the engagement between the U.S. Navy man-of-war, *Bon Homme Richard* and her British frigate opponent *Serapis*. Captain John Paul Jones commanded the *"Bonnie Dick"* and Captain Richard Pearson commanded *Serapis*. The famous naval engagement occurred off Famborough Head in the North Sea on September 23rd 1779. The Yankee ship had taken a pounding from her British opponent to the point that it began to founder. Captain Pearson shouted across the narrow expanse of water separating them, "Do you strike your colors, sir?" This would entail Jones hauling down the American flag as a gesture of surrender.

As history tells us, and as every American knows, Captain Jones had other plans. He broke out the grappling hooks and shouted his time-honored reply, "I have not yet begun to fight." With that his sailors boarded the other vessel and a violent hand-to-hand battle ensued punctuated by saber thrusts, cutlass slashes, pistol reports and a deadly hail of sniper fire from his best Marine marksmen in the rigging. The epic battle ended with Captain Pearson striking *his* colors. Jones took command of *Serapis* just as *Bon Homme Richard* was sinking. John Paul Jones went down in the history books as epitomizing all that is ideal in the meaning of command at sea.

Unfortunately, not all U.S. Navy commanding officers have been sufficiently imbued with Jones' principles to show they have *cojones* as big as his. Such was the case when the U.S.S. *Pueblo,* an electronic intelligence-gathering ship, was boarded by the North Korean Navy in 1966. As any experienced seaman will tell you it is virtually impossible to board a ship that is underway and it can be deliberately maneuvered in such a way as to discourage boarders. Had Bucher ordered his men to return any enemy fire with the few automatic weapons he had on hand, rung up flank speed (13 knots), turned away from the Korean coast and maneuvered as necessary to deter the boarding party, the *Pueblo* most probably would not be still sitting tied up to the pier in Wonsan 39 years later, an embarrassing monument to trepidation and command indecision. Yes, lives might have been lost. Yes, the ship might have been sunk. But, it is also possible that such a show of determination might well have convinced the North Korean senior officer present to back off for fear of losing some of his own men in a futile attempt to capture the ship.

Whatever Bucher's mind-set was in those terrible moments of indecision, it couldn't have been as bad as the long, painful 11-month imprisonment, torture and worse, the years of disgrace, which his action brought upon himself, the service and his country.

In November 1962 a U.S. electronic intelligence-gathering EP-2 airplane was flying a mission off the northern coast of Cuba. Its pilot, a naval academy classmate of mine, was carefully observing the 12-mile limit and therefore was in international airspace. I was officer-in-charge of a hot-pad detachment of F-8 fighters based only 60 miles north of him at NAS, Key West. Our mission was to protect him and his crew against Cuban fighters. On that particular day the Cubans launched two MiG-17 fighters to intercept him. The first warning we got was a terrified MAYDAY call from him on Guard (emergency) channel telling us he was being harassed by the Cuban fighters. One minute and forty-five seconds later two Crusaders roared down the runway and turned toward the EP-2 which was now headed for Key West at full power. The Joint Aerial Reconnaissance Control Center (JARCC) at Key West had all five airplanes on their radar and within a few minutes the plots merged.

The last transmission from the EP-2 was that, in accordance with the rules of engagement, he was headed for Key West as fast and as low as he dared fly the airplane. In spite of the low altitude (estimated to be about 100 feet), one of the MiGs approached him from behind at high speed, flew directly under the EP-2 and pulled up immediately in front of it. The clearance between the top of the MiG's vertical fin and the bottom of the EP-2 had to be no more than a few feet. The MiG pilot must have been either a raving maniac or a very skillful and intrepid aviator. Then the two MiGs joined up in a combat spread formation totally unaware of the presence of the two Navy fighters.

The two Crusaders slid in behind the two MiGs, one on each, with their master armament switches on and a Sidewinder growl on their headsets indicating the seeker was locked on, and requested permission to fire. The moment was pregnant with high drama. The Crusader pilots were told to "wait one" while clearance from higher authority was being sought. Seconds ticked agonizingly by as the two pilots waited, fingers curled about triggers sitting in the heart of the Sidewinder's firing envelope. Unfortunately, the Cuban ground control intercept radar was also watching the engagement and recalled the MiGs to Cuban airspace.

We have often wondered what would have happened if the Crusaders had fired and downed the MiGs. Our conclusion was that their Distinguished Flying Cross award recommendations would have cancelled out their court martials, or vice versa!

We now fast-forward to the recent intercept off the EP-3 by Chinese fighters in the Sea of Japan in international airspace. Based upon the published statements of several of the crew members, the hazardous pass by one of the fighters resulted in what was a horrible but accidental mid-air collision. I am not privy to the rules of engagement existing for EP-3 missions in that arena, but I knew them well when they first began flying their missions, and suspect they haven't changed substantially. Nonetheless, I doubt that they included the option of landing on Hainan.

The harassment could, and perhaps should, have been interpreted by the pilot at the time as an act of war because that is exactly what it would have seemed from his perspective. Therefore, the subsequent landing at Hainan was an act of surrender, "striking his colors." The EP-3 pilot had the option of running for it in much the same way as the EP-2 pilot did 39 years earlier off the coast of Cuba. He had the unique, once-in-a-lifetime opportunity to become a modern day John Paul Jones. Instead he chose to be a modern day Lloyd Bucher.

There is a litmus test I applied to this incident which seems to clear things up for me. Assume, for the sake of argument, that the EP-3 had been instead an armed fighter plane. What would have been his instantaneous answer is simple. He would have tried to shoot down the other fighter as an act of self-defense without asking permission from anyone. That is a basic element for all of the rules of engagement I have been aware of for the last 40 years, and it pretty well establishes why a landing at any other place including the water would have been preferable to China.

I am enormously impressed by the flying skill of the pilot in recovering his airplane from the moments of out-of-controlled flight that followed the mid-air collision. I can also share the concern he had for the safety of his crew of 23 other men and women. But, having acknowledged all of this, his primary concern still should have been for mission accomplishment first and crew safety second. Mission accomplishment would call for "getting out of Dodge" as fast as he could. Turning one's airplane over to a country that has just tried to kill you and your crew and destroy your airplane, and giving them 24 hostages to boot, can hardly be described as mission accomplishment. That is not even arguable.

There has been much written and said by uninformed pundits about the hazards of ditching an EP-3 in the open ocean and the dangers of parachuting into it. However, as some one who has survived an ejection into the Pacific, I feel comfortable stating that bailing out was definitely an option. That the pilot ruled out both of these options, tells me that he had his top two priorities reversed.

The same pundits have argued that Hainan was a permissible landing option for someone who was having such difficulties keep his airplane under control. I would remind them of several friends of mine who went through far greater difficulties flying their airplanes over many miles of North Vietnam so that they could eject over the Gulf of Tonkin. None of them ever even considered landing at an airfield in North Vietnam. So much for priorities and options!

The whole incident and the ensuing debate by those who have never put their lives on the line for anything has been sickening. To make matters worse, our leadership didn't have the *cojones* to hold the pilot accountable and chose instead to award him the Distinguished Flying Cross.

John Paul Jones must have turned over in his grave!

The final vignette in the litany of failures is the most egregious because it is a failure of leadership at the very top of the pyramid, pure and simple. I am referring to the suicide of the Navy's 25th Chief of Naval Operations on May 16th 1996, shortly after that gentleman, also an acquaintance of mine, allowed himself to be rolled over by the oldest ploy in town by one of our distinguished members of congress. It was a silly game, in the lawmaker's words later, to threaten to withhold approval on the appointment of one of Naval Aviation's stalwarts to a four-star command in exchange for some other congressional consideration. The CNO folded, and withdrew the nomination bringing down on his head the wrath of almost everyone in the military establishment.

But the problem went beyond that particular loss of intestinal fortitude. This particular CNO was being lionized by the media because he was the first to achieve that exalted position after starting out his naval career as an enlisted man.

When the Chief of Naval Operations committed suicide in the back yard of his quarters at the Washington Navy Yard, the political pundits had a heyday with it. Most of them got it all wrong. But the one who got it the most wrong was the journalist who characterized the act, in a Washington Post OpEd, as "the warrior's way out." The pundit went on to say that the Admiral, the first enlisted man to ascend to the position of Chief of Naval Operations, must therefore have been a warrior. He equated enlisted status to warrior status by some mystifying train of logic which escaped all of us who knew the gentleman. In actual fact, he was not a warrior any more than many of his contemporaries and that may well have been the problem.

With all due respect to his family, suicide can only be described as a cop out. It is never a warrior's way out! In actual fact, it turns out that this gentleman, when he was executive officer of a destroyer operating off the coast of Vietnam, engaged in a combined operation called, "Rolling Thunder." He decided to wear a small device called a combat "V" on his Vietnam Campaign ribbon. In this case the device would have meant that the ship on which he was serving had either engaged the enemy (North Vietnamese shore batteries) or been taken under fire by them. In truth, neither was the case. For years thereafter the gentleman wore that device on his ribbons. It was only after he had been informed that a reporter was researching his awards that he stopped wearing the device. On the particular morning of his demise, the gentleman had been further warned that the subject of the device was going to be brought up by another reporter with whom he was scheduled to be interviewed that very afternoon.

A good friend of mine, a highly decorated retired Rear Admiral, happened to be at the National Naval Medical Center awaiting a prescription when he overheard the terrible news and saw a cluster of hospital corpsmen discussing it in a passageway. He went over to them, identified himself and asked them for their reaction. One of them spoke up and voiced what he believed to be the general consensus of opinion among all active duty personnel regardless of rank. "We feel cheated," the young man said.

The United States Navy seems to have metamorphosed from leaders, the likes of John Paul Jones, to the likes of a man who took his own life over the issue of a small, unauthorized piece of tin attached to a ribbon he wore on his chest.

As I examined this series of supposedly unrelated events over the last 200 or so years of naval history there seems to have been a slow, almost imperceptible change from the black and white world of John Paul Jones to the increasingly numerous shades of gray that seems to have pervaded our modern society where an acting President could actually stand before a television camera and obfuscate to the world over the meaning of the word, "IS." Is it any wonder that our military leaders, who are spawned from our society, reflect the values of that society?

Our military academies continue to teach the traditional warrior concepts of Duty, Honor and Country. But, can they permanently instill into our young midshipmen and cadets those values? Do these young people, as they advance through their military careers, find these exalted concepts eroded by the reality of present day life in our military establishments and our society?

In answer to all of the above questions, I believe that we are all at fault. Did we say "No" to our children often enough as they were maturing under our tutelage? Did we impose sanctions rather then make hollow threats? Did we demand accountability of our children as they passed through their teen years? Did we give good example to them by our own behavior? Did we worry too much about their self-esteem and not enough about instilling a little "iron" into their characters? Do they seem to be imbued with the desire to make us proud?

If the answers to most of these questions are negative, then we are the problem! If this wonderful country of ours is to lead the world into a more enlightened era free from the tyranny of terrorism where peace can be enjoyed by the majority of us, then we must not let our society develop feet of clay!

The last line of the (original lyrics) of the United States Naval Academy's anthem, "Anchors Aweigh" comes to mind as an appropriate way to end this reflection:

"Faith, courage, service true, and honor over, honor over all."

EPILOGUE

After we had reviewed the results of our efforts we came separately, to the same curious conclusion: the Good Lord had put us on this earth for a reason. Both of us could, and should have, succumbed to the combined effects of our own stupidity and the harrowing circumstances into which we had repeatedly allowed ourselves to be led.

Did the Good Lord have a purpose in keeping us alive...again and again? As we approach the winter season of our lives, we wondered what, in heaven's name did He have in mind? Surely, neither of us was going to find a cure for cancer. Neither of us was going to solve the terrible problem of feeding the starving in Darfur. Neither of us was going to solve the global problems of war, pestilence, starvation, genocide and mindless racial hatred. What then? Why are we here? Is it all just a cosmic accident?

Bob sat every evening with his wife Anne in New York in front of his *chiminea* pondering these imponderables and I, three thousand miles to the westward, sat in my jacuzzi, puffed on a Cuban cigar and went through the same philosophical quandary: What, if anything, does the Good Lord expect of us?

Are we endowed with some curious sense of prescience? What is it that we are supposed to do? We stay in close contact and share the closest contact with each other on these weighty issues.

Should our readers get this far without throwing the book down they will probably have drawn some fairly obvious conclusions:

a. Life isn't always fair; and it probably wasn't meant to be.

b. We should play the hand that was dealt us, with as much skill and enthusiasm as we can muster up, because there won't be another. Then we should accept the results with equal *noblesse*.

c. Regardless of the temptation to do otherwise, always stay on the high road in dealing with opposing ideas/opinions/theses.

d. Everything we do, should be done with dignity and class.

e. When the time comes for us to depart this world we will hopefully have left behind a reputation for honor, integrity, accountability, good humor and truth.

f. If it hasn't been fun, then we have been doing something wrong.

g. Kicking ass and taking names ought to be the best vengeance

h. We should have created the circumstances for one good belly laugh every day.

i. Each of us have been provided with an inestimable opportunity to do good; Let us hope we did our best to take advantage of that opportunity.